HOW IT ALL BEGAN

Penelope Lively

D0067398

PENGUIN BOOKS

To Rachel and Izzy

PENGUIN BOOKS
Published by the Penguin Group
Penguin Group (USA) Inc., 375 Hudson Street,
New York, New York 10014, USA

USA | Canada | UK | Ireland | Australia | New Zealand | India | South Africa | China
Penguin Books Ltd, Registered Offices: 80 Strand, London WC2R 0RL, England
For more information about the Penguin Group visit penguin.com

First published in Great Britain by Fig Tree, an imprint of Penguin Books Ltd 2011
First published in the United States of America by Viking Penguin,
a member of Penguin Group (USA) Inc. 2012
Published by Penguin Books 2012

This Read Pink edition published in Penguin Books 2013

THE LIBRARY OF CONGRESS HAS CATALOGED THE HARDCOVER EDITION AS FOLLOWS:
Lively, Penelope.
How it all began : a novel / Penelope Lively.
    p. cm.
ISBN 978-0-670-02344-8 (hc.)
ISBN 978-0-14-312516-7 (pbk.)
1. Life change events—Fiction. 2. London (England)—Fiction. I. Title.
PR6062.I89H69 2012
823'.914—dc23   2011032994

Printed in the United States of America
10 9 8 7 6 5 4 3 2 1

ALWAYS LEARNING   PEARSON

PENGUIN BOOKS

HOW IT ALL BEGAN

Penelope Lively is an award-winning novelist and author of children's literature. She received the Booker Prize for her novel *Moon Tiger* and wide acclaim for *The Photograph* and *Family Album*. Lively is a Fellow of the Royal Society of Literature, a member of PEN and the Society of Authors, and a recipient of the OBE and CBE. In recognition of her contributions to British literature, she was recently elevated to Dame Commander of the Order of the British Empire. She lives in north London.

Praise for *How It All Began*

"A vital new novel . . . Writing with her usual poise and cutting cinematically from one character's story to another's, Ms. Lively elegantly orchestrates these events while using them as a setup for another series of developments. . . . As she's done in so many earlier books, Ms. Lively writes with an astringent blend of sympathy and detachment, emotional wisdom and satiric wit, and the result, here, is a Chekhovian tale that's entertaining, even funny on the surface, but ultimately melancholy in its awareness of time and lost opportunities, its characters' apprehension of mortality, and the limits to their dreams."
—Michiko Kakutani, *The New York Times*

"Since the mid-1970s, Lively has been folding philosophical contemplation into the psychological analysis of her characters, melding the novel of ideas with the droll novel of manners. . . . Her gift is for delving into the roiling uncertainty beneath our seemingly mundane choices and for rendering the consequences of those choices in crisp yet subtle terms. She extends our ways of trying to comprehend, if not to answer, life's big questions. . . . Here, one of our most talented writers has written an elegant, witty work of fiction, deceptively simple, emotionally and intellectually penetrating, the kind of novel that brings a plot to satisfying closure but whose questions linger long afterward in the reader's mind."
—*The New York Times Book Review*

"In this mischievous novel, Lively traces the genealogy of randomness that messes up the lives of strangers. . . . Moving skillfully between streams of consciousness and a wry omniscient voice, Lively investigates her characters' motives and afterthoughts with precision and tenderness. The happy ending is deceptively simple—the novel not only establishes that beginnings and endings are arbitrary points on a timeline of unintended consequences but also hints at the profound mystery with which life untangles itself."
—*The New Yorker*

"The masterful and prolific Penelope Lively has traced several decades of social change in England in comic novels that capture the edginess and nuance of human behavior with wit and empathy. Sentence by sentence she is superb—crisp, clear, pared to the essence. She seems preternaturally alert to the echoes of the past in the clamorous present and perennially fresh in her themes. . . ."

How It All Began is another virtuoso performance, our spectacle, in almost real time. I found it even more delightful a second time through, appreciating once more the elegance of Lively's design, the grace notes of thematic underpinning shining through—and yes, the shadowy presence of that mugger. . . . In her own late seventies now, with a legion of regular readers and newcomers with every book, Lively continues to surprise and illuminate, writing to ever more dazzling effect."
—*The Boston Globe*

"The ever productive, ever graceful Penelope Lively returns to several pet themes—memory, history, and the powerful role of happenstance in reshaping lives—with a fresh and charming novel. . . . She has provided a golden passport that will sweep you through the border control of other people's lives."
—*The Washington Post*

"A spellbinding surprise . . . *How It All Began* is a revelation. While Lively's novels always feature intelligent people who use their brains to negotiate their way through a complex and sometimes perilous world, *How It All Began* is also about feeling. . . . Lively reminds us of the earnest, obtuse fumbling that constitutes most of what happens in a human life, the coincidences and accidents that are as much in charge as are the explicit decisions. . . . Every small twist in the road in this superbly well-plotted novel sheds ever widening concentric rings of consequences."
—*Chicago Tribune*

"The idea of human choice vs. fate lies at the core of much fiction. Penelope Lively, one of England's most talented novelists and a writer whose works combine narrative intensity and artistic control, has explored this notion repeatedly. . . . Lively's novel is skillfully constructed, with a thoroughly engaging plot. It also has much to say about the role of chance in human affairs, the aging process, and the importance of memories."
—*Minneapolis Star Tribune*

"Lively is a consummate storyteller who once again illuminates the ways that the vagaries of chance bring powerful alteration to the ordinary plans of ordinary people. . . . The characters in this novel are, each and all, well drawn and fully conceived. . . . Everyone in this elegantly told tale is connected by chance and the power of story."
—*The Seattle Times*

"Startling and soothing, uncommonly paced, this is a book to treasure. . . . To a person, each character is wholly developed, and the trajectory of all the chaotically intersecting lives moves forward. Ms. Lively attends to these with great care, and with every detail and keenly observed moment, the reader accrues more information about where it all leads. There are consequences to missteps and random acts. . . . Three cheers for this gorgeous writing."
—*The Washington Times*

"In this densely patterned novel . . . Lively reminds us how tentatively we actually control our fates. . . . *How It All Began* is a novel of the recession—as in previous books, Lively here describes social systems in addition to social lives—where money is practically a character on its own. . . . She observes how the 'strange notional movements' of world economies can 'wreck individual lives.' This novel shows that if minor events wreak major effects, so can grand systems shape our own small ends—and our beginnings, too."

—*San Francisco Chronicle*

"With grace, wit, and wisdom, Booker Prize winner Lively has crafted a highly readable tale about fates intersecting amid the chaos of modern life." —*People*

"Wonderful . . . British treasure Penelope Lively examines the effects of a seemingly random crime on a group of London acquaintances and strangers."

—*Marie Claire*

"Lives intersect in unexpected and comical ways in this breezy, engrossing novel. . . . Lively infuses her motley cast of characters with a blend of pathos and sharp satire. . . . This deftly paced novel remains compulsively readable throughout."

—*Entertainment Weekly*

"A clever and fun romp, where we the reader get to play peeping tom, peeking into ordinary lives turned sideways by one incident. . . . *How It All Began* is more than just a lovely and engaging story. It is a deeply incisive explanation of how we all begin, how we plod on, and how we approach the end. . . . We come to like, even love, this band of travelers and we wish them Godspeed and a bit of happiness, before the next flip of fate." —*The Huffington Post*

"That rarest of things, a book that is both smart and cheerful. . . . I found myself smiling again and again, mostly at the character Charlotte's thoughts about books and the comfort she takes in reading. . . . All the various threads in the novel wove together beautifully. This is a hard thing to pull off, trust me."

—Ann Patchett

"This delightful, absorbing novel relies on a sophisticated and skillfully realized structure to introduce and then follow its endearingly ordinary characters. . . . The interdependency of the characters' lives, which they remain largely unaware of, builds intriguing momentum, and the pace quickens as the novel develops. Throughout, prolific Booker Prize–winning author Lively illustrates her knack for charming familiarity and just the right dash of surprise."

—*Publishers Weekly*

"The ruling vision of master British novelist Lively's latest delectably tart and agile novel is the Butterfly Effect, which stipulates that 'a very small perturbation' can radically alter the course of events. . . . Throughout this brilliantly choreographed and surreptitiously poignant chain-reaction comedy of chance and change, Lively shrewdly elucidates the nature of history, the tunnel-visioning of pain and age, and the abiding illumination of reading, which so profoundly nourishes the mind and spirit." —*Booklist* (starred review)

"Explores the far-reaching effect of happenstance, as individual circumstances shift, lives change, and the known is perceived in an altogether new light. . . . Lively delivers her story about these intertwined lives with faultless dexterity, sly humor, keen insight, and deft economy. . . . A feel-good masterpiece that will delight faithful fans as well as those new to the work of this consummate storyteller."   —*Library Journal* (starred review)

"Lively is now nearly eighty but, as *How It All Began* shows, there is no diminution in her skills. It is an autograph work in which she shuffles her familiar topics as adroitly and satisfyingly as ever."   —*Financial Times*

"More stylish than many writers half her age . . . Lively knows a thing or two about storytelling. Her veteran understanding of the function of narrative in our lives is impressive but lightly worn. . . . Her candor is refreshing, and reminds us that you don't have to lie to yourself to live life finely until the very end."   —*The Times* (London)

"As always, Lively has a precise control of the comic, and an ear for dialogue honed over more than forty years of writing."
—*Independent on Sunday* (London)

"Lively remains a sublime storyteller. . . . She has us riveted with curiosity as to what will happen next, yet also keeps us consistently aware of the nature of the illusion."   —*The Guardian* (London)

"A deftly constructed, always enjoyable novel." —*The Sunday Times* (London)

"Approaching her eightieth year, Lively's sense of humor lives up to her name. . . . Whatever your age, *How It All Began* is a splendid tonic."
—*Sunday Telegraph* (London)

"A kaleidoscopic picture that disintegrates and then reassembles itself, in a manner that is surprising and completely satisfying . . . Lively's style has a beautiful economy, and she can be wickedly funny. . . . This is classic Penelope Lively— deeply comical, essentially kind-hearted, wonderfully written, and seasoned with a rare wisdom."   —*The Literary Review*

To access Penguin Readers Guides online,
visit our Web site at www.penguin.com.

The Butterfly Effect was the reason. For small pieces of weather—and to a global forecaster small can mean thunderstorms and blizzards—any prediction deteriorates rapidly. Errors and uncertainties multiply, cascading upward through a chain of turbulent features, from dust devils and squalls up to continent-size eddies that only satellites can see.

—James Gleick, *Chaos*

CHAPTER ONE

The pavement rises up and hits her. Slams into her face, drives the lower rim of her glasses into her cheek. She is laid out there, prone. What is this? Voices are chattering above her; people are concerned. Of course.

Bag.

She says, "My bag."

A face is alongside hers. Woman. Nice woman. "There's an ambulance on the way, my dear. You'll be fine. Just keep still till they come."

Bag.

"Your shopping's right here. The Sainsbury bag."

No. Bag.

Bag is not. She'd known that somehow. Right away.

Another voice, up above. Man's voice. "She's been mugged, hasn't she? That's what it is."

Ah.

Voices discuss. She is not much interested. Nee-naw, nee-naw, nee-naw. Here it is. Know for whom the bell tolls.

Expert hands: lifting, bundling. In the ambulance, she is on her side, in some sort of rigid tube. She hurts. Where is hurt? Don't know. Anywhere. May as well try to sleep for a bit.

"Keep your eyes open, please. We'll be there in a few minutes."

Trolley-ride. On and on. Corridors. People passing. Right turn. Halt. More lifting. They take the tube away. She is on her back now.

Nurse. Smiling but business-like. Name? Address?

Those she can do. No problem.

Date of birth?

That too. Not a good date of birth. Rather a long time ago.

Next of kin?

Rose is not going to like this. It's morning, isn't it? Rose will be with his lordship.

Next of kin will be at work. Not bother her. Yet.

On Mondays, Rose arrived at the house later than usual, having stopped off at the bank to collect some cash for her employer and to pay in any checks that might have arrived the week before. Henry did not care to fiddle with cash dispensers and could not be doing with the electronic transfer of money. He insisted on paper in the hand, for minor payments such as lecture fees or book reviews. E-mail too was beyond his remit; Rose dealt with that. Probably Henry did not know how to turn on the computer. Though you wouldn't put it past the old devil to be cruising cyberspace once she was out of the house, Googling old friends and enemies.

"I propose we drop Lord Peters and Mrs. Donovan, Rose. All right with you?" Her second week with him, way back, and actually it hadn't been all right, not at first. She had called him "you" for months. He was after all her mother's generation, never mind what else he was, or had been. She called some of her mother's friends by their first names? Yes, but she'd known them all her life and they hadn't been Regius Professors and head of Royal Commissions and adviser to a prime minister and what have you. String of letters after his name; people sometimes glancing at him, thinking: why do I know that face? Shirty enough if anyone looked like taking liberties: "Curt letter, Rose, saying Lord Peters does not provide puffs for other people's books, and if you're feeling expansive you could add that no, Lord P. does not recall his conversation with the author in 1993."

Well, in ten years a relationship tends to solidify. The newly retired, brisk and self-important Henry for whom she had first come to work had mutated into a querulous, though still self-important, seventy-six-year-old with a gammy knee, a high consumption of claret and certain unpredictable behavior patterns. You trod carefully. Occasionally you considered chucking in the job. Except that it was extremely convenient, he'd always paid a nice little bit above the odds, and you never knew what might happen, which was better than a desk in an office. And at the beginning, it had been the answer to a prayer: part-time, mornings only, she could be home to get the children from school, free to be theirs for the rest of the day.

Now, of course, that wouldn't matter—James in Singapore, Lucy at college.

Over half an hour late. There had been a long wait at the bank, to get that check in. He'll be tetchy. Opening the post himself, grunting over each sheet of paper. Or purring: "Rather a nice letter from Cornell, Rose. They want to give me an honorary degree. What do you think—shall we go over and collect it?"

He did not like to travel alone now. From time to time she was prevailed upon to escort him. Swings and roundabouts: you got a trip to somewhere you wouldn't otherwise have been; but the trip was with him, who could be a pain. One became "Mrs. Donovan, my PA," and there was a lot of hanging about and making small-talk to strangers or no talk at all. The hotels could be a bit of a treat. And because someone else was paying it, was business flights, or first-class rail.

She walked the last few hundred yards away from the bustling road and onto his leafy quiet street with the smart white stucco houses. Expensive houses. Academics are not usually well-heeled, apparently, but Henry's father had been some sort of industrialist; money had filtered down to Henry—hence the house in a grandish part of London. Distinctly grand if you yourself live in a semi in Enfield, and grew up modestly enough in the suburbs of St. Albans, daughter of two teachers. Henry was kindly patronizing about her parentage, on occasion: "Accounts for your exemplary syntax, Rose. Breeding will out."

Her mother had ever been crisp about Henry. His lordship.

Needless to say, they had never met. Her mother was entertained by the stories that Rose could tell of his lifestyle and his remarks— gleeful, indeed, sometimes—but Rose was well aware that she considered the job menial. Rose could have done better than that. The subject was never raised—comment and counter-comment remained unspoken: "Literate, numerate, efficient—there'd have been all sorts of options"; "But I never *wanted* a career. I *chose* this."

And thus had one chosen Henry also, though unwittingly, a blind date as it were. Face to face at that initial interview, across the now so familiar large desk with the tooled leather top: he seems nice enough; rather grand, lovely house, never seen so many books (thought *we* had quite a few); salary's good, actually.

"Do sit down, Mrs. Donovan. Suppose I start by outlining my requirements."

Correspondence . . . diary . . . travel arrangements . . . protect me from the telephone . . . my memoirs.

My memoirs. *My Memoirs* were but a gleam in his eye then, and remained so for several years. Only relatively recently—"Commitments thank goodness, being less consuming"—has the spiel gathered pace, the handwritten sheets waiting each day for her to type them up. "Here you go, Rose, this morning's offering. You may be amused at what I have to say about Harold Wilson." Chuckle, chuckle. There'll be quite a few people distinctly unamused when the spiel at last achieves publication; good thing Harold Wilson's dead.

"Now tell me a bit about yourself, Mrs. Donovan."

What had one told? Secretarial experience, period as PA to a company chairman (who tried to put his hand up my skirt, so I walked out, but no need to tell that), five-year break for family reasons.

Henry does not have children. Dear me, no. A dad figure he is not. Never a wife, either. But not gay, it would seem. There have been ladies, occasionally wined and dined or taken to the theater, but clearly none have managed to adhere. So Henry is a lone spirit. He had a sister, who died a few years ago, and he appears to have some affection for her daughter, Marion, who is a businesswoman and visits from time to time.

About once a year Henry remembers to ask after James and Lucy.

He never displays interest—assumed or otherwise—in Gerry, who is evidently beyond his horizon. "Ah, your husband . . ." in vaguely baffled tone, when once Rose mentioned him (with pneumonia, as it happened, requiring unusual attention).

Gerry is not interested in Henry, either. Gerry is interested in local government, carpentry, sacred music and a spot of coarse fishing. Gerry is fine. Who'd want a husband who would run you ragged?

She climbed the steps to that handsome black front door with the pillared portico, took out her keys, opened, entered. She went through to her own office, hung up her coat, removed the cash from her bag, and knocked on the study door.

"Come in, come in." Tetchy, yes. "Ah, there you are. A whole lot of stuff from the insurance company that I don't understand and don't want to. Deal with it, would you? Some other bits and pieces we can see to together—here's a fellow I barely remember asking if I'll stand as a referee. He's got a nerve. The rail tickets for the Manchester trip have come. Why are we going so early? Nine-thirty at Euston. Christ!"

"There's a lunch before your lecture—they'd like you there by twelve-thirty."

"Inconsiderate of them. Oh—there was a phone call for you. Some-one from a hospital. Can you call them back—here's the number. About your mother, apparently. Unwell, is she? And, Rose, I'm dying for a cup of coffee."

She thought about the mugger. Her mugger. This faceless person with whom she has been in transitory, intimate relationship. Him. Or pos-sibly her. Women muggers now, no doubt; this is the age of equal opportunities. Person who was here one moment, gone the next. With my bag. And my packet of Kleenex and my Rennies and my comb and my bus pass and my rail card and three twenties I think and some change and the Barclaycard. And my keys.

Keys.

Oh, Rose has seen to that. She said. Changed the locks. And the card. Stopped. Goodbye to the three twenties and the change.

What will he/she buy with the sixty-odd quid I've so kindly given him/her?

A handful of Three for Two's at Waterstones? A ticket to Covent Garden? It'll have to be Upper Circle, I'm afraid. A subscription to the Friends of the Royal Academy?

Drugs, they say. Day's supply of whatever is their particular tipple.

No. I prefer to imagine my mugger as a refined soul. Just a rather needy refined soul. Our brief relationship is more tolerable that way. Maybe there's a *Figaro* on offer—that would perk him up. Him or her. German Expressionists at the Academy, I think. Hmmn. The new Philip Roth is good. And there's this book on Shakespeare.

Hip. Hurts. Despite painkiller. Does not kill. Makes you woozy. As though hallucinating. No—sod you, mugger. Why didn't you just ask nicely? Sod you. Go and slurp your heroin or whatever it is. No *Figaro* for you.

Rose had had to call Henry from the hospital to say that she would not be back that day. He did remember to inquire after her mother, when she arrived the next morning.

"They're looking after her well, I hope? No joke—broken bones at our age. Now . . . we're drowning in paper, Rose. Two days' post not dealt with."

She explained that it was possible she would not be able to accompany him to Manchester. It would depend on the date of her mother's release from the hospital, not yet decided. "I'll need to bring her home and settle her. She'll be coming to us for a while."

Consternation. "Oh dear. Well, let's face that when we come to it. I suppose at a pinch Marion . . ."

Rose's spare room.

"For a month or two, Mum. At least till you're off the crutches."

"I'd manage . . ."

"No. And anyway, the hospital is quite firm about it. So there."

So. Just what one didn't want. Being a burden and all that. What one had hoped to avoid. De-railed. Thanks a lot, mugger.

Sorry, Rose. And Gerry. And bless you. Let's hope this won't blight a beautiful relationship. It's the classic situation: tiresome old mother moves in.

Old age is not for wimps. Broken hip is definitely not for wimps. We are crutch-mobile now. Up and down the ward. Ouch. Sessions with delightful six-foot New Zealand physiotherapist. Seriously ouch.

Of course before the hip there was the knee, and the back, but that was mere degeneration, not malign external interference. The knee. The back. And the cataracts. And those twinges in the left shoulder and the varicose veins and the phlebitis and having to get up at least once every night to pee and the fits of irritation at people who leave inaudible messages on the answerphone. Time was, long ago, pain occasionally struck—toothache, ear infection, cricked neck—and one made a great fuss, affronted. For years now, pain has been a constant companion, cozily there in bed with one in the morning, keeping pace all day, coyly retreating perhaps for a while only to come romping back: here I am, remember me? Ah, old age. The twilight years—that delicate phrase. Twilight my foot—roaring dawn of a new life, more like, the one you didn't know about. We all avert our eyes, and then— wham! you're in there too, wondering how the hell this can have happened, and maybe it is an early circle of hell and here come the gleeful devils with their pitchforks, stabbing and prodding.

Except that life goes on in parallel—real life, good life with all its gifts and graces. My species tulips out and blue tits on the bird feeder and a new book to look forward to this evening and Rose ringing up and a David Attenborough wild life program on the telly. And the new baby of Jennifer next door. A baby always lifts the spirits. Rose certainly did, way back. Pity there were no more, despite trying. But her own, in due course, thanks be.

Charlotte views her younger selves with a certain detachment. They are herself, but other incarnations, innocents going about half-forgotten business. One is not nostalgic about them—dear me, no. Though occasionally a trifle envious: physically spry, pretty sharp teacher, though I say it myself, all my lot got A's at A level, no question.

And further back yet, young Charlotte. Gracious, look at her—stepping out with men, marrying, pushing a pram.

All of which—all of whom—add up to what we have today: Charlotte washed up in Ward C, learning laboriously how to walk again. Ward C is full of breakage—legs, ankles, arms. The elderly fall off steps, trip over curbs; the young pitch off their bikes, exercise too carelessly. People are grounded, heaped up here together, an arbitrary assortment of misfortune: middle-aged Maureen who borrowed a neighbor's stepladder to put up her new curtains, with disastrous consequences; young Karen who tried to overtake a bendy bus on her scooter; old Pat who braved an icy pavement, and should not have done. Ward C is exhausting—noisy, restless, you don't get a lot of sleep—but also perhaps in some ways an expedient distraction. You don't fret so much about your own distress when surrounded by other people's. You endure, but also observe; you become a beady eye, appreciating the spectacle.

"Like watching *Casualty*," says Rose. "Only you're in there too."

They are in the patients' Rest Room, to which the crutch-mobile shuffle, to receive their visitors. They have had the spare room conversation, Charlotte and Rose. The thing is settled; Rose is firm, Charlotte resigned. Charlotte is leaving the hospital next week; Rose will fetch her and install her in the spare room, which is being prepared, her clothes and other necessities brought from home.

"It's the day I was supposed to be going with Henry to Manchester," says Rose. "I've told him I can't."

"His lordship will be put out."

"He was." Rose is unperturbed. "It's all right—he's roped in his niece, Marion. The interior designer. She's got to do duty."

"Is she the heir?" demands Charlotte, who calls a spade a spade.

Rose shrugs. "No idea. Well, someone has to be, I suppose."

"Nice girl?"

"No girl, Mum. She's my age."

Charlotte sighs. "Of course. Talking of heirs, when I hand in my dinner-plate I want you to give a little something to Jennifer next door for her baby—a couple of hundred for his piggy-bank."

"Mum . . ."

"Not *much* . . ."

"Don't talk like that. You're not going to . . ."

"Well, not this afternoon, or indeed tomorrow, probably. But bear it in mind. Is she competent, this Marion? Will she get him there and back in one piece?"

"She's very organized. Runs a business. Doing up rich people's houses. She's got this showroom in her house—all too elegant for words. You can see her shuddering when she comes to Lansdale Gardens." Rose grins.

Charlotte has never been to Lansdale Gardens. "I thought it was quite grand?"

"There are some nice *things*. And the house is. But it's all a bit seedy, too."

Charlotte shifts in her seat, grimaces. Hip is giving her stick. Marion what's-her-name is a distraction. "People *pay* to be told what color their curtains should be? I'm on his lordship's side. Mail order ready-made always did me fine. Is she rich?"

"Nice clothes," says Rose. "But I really wouldn't know."

Marion is doing money at the desk in her office next to the showroom; she is also awaiting a call from her lover, and remembering that she has a client due in half an hour. Marion is good at doing money— careful, efficient, numerate—but is not in fact rich. Comfortable, yes, an adequate sufficiency, but one needs always to keep a sharp eye on the figures, on that irritating but manageable overdraft. Right now she is checking suppliers' bills and running through last month's bank statements and hoping that Jeremy will ring before she has to put the phone on answer while the client is here. Her mind is flicking also to Henry, and this tiresome matter of the Manchester trip next week, when she really cannot spare the time.

Thinking of money, she considers for a moment Henry's resources.

He is of course well off. That house. The lifestyle—his club, the pricey restaurants to which he goes from time to time. The minions—Rose, Corrie, who cleans and shops and does some cooking. Henry is . . . getting on. And has no relations except for Marion. Eventually someone has to inherit, unless all is destined for Oxfam or a cats' home.

Not that Marion considers this. Of course not. She has an affection for the old boy, he is after all her uncle, her only uncle. She respects him, too, he is something of a grand old man, no question; she has not been above dropping his name from time to time. If only he would let her do something about the Lansdale Gardens house; every time she goes there she shudders at that fearful old chintz sofa, those leather armchairs, the murky brown velvet curtains. As for the kitchen . . . But Henry dismisses the least proposal of change; Marion has not been able to infiltrate so much as a cushion.

"I am beyond the reach of good taste, my dear." A chuckle; good taste itself is in question, it would seem.

Marion rejects the term, of course. Hackneyed, meaningless. Effective decor is a matter of surprises, coordinations, contrasts; the unexpected rug, those interesting colors, that mirror. But no point in trying to explain this to Henry, for whom her trade is an amusing diversion, something with which she fills her time, an activity beyond his horizon. Henry is interested in powerful people, past and present, in good claret, in academic gossip, in writing his memoirs, and perhaps still, marginally, in eighteenth-century party politics, his original field of study. All of these are the central and seminal issues, so far as Henry is concerned; anything beyond can be a matter for idle and transitory comment but nothing more. Searching for conversational departures, Marion has sometimes talked of her clients; if they are prominent in some way Henry will be intrigued, even if their prominence is in areas unfamiliar to him. "Goldman Sachs? I've heard of it. *What* did you say this man earns? Outrageous!" Actors catch his attention: "The name rings a bell—not that I get to the theater so much these days. Of course I knew Alastair Sim at one time—did I ever tell you that?"

Henry has known many people. His conversation is laced with

names, most of them unknown to Marion, though there pops up the occasional recognizable celebrity. Henry has hobnobbed with leading politicians, has consorted with men and women of letters, he has known everyone who was anyone in the academic world.

Macmillan consulted him, as did Harold Wilson; he has tales to tell of Stephen Spender; Maurice Bowra was a chum. Oh, there is fuel enough for the memoirs, even if Marion's eyes glaze over, periodically, during tea or one of Corrie's rather awful lunches (Scotch broth, steak and kidney pie, treacle sponge pudding—Henry is a culinary conservative; Marion used to wonder how he managed in those posh restaurants to which he goes, but it seems that he knows the ones that cater for gastronomic retards). The names flow forth, and are rubbished or extolled, while Marion declines a sandwich or asks for a small helping, and wishes she could sneak in a new tablecloth. Sometimes, with Henry settled into cathartic discourse, she wistfully designs the entire room, sources wallpaper and curtain material, installs a lovely old Provençal table.

Marion has her own style, of course, her signature style, but where clients are concerned she is flexible—she wants to know what sort of thing they have in mind and then infuses that with her own suggestions and ideas. And of course they will have sought her out in the first place because they fancy the sort of thing she does—that fresh, appealing marriage of New England simplicity—the blues, the buffs, the painted floorboards—with French rustic and a touch of Kettle's Yard: the Arts and Crafts chair, the clever arrangement of shells or stones on a sill, an intriguing painting above the mantelpiece.

Marion's own house is the expression of all this. It is also her showcase: clients come there to be shown, and also to wander around the big ground floor room which displays fabrics, wallpapers, paint colors, objets d'art that Marion has picked up, the odd chair, table, lamp that nicely tunes in with the house style. Henry has seldom been here; when he has come he appeared to notice nothing. He would ensconce himself in one of the pretty pale linen-covered armchairs in the upstairs sitting-room, and hold forth as if in his own habitat. Henry does not see what does not concern him.

As someone who sees compulsively, Marion finds this both irritating and incomprehensible. Her mother shared her own interest in domestic interiors—home was elegant and considered. How can her brother be so entirely impervious? His own childhood backdrop was rather imposing—a Dorset country house stiff with antique pieces, good rugs, silver, the works. Not especially considered or contrived, but effective in its way. A few objects from there have fetched up at Lansdale Gardens, looking out of place: the seventeenth-century Italian cabinet amid the sagging leather armchairs of the sitting-room, the Regency mirror against the floral flock wallpaper of the hall. They are there not because Henry particularly appreciates them but because they are furnishings.

Marion's clients are people who furnish as an occupation. They have become rich by one means or another, they may as well spend the dosh, and their surroundings are of prime importance to them. They change house frequently, each new abode will require dressing from top to toe, and even if they stay put periodic make-overs will be necessary. Prime spenders will lay out many thousands on a single room; even Marion is sometimes surprised at their capacity, while grateful. She will find herself supervising the disposal of a whole lot of stuff not that long installed because the client got tired of swagged curtains and urban chic and likes the idea of Marion's calm palette and elegantly casual compositions. Sometimes sofas, chairs, hangings can be sold back to the original suppliers, who will be unsurprised. There is a cargo of interior adornments forever on the move, filtering from one mansion flat or bijou Chelsea terrace house to another.

This is how Marion met Jeremy Dalton—sourcing, not disposing. She was in need of the perfect fire surround for a client and had heard of this new place, just opened, in south London—an emporium, apparently, a cut above reclamation, just crammed with good things, run by some man with a genius for acquisition. So she had ferreted her way through an unfamiliar area and found this immense warehouse—a wealth of fire surrounds, Georgian through to art deco and beyond, you name it; stained glass panels, claw-foot baths, some mouthwatering Arts and Crafts pieces. And presently there was this man at her side, Jeremy someone—helpful, charming, funny, absolutely on her wavelength. They spent ages talking, then coffee in his office, with just the right fire surround sorted, and she'd have to come back when she'd had a further think about the little cane settee . . . And so it all began, the way things do.

That was nearly a year ago. Jeremy's wife Stella was not working with him in the business. She lived in Oxted, where he had had his previous, smaller, outlet, and was a doctor's receptionist. There were two teenage daughters. Complications, then. Marion herself was uncomplicated, being childless and tidily divorced a while back.

The situation must be kept under wraps, they agreed—at least for the foreseeable future: the daughters; Stella, who was excitable and had had a depressive episode in the past. But with Jeremy in London most of the time, spending many nights in the small rented flat near the warehouse, there was really no problem about seeing each other. Of course, he was away quite a bit in pursuit of stock, but that had made for several happy periods deep in Wales or up in Cumbria, with Marion snatching some time off. There were plans for an excursion to Provence in the summer, in search of old armoires and bedheads.

CHAPTER TWO

The Daltons' marriage broke up because Charlotte Rainsford was mugged. They did not know Charlotte, and never would; she would sit on the perimeter of their lives, a fateful presence.

The mobile phone was the smoking gun—Jeremy's mobile phone. He was at home in Oxted, unknown to Marion, when she left the message; she had thought him to be in the flat, had left a message on the mobile, which as it happened was in his coat pocket in the hall of the family home in Oxted. Jeremy had gone home for the night, at Stella's behest, to sort out a problem with a blocked wastepipe; Stella had a tendency to get in a state about minor domestic mishaps.

Jeremy had found himself without a requisite tool, and had driven off to see if a neighbor could help (the Daltons lived down an isolated lane). Meanwhile, Stella was anxious about the daughters, who were late back, and had discovered that the land-line was out of order. She searched for her own mobile, and realized that she had left it at the surgery. She would have to use Jeremy's to try to locate Daisy and Emma. Taking it from his coat pocket, she went first to Messages: conceivably they would have left a message here, foiled by the errant land-line and Stella's own not-answering phone.

Thus, Stella found Marion's message: "I can't make it on Friday. Have to escort Uncle Henry to Manchester—his PA out of action. Bother, bother. I'm so sorry. Love you."

It was the "love you" that did it, of course. Otherwise—just a message from some female associate who might not have given pause for thought (though perhaps a bit intimate in tone . . .).

Oh, this betraying technology. Jeremy deletes his messages; he is assiduous about this, given the circumstances, but this time the technology was one step ahead (just doing its job); he has not had the chance. When he returned, Stella was waiting by the door, and all hell broke loose.

Marion arrived at Lansdale Gardens in a taxi to collect Henry and go on to Euston for the Manchester train. She was slightly late, and much distracted. She had slept badly, unsettled by a long phone conversation with Jeremy the evening before. Apparently Stella had initially tried to throw him out, there and then, charging back upstairs to hurl his clothes into a suitcase. He had managed to talk her into a holding position (the girls would be back at any moment, simply not fair to upset them, talk things through tomorrow, stupid to rush into something they might regret) but the position had not held: Stella had gone on the rampage the next day—hysterical outbursts, tearful phone call to her sister, renewed demands for his departure. Jeremy was now in London, continuing to negotiate with the increasingly volatile Stella. She was talking lawyers. Her sister had got on to Jeremy and told him that he would be held responsible if this situation compromised Stella's fragile mental equilibrium: did he not remember that breakdown four years ago?

Marion had tried to be soothing and level-headed. She felt her own situation to be eminently undesirable. No one wants to break up a marriage; no one wants to be seen as the blunt instrument. Both she and Jeremy had thought that the status quo could go on indefinitely; both were a touch uncertain that this relationship was forever, though neither would have admitted as much to the other, at this relatively early stage. Time would tell, both had been privately thinking, while enjoying an invigorating liaison, an unexpected tonic. But now they were scuppered.

So Marion lay awake, then plunged into fitful sleep at five in the morning, and surfaced to a rushed shower and breakfast. When she reached Lansdale Gardens she felt light-headed; Henry's robust welcome was jarring. Here was a man who had clearly had a good night's sleep and was looking forward to the day ahead.

"Hello, hello. Taxi all set, is it? Rose has left the tickets and everything on my desk—just a question of grabbing them and we're off." He vanished into the downstairs cloakroom. Marion looked at herself in the Regency mirror, yawned, attempted a quick makeup repair. Henry emerged, fussed around the house looking for his keys and getting into his coat, and they went down the front steps to the waiting taxi.

At Euston, Marion looked at the departure board, and turned to Henry for the tickets. At which point both realized what had happened. Each had assumed that the other had taken the tickets from Henry's desk. Along with the letter from the university about where to go, and Henry's lecture notes.

Consternation and exasperation were gracefully contained: this was a public place. "My fault *entirely*," Marion (inwardly cursing him). "I didn't make myself clear," said Henry (feeling that he damn well had—oh, Rose, where art thou?). Marion set about quick remedial work: replacement tickets, assurances to Henry that she could get through to Manchester on her mobile for instructions, once they were on the train. Henry said grimly that he would have to spend the journey putting together some emergency notes; one had after all given this particular lecture God knows how many times before. "Politics and Personalities in the Age of Walpole" should more or less trip from the tongue.

Once settled in the train both fell silent. Marion had found a notepad in her bag for Henry to use; he delved for his pen and stared frowning at the paper; she set to work on the mobile and eventually achieved a helpful voice at Manchester University.

The midlands rolled by. Henry made the occasional note. Marion appeared to be reading the paper but was far too distracted to concentrate. She was thinking of the Jeremy situation, and realizing that this could not have come at a worse time. Both she and Jeremy had problems already, over and above the pressures of a clandestine love affair.

Marion was experiencing a sharp fall in client numbers; Henry's portfolio was nothing like as plump as it had been, and Jeremy was having difficulty in borrowing from the bank to fund his recent business expansion. The indigent couple (and the many others like them) do not come into this story; they are relevant, but they are hunkered down nameless out of sight, much as Charlotte Rainsford lurks on the perimeter of the Daltons' lives. Were it not for them, things would have been different.

Henry was not much bothered about the depletion of his portfolio; he had a nice index-linked pension, and plenty of cash on deposit. Marion, on the other hand, was worried. She had only a couple of serious money clients on her books at the moment; the phone rang less often, fewer people looked in at the showroom. Even the well-off were tightening their belts, it would seem. Smaller bonuses to fling around, other businesses feeling the pinch, just like her own; no make-over of the house this year, no holidays in the Seychelles, Bermuda and Klosters. Without work in hand, the overdraft—hitherto nicely under control—would start to climb. The notion of debt scared Marion; solvency was decency.

Jeremy had borrowed heavily to acquire the warehouse; he now needed more cash for some improvements and repairs. He had rushed to get the place up and running, to install stock and bring the punters in, and was now realizing various deficiencies. The derelict junk-yard needed to be made into a viable car park—customers were complaining about the lack of parking in the area. They were complaining equally about the disagreeable toilet facility, and you could see them always looking around for somewhere to sit down for a few minutes. Jeremy was determined to do up an elegant customer reception area, and install a proper cloakroom. The banks were less enthusiastic.

Henry found that note-taking became tedious. He dozed off a couple of times, woke to jot down a few more points, accepted another coffee from the trolley. He was not too concerned, confident enough that the complexities of eighteenth-century politics would spring readily to mind once he was on his feet in the lecture theater, though he was annoyed that the wording of a particular witticism escaped him for the moment. Never mind, it would arrive once he was under way, in full flow. He was after all known for his fluency and spontaneity—not for nothing had he been in demand as a speaker on both sides of the Atlantic. All the same, it was tiresome not to feel that he had the ballast of his old outline of this lecture; Rose would have seen to it, too bad she had had to let him down, good of Marion to come but so far her performance fell short. Henry made a few more notes, irritated now, and then sat back to stare at the passing scenery, and doze again.

They arrived in Manchester and progressed seamlessly from the station to the university, where suitably deferential officials were standing by to conduct them to the lunch. Henry cheered up. He always enjoyed being lionized. There were twenty or so people for the lunch party; it had clearly been made an occasion for the university to entertain some of its supporters. Captains of industry, Marion saw, skimming down the guest list, local bigwigs. This was an annual event; the lecture by a visitor of distinction.

Henry had the Vice-Chancellor to one side of him, and a Professor someone on the other—a youngish man to whom he turned with a benign inquiry about his field of interest: "Know your name, of course," (he didn't) "but can't for the moment recall . . ."

The man grinned. Said that he believed Henry would have known his old tutor, way back—contemporaries, he rather thought. He mentioned the name, a smile still on his lips. He knew all too well of what he spoke: this was one of Henry's archenemies, a man with whom he had waged intellectual war for many a year. Henry represents—with pride, let it be said—the last gasp of the Namier school of history, the insistence that events are governed entirely by politics and persons. The old enemy was an ideas man, a political theorist, nicely contemptuous of that reductionist vision of how the world works. And now here was one of his disciples, one of his acolytes. The old enemy was dead, so Henry had the advantage of him there, but he was serving up this ace from beyond the grave. His protégé had a Chair. A rather prestigious Chair, indeed: Henry had managed a glance at the guest list.

The day was now tarnished. Henry made a few chill remarks to the man, who was polite—urbane, indeed—self-confident, and appeared to be suppressing amusement. Henry abandoned him as soon as possible and took refuge in the Vice-Chancellor.

Marion, meanwhile, was doing rather better. She had engaged at once with the man to her right, who introduced himself as "George Harrington—a pleasure to meet you, Mrs. Clark. I gather you're looking after our distinguished visitor. And are you also in academic life?" Marion told him what she did; her trade sounded distinctly lightweight in the context of the occasion and the company but Harrington displayed interest, asked questions.

"How satisfying—creative and constructive. I'm just a money man, I'm afraid." He named a financial institution. "One of those people everyone hates at the moment." A wry smile. "Though actually I do have a little personal sideline that is more in your area."

He bought and restored flats in London for rental purposes, it emerged. "It's a sort of hobby, I suppose, a diversion. I even see it as vaguely creative"—an apologetic laugh—"making something pleasant out of something neglected. I cater for the top end of the market—foreign diplomats, businesspeople. It's pretty low down the creative scale, but an antidote to the day job—figures, figures, figures. But my creativity is limited—I'm good at the bricks and mortar side but I can be all at sea when it comes to bathroom fittings and curtains. My PA helps out but I'm not sure she always gets it right."

Marion was paying close attention. She liked this man: his self-deprecating manner, which masked, she suspected, considerable status within his own world. This was some rather high-up money man, for sure. He had a certain charm, but not too much—Marion was well aware that charm can be both self-serving and deceptive. His talk was entertaining: a recent visit to China and the disconcerting food encountered, the temporary loss of his BlackBerry a few days ago, rendering him "helpless and useless, a salutary experience, we are only as good as our technology these days." His financial institution had funded some new IT installations for the university, which was why he had been invited here: "Though after the BlackBerry event I wonder if we are doing them a favor." He encouraged Marion to talk of her own life, was amused by her account of the search for a marble bath to meet the requirements of an opera singer. "I can see you have to be versatile—take the client's deplorable taste on the chin. I too have to pander to clients, but at least it doesn't involve marble baths."

Both paid token attention to their neighbors on the other side, but resumed the conversation as soon as possible. It came as no surprise to Marion when George Harrington said, "You know, I am wondering if perhaps you might be the answer to a prayer."

Marion, who had been wondering the same thing, inclined her head gracefully. This could be interesting. She was not taken in by the "hobby" talk. His was an investment project, she could see—buy to let, no need to get fancy about diversions and creativity. George Harrington was using his handsome bonuses to build up a property portfolio. Fine. A sensible thing to do, no doubt, if you've got surplus cash.

"Let's have a talk, back in town," he said. "I think we could work out some rather nice arrangement. Give my PA a break—the poor girl's overstretched looking for sofas and I don't know what. Can you do—you know, that business where you have just one elegant chair and a glass table with a vase on it, and goodness knows where they're supposed to put down their newspaper?"

"Minimalist," said Marion. "Yes, I can do minimalist, if pressed. And oriental—Chelsea Arabian Nights. And Cotswold manor. Traditional American a specialty."

George Harrington beamed. "This is most exciting. What very good luck that Manchester brought us together in this way."

"It's only by chance that I'm here," said Marion. "My uncle's secretary's mother . . . Oh, we needn't go into that." She too was smiling.

Cards were exchanged. The lunch drew to a close.

Once in the lecture hall, Henry's spirits rose somewhat. This was after all his natural habitat. He listened appreciatively to the Vice-Chancellor's introduction, rose and moved to the lectern during the audience's suitably welcoming applause, smiled around the room, said what a pleasure and an honor to be here today, so forth and so on, and launched into the eighteenth century.

For the first few minutes, fine. He was on autopilot—the introductory stuff. The general picture, the setting of the scene. Then to the detail: the defining political moves, the names. That was when everything came unstuck. This infinitely familiar scene dissolved into mist, this period that he knew better than his own time, the age in which he moved with absolute confidence, became uncertain, betraying; the chronology escaped him, he started to get things in the wrong order. The notes he had made in the train were useless; they merely confused him. And the names, the names . . . He would begin to speak of a key figure and the man's name would have vanished into a black hole. Henry hesitated, he stumbled, he corrected himself. He had to resort to the most appalling, blatant circumlocutions: "Walpole's confidant . . . Walpole's right-hand man . . ." He had lost his grip on the contents of his own mind: he *knew* these names, he *knew* the events, they were the element in which he lived—had lived—but now, suddenly, they had slithered into some pit from which he could not retrieve them. He waffled, he digressed, he gave himself pauses in which to retrench, to delve wildly for that *name*. He was fighting his way through a nightmare; from time to time he sensed an audience that was both restless and embarrassed. The Vice-Chancellor, in the front row, stared ahead with a fixed expression. Next to him, Henry's other lunchtime neighbor looked down at his own shoes, concealing perhaps a smirk.

At last, Henry managed to bring things to a close. Polite applause. The Vice-Chancellor joined him on the platform. Would Henry care to take a few questions? Henry would, with clenched teeth.

The first question he could deal with, just. And then someone wanted to quiz Henry on the later part of the century. Would Henry like to comment on the relative roles of the prime minister before and after 1750?

Henry began to speak. And as he did so he realized with horror that he could not remember the names of the late eighteenth-century prime ministers. The Elder and the Younger. Elder and Younger *what*?

Name. The name? He spoke; he avoided, he danced away from the crucial word, he sounded odder and odder, he skirted, he fluffed, he knew that it was becoming obvious. And then at last the name surfaced: Pitt, Pitt, Pitt. He flung it out, triumphant, but too late: the puzzled faces before him told him that.

Almost never before had Henry experienced humiliation. Occasional embarrassment, yes—moments when one had been at a loss, or when one was aware that one had not performed quite up to scratch. But not this total, absolute chagrin. He felt as though he had been flayed, mercilessly exposed to the scornful gaze of all those strangers. He wanted only to get away from this place, to end this horrid day, to be on the train, heading home, but was obliged to proceed to a room where tea was on offer, and submit himself to strained conversation. He could see only derision, he thought, in the eyes that he tried to avoid. His old enemy's protégé came up, smiling sweetly, and made some comment about a recent publication on eighteenth-century politics that Henry had not read. Henry sipped his tea, inclined his head, and was silent. From somewhere far away, the old enemy was jeering.

At last, he and Marion were back on the train. It suddenly occurred to Henry that she had not previously heard him lecture; perhaps she thought it was always like that.

He said, heavily, "I suppose you realize that that was a disaster."

She had. She could not think what to say. "Not a *disaster*, Uncle Henry. I did feel those bright lights must have been rather distracting for you . . . And those people who came in late . . ."

"A disaster," said Henry.

"Your notes," sighed Marion. "*All* my fault."

"No," said Henry, surprisingly. "Not your fault. Anno bloody domini. Suddenly I knew nothing—nothing—about the eighteenth century. Can you conceive of that?"

That period, for Marion, meant certain furnishings and styles: Chippendale, Hepplewhite, Robert Adam. Stripes. Tottery little tables. The names so devastatingly lost to Henry would have meant nothing to her anyway. One had got through life quite easily knowing nothing much of the eighteenth century.

She suggested a drink. She would look for the chap with the trolley.

Fortified with a half bottle of Virgin Trains red wine ("What is this fearful stuff?"), Henry became eloquent. "Let me tell you something, my dear. Old age is an insult. Old age is a slap in the face. It sabotages a fine mind—though I say it myself—until you can appear as ignorant and inarticulate as some . . . some assistant lecturer at a polytechnic." Henry ignored the fact that the polytechnics were long since laid to rest—they remained a term of abuse. "Some paralysis of the brain occurs. It's like . . . like being thrown into the pitch dark and you can't find the bloody door but you know it's there. Pitt, for Christ's sake! I couldn't remember Pitt's name. I couldn't remember anything about the South Sea Bubble. It's a suffocation of the intellect. One's mind—one's fine mind, if I may say so—becomes incompetent. Impotent. Yes, impotent." Henry stared intently at Marion, as though she might not be following him. "One cannot perform. One is emasculated. One . . ." Perhaps this line had gone far enough. "The long and short of it is that you can't bloody well remember what you were going to say next when you know perfectly well what it was."

"Poor Mummy used to ring up and then forget what she'd rung about," murmured Marion.

Henry waved a dismissive hand. "All right. The human condition. Which is no reason why one shouldn't protest. Which is what I'm doing. Vehemently. I have been made to look stupid through no fault of my own. That is an outrage."

Marion nodded. She agreed, with fervor. She made a little moue of sympathy. At the same time, she was thinking of George Harrington, with a certain complacency. This might turn out to have been a rather fortunate encounter; at best, a solution to her declining revenue. Work; lucrative work, maybe. A bit of luck, really, that Uncle Henry's Rose had had to "let him down" today.

Henry finished his wine and fell into a doze. Cruising that interface between sleep and wakefulness, he found himself in a seminar room, required it seemed to discuss Hobbes and the concept of liberty.

His old enemy stared at him expectantly, flanked by acolytes. The room they were in was rocking and swaying. One of the acolytes rose to his feet and said that the buffet car was now serving hot and cold drinks, sandwiches and snacks. Henry surfaced, to a splitting headache and a certain sense of relief. Hobbes—Christ!

Jeremy Dalton also had a disagreeable day. He made further attempts at conciliation with Stella; she either hung up on him, or wept hysterically. By late afternoon her sister was with her, and came on the line to say briskly that Stella was in no condition to talk and that Jeremy had better not get in touch for the moment. She, Gill, the sister, might contact him in a day or two. Stella had seen her doctor and was on tranquilizers.

Jeremy was not accustomed to adultery. He had done it a few times before, but these had been transitory matters. Now, he was branded, condemned, sentenced, and all because of a change of plans and a message. So . . . so fortuitous. So unfair, in a way. The situation as it was—had been—really wasn't hurting Stella. Their married life was going on as it ever had done; he was home as much as his work allowed, he was an attentive father, he and Stella—well, when you've been married nearly twenty years you're not in the first flush of passion, are you? But there was nothing basically *wrong*; Stella of course was inclined to fits of depression, and frequent manic reactions, he'd learned to live with that, to manage her, in a way. She was needy, he knew that, you had to pander to that, but all in all they got along well enough; sexually, things were fine, unless Stella was in one of her states, and anyway he wasn't a man who always felt the grass would be greener elsewhere. Until Marion hove on the scene, and he found her most attractive, and so invigorating, and there was always so much to talk about and . . . well, before he knew what was happening he was entirely involved with her, in bed, out of bed, and not really feeling all that guilty because this wasn't going to interfere with his life with Stella and the girls. Almost certainly not.

But now it had. Everything had gone up in smoke; that blasted woman Gill had muscled in, Stella was allegedly heading for another breakdown, the girls had been told that Daddy would be away indefinitely on business. Marion had been a comfort, on the phone; rational, soothing. Look, just take things day by day, try to get past this tiresome sister, talk to Stella when she's calmed down, everything always looks a bit different after a week or two. She wasn't saying—well, there's us to think about too, you and me, what do *we* want? And he was grateful for that; he didn't really know what he did want, except that he was a man who didn't care for upheaval, and things weren't good at all on the financial front, and he certainly couldn't let himself in for anything that involved expense. Let alone divorce.

Jeremy may seem a somewhat contradictory figure. Here is someone whose occupation is the acquisition and disposition of a superior form of junk—reclamation, after all, is just that—who spent most of his days scouring the landscape for the antique doors, wash basins, chimney pots, old brewery signs, cast iron radiators that one person did not want but another would, and the rest of his time prowling around amid the heaped, piled, stacked confusion of his wares; a man who worked with random chaos, but for whom a stable and orderly base was a necessity. He liked to know that the carefully restored farmhouse in Oxted was always there. And his girls. And Stella.

Jeremy did not see his wares as superior junk, or himself as a serendipitous junk-hunter. Of course not. He saw himself as a connoisseur, as a skilled investigator. He knew how to study sales catalogues and estate agents' Web sites; he could smell out any mansion prime for stripping and be there at the point when the builders got going. He knew just how casual an interest to display before handing over a wad of notes and getting on the phone to the guys who did the heavy work for him. He knew the thrill of the chase, the discovery: the overmantel spotted jutting from a pile of rubble, the stained glass panel behind some smashed-up kitchen fittings. You never knew what might surface, but when you saw it you recognized it at once: that supposedly redundant artifact which could be given a new lease on life, that could spark acquisitive fire in a customer. The railway waiting-room clock, the wrought iron gate, the intriguing tiles, the church pew.

Jeremy had passion—that overworked word of the moment. Passion for his stock, passion for the pursuit of stock. Passion is infectious; Jeremy's enthusiasm, his stream of comment and information, could fire up a customer so that suddenly they realized they could not live a moment longer without that Victorian grate. Jeremy was not so much a salesman as an evangelist; he wanted others to share his fascination with the stuff that time discards. People came away from the warehouse (with the Victorian grate, the Edwardian glass) feeling not that they had been sold something but that they had understood how to see and appreciate.

It was this quality that had attracted Marion, initially. She had enjoyed drifting with him through the warehouse as he pointed things out: ". . . last week from this extraordinary castle place in Wales, I hope nobody wants it, I can't bear to part with it . . . and just *look* over here . . ." She too knew the excitement of discovery, of recognition, the rush you get from your own discerning eye. She warmed at once to Jeremy; this was her kind of man. Why hadn't Harry been like that? But Harry, ex-husband, was history. To be honest, she did not that often think of him. Nor had she been in the market for a replacement until Jeremy appeared. And even then . . . She had seen the situation as a delightful, unexpected adventure. But now they were compromised, forced into something darker, more guilty, by Stella's extravagant reaction.

And what of Stella?

Jeremy is relaxed, pragmatic, he deals unfazed with what comes along. Stella is clenched, strung tight as a wire, waiting for the next inevitable blow: the girls will break a limb, Jeremy will get cancer, the house will fall down. And when these hold off, so far, there is always winter flu, the car packing up, the cat run over, a blocked pipe. Ah, that blocked wastepipe.

In fact, nothing much has ever happened to Stella. She has seldom been ill, has never been seriously short of money, her children are healthy and compliant. Jeremy courted and married her because she was small, neat and so pretty, and she came along at the right time—the conjunction of availability and the moment that triggers most marriages. He told her he adored her, which he did, right then; she was happy to adore back.

Twenty years ago. Since when both Jeremy and Stella have discovered her propensity to collapse. Disaster is not necessary; Stella can go into meltdown for no very evident reason. There was that major event a few years ago, requiring alarming medications and specialist treatment. She is basically vulnerable, said the sister, staring hard at Jeremy. Stella herself admits as much. I just don't know what happens, she says—mystified, mortified—I don't seem able to hang on. You will need to watch her, Gill orders Jeremy—the responsible older sister; no stress, no shocks.

So Stella's present state is Jeremy's fault entirely. He acknowledges this, with a few wry thoughts about that betraying mobile. Offstage, Charlotte Rainsford, catalyst, is settling into her room at Rose's house and, elsewhere, a juvenile delinquent is going about his (or her) business.

CHAPTER THREE

Henry has lived in London for years, or rather, he has existed on a particular one of London's planes. He lives in his white stucco house in an expensive postcode, and goes forth to his club in Pall Mall, to Wiltons or Rules, to Covent Garden (a couple of times a year), to the Royal Academy and the Tate and the British Library and the British Museum. He visits the House of Lords less and less frequently; the debates are tedious, the company dismayingly mixed nowadays, and the food appalling. He uses buses whose routes are familiar to him, finding the Freedom Pass that Rose obtained most satisfactory (one doesn't need to fumble for change). On the buses his plane intersects with those of many others—people who are ignorant of the British Museum and the Royal Academy, whose own London backdrop would be as alien to Henry as a North African souk or downtown Moscow, just as the destination of many of the buses are entirely mysterious to him—Clapton Pond, Whipp's Cross, Hackney Wick.

London is said to be an agglomeration of villages; not at all, London is a vast entity within which people move around, each upon their own exclusive level, ignoring all that is unknown and irrelevant. In the buses, Henry is sometimes aware that there do not seem to be many others like him—elderly white male wearing suit and tie, with raincoat over arm, and that the bus speaks in tongues, most of them unfamiliar to him. In his youth, the Britain of fifty years ago, he recognized the class divide, both as a social phenomenon and something you were aware of all around you; there were distinct planes of existence then, oh dear me, yes. But today's disparate and polyglot populace is another matter; you cannot place anyone in context, you cannot judge prosperity, hazard a guess at occupation, know if this person would speak English, Russian, Bulgarian, Serbo-Croat, Urdu, Pashto. From time to time, Henry stares at his fellow travelers on the bus and feels disoriented. What has gone on here? The society of his youth was a familiar territory; you knew where you were with it, and moreover it related to history: he saw also from whence it sprang, he saw its origins in the nineteenth century, and in his own personal patch, the eighteenth. Behind and beyond it lay the long slow metamorphosis of this country. In the mind's eye, the centuries were laid out, heading toward today, with significant developments flagged up: Civil War, Reform Act, universal suffrage. But none of that could have been seen to lead to this.

Truth to tell, Henry is not that interested. His professional concern has been the past, and the present has caught his attention only when relevant to himself: who was what in academia, and beyond it the people he knew or felt he should know, or had heard of. He has devoted himself to intense scrutiny of eighteenth-century political life but his fellow citizens and their circumstances are not, on the whole, of much concern to him. He keeps up with political affairs, of course, has always made sure to be acquainted with a few key people at Westminster; he would have views on most issues of the day. But he is without curiosity, when it comes to those around him; they exist, and that is all there is to it. Crucial political factors, of course, in a democratic society, but without individual significance.

Today, Henry is on the 19 bus, heading for the Royal Academy. It is a few days only since the Manchester debacle, and he has not recovered. He seethes still with humiliation. He sees again and again the complacent face of his old adversary's protégé. He replays the Vice-Chancellor's words of farewell, and detects patronage, even, possibly, mild contempt for one whose day is done. The situation is unbearable; one made a fool of oneself—was made a fool of, by anno bloody domini.

He must do something. He must redeem himself. He must demonstrate capacity, power, prestige. Publish something.

Publish what?

Well, the memoirs, in due course. But they are far from comple-
tion, and some immediate measure is required.

A letter to *The Times*? One has written many letters to *The Times*,
over the years; always a good idea to keep one's name in the public
eye. But *The Times* has lost its clout, and anyway on what would one
write?

No, something more substantial is required. A long piece in *The
Times Literary Supplement*, or a leading academic journal, demonstrating that one is still very much a figure to be reckoned with. Something provocative, contentious even, to set people talking. A new slant
on some aspect of the eighteenth century.

What slant? Henry is in fact out of touch with the eighteenth century. He stopped thinking much about it a number of years ago, he
has not kept up with new publications. The eighteenth century has
moved on, leaving him behind. History is a slippery business; the past
is not a constant but a landscape that mutates according to argument
and opinion. Henry is well aware of this, and aware that the eighteenth century has disappeared over the horizon so far as he is concerned, reconstructed, reinterpreted.

No, better not stick one's neck out. Could be cut up by some young
turk. Not that one's own work does not remain the basis of Augustan
studies, in the opinion of any reputable scholar. Most reputable scholars, anyway.

She can crutch it to the bathroom. Rose and Gerry's spare bathroom;
their own is en suite, thanks be, so she is not getting in their way. She
can crutch it down the stairs, just, Rose and Gerry's stairs, waiting till
both have gone to work, and Rose will have left breakfast on the table,
Rose and Gerry's kitchen table, having brought up a cup of tea earlier, to
check that one has not croaked during the night. Rose is being kind,
tactful, she brings tears to the eyes; Gerry too is doing his best, he insists

that one has his end of the sofa, from whence the TV is best viewed, he is always offering the newspaper.

Charlotte is doing what she would not wish to do—living with her daughter and son-in-law. She is filled with resentment and compunction. The resentment is not directed toward Rose, whom she loves to distraction, but toward the malign fate that has forced her into this situation. The compunction is because Rose and Gerry are obliged to do this, to have their marital privacy invaded, to have this perpetual third in their home. Yes, yes, Rose is doing it not just because she knows she ought to, but also because she is concerned, feels responsible and probably loves her mother back, though this is not a matter that is ever bandied around between them. Neither are people who brandish affection.

That said, all this should not be. Charlotte should be in her own home; out of sight although not out of mind, of course not. Rose and Gerry should be enjoying the intimacy of marriage, if enjoy is what they do and one has always hoped and prayed so. The days when the indigent, dependent old had to be stacked up by the fireplace, fed, grumbled at, nudged toward the grave, are long gone. There are arrangements now, state provision.

"Home help," she had said. "Coming in every day . . ."

Rose had had that set look, long known, experienced first when Rose was three, four, five. "No."

"Really, that would be fine."

"*No.*"

Rose was a good child, she never gave trouble, but there was always that small, firm core of resistance. If she wasn't going to, she wouldn't, and you didn't bother pushing the matter. Later, grown up, she did what she intended to do, and you knew better than to go on at her with disapproval or alternatives. She chose to go to one of the lesser universities because a friend was going there; Charlotte made a protest, and then subsided, knowing herself ignored. Then there was office work that was leading nowhere, and then the children, who were fine and thank heaven for them, and at that point his lordship did indeed seem a useful interim job while the children needed Rose, but there she still is, interim it apparently was not. So Charlotte eyed Henry with a certain disdain, he who has consumed Rose's working life, had her dance attendance on him when she might have . . . Oh, I know, I know, says Charlotte, hearing what Rose has never said, I know you never wanted a *career*, but even so . . .

Charlotte had not known that she herself wanted a career; she fell into one because she was so good at what she did. She began to teach, with her nice new shiny degree in English, back in the heady 1960s, which for some were all about miniskirts and the Beatles (and indeed Charlotte wore a miniskirt), but for her this was the time of liberation (yes, the word of the day) and the realization that there was something she could do, and do very well, and enjoy. She could persuade young and pliant minds to appreciate reading in the way that she did herself; she could take the set texts on an exam syllabus and bring them alive, she could stand in front of a class and see attention on every face. She could glow with satisfaction as she read an appreciative, intelligent essay. She rose through the system; she moved to a more celebrated school. She could have had a headship but did not want one; she wanted to be in the classroom. She ended up as Head of English at one of the most prestigious of girls' schools in north London, showering her pupils around the nation's universities, a legend to many of them: Mrs. Rainsford who could have you mesmerized by *Macbeth* on a wet Monday afternoon when you had a cold and your boyfriend had dumped you and A levels were only a month off.

So there it was, there it had been, a teaching life, a career if you must call it that, and Charlotte now looks back on it with a certain satisfaction, and then scolds herself for being smug. I was a conduit, she thinks, that's all. I was lucky enough to have the knack of transmission—I could get them to see and hear a poem, to absorb a novel. The power is in the stuff itself—language; all you have to do is show the way.

In Rose and Gerry's house, Charlotte misses her books. Her familiar walls, lined with language. Rose and Gerry have books, of course, but not so many, nothing like, and some of them are wonderfully obscure, to her eye, and that is in itself a challenge. She has spent a morning with Gerry's *Handbook to Coarse Fishing*, and learned a lot. Equally his manuals on carpentry and home repairs, though here her eyes began to glaze over after a while.

Gerry is fifty-four, and seems to have been that since he was twenty-seven, when he and Rose were married. He was one of those young who are not, in whom you spot already the older self, peering out, waiting to take over. He was cautious, reserved, pragmatic. She and Tom had told each other that he was a nice, sensible chap, he'd do fine for Rose, stable, not someone who'd go off the rails. Neither wished to find fault; any doubts were unspoken. Is he a wee bit dull? Charlotte had wondered. Of course, one doesn't really *know* him.

She does, now, probably. In so far as one knows a person. She knows Gerry's political views (temperate), his tendency to indigestion, politely concealed, his reluctance to get into argument, his worry that he may be going bald (he is), his few intense dislikes (unpunctuality, garlic, Spain, the tabloid press, German shepherd dogs). The aversion to Spain stems from a family holiday there many years ago, when it seems there was a contretemps with a Spanish hotelier about inadequate facilities. The German shepherds would appear to have to do with his childhood—better not to inquire.

Charlotte is entirely used to Gerry. He has been a part of the landscape of her life for a long while now. He is Rose's husband, and that is that. Occasionally she thinks of her own dear man, by contrast, and then pushes the thought away. Tom who was vigorous, spontaneous, filled with energy and curiosity, who, like her, could teach the socks off most of his peers, who was head-hunted from school to school. Tom who was unfairly snuffed out at fifty, one of those beastly galloping early cancers, nothing they could do, just the two of you holding hands a lot, moving from day to day, waiting.

Charlotte sits in Rose and Gerry's kitchen, eating breakfast and reading Gerry's *Telegraph*, which in fact reads pretty oddly, if you are used to the *Guardian*. The hip aches, but not unbearably, one has known worse, much worse. Later, she will attempt a hike to the front gate, though Rose would prefer that she did not, for fear of falling, and Rose will not be back till half-past one, when she has done with his lordship.

If Charlotte was at home, her day would be filled. Getting up with *The Today Program* (occasionally interrupting John Humphrys), breakfast with the *Guardian*, tidy the kitchen, do a bit of cleaning, put on a wash, walk to the shops, lunch with a book propped up in front of her—one of the few mitigating factors of life alone is that you can read during meals without giving offense—a rest on the sofa, then whatever needs doing in the afternoon—letters, a spell in the garden, her shift at the adult literacy class on Tuesdays and Thursdays, then the evening with plenty more reading time and whatever is acceptable on the telly.

None of that now, except the reading. She has a stack of books from home with her, and has commissioned Rose to get a new paperback she wants. So the most important thing is still available, though somehow reading was more savored when kept for those special periods in the day. When you can do it any old time it is less cherished. And her concentration is all askew: the medications, the nagging hip.

Forever, reading has been central, the necessary fix, the support system. Her life has been informed by reading. She has read not just for distraction, sustenance, to pass the time, but she has read in a state of primal innocence, reading for enlightenment, for instruction, even. She has read to find out how sex works, how babies are born, she has read to discover what it is to be good, or bad; she has read to find out if things are the same for others as they are for her—then, discovering that frequently they are not, she has read to find out what it is that other people experience that she is missing.

Specifically, she read bits of the Old Testament when she was ten because of all that stuff about issues of blood, and the things thou shalt not do with thy neighbor's wife. All of this was confusing rather than enlightening.

She got hold of a copy of *Fanny Hill* when she was eighteen, and was aghast, but also intrigued.

She read Rosamond Lehmann when she was nineteen, because her heart had been broken. She saw that such suffering is perhaps routine, and, while not consoled, became more stoical.

She read Saul Bellow, in her thirties, because she wanted to know how it is to be American. After reading, she wondered if she was any wiser, and read Updike, Roth, Mary McCarthy and Alison Lurie in further pursuit of the matter. She read to find out what it was like to be French or Russian in the nineteenth century, to be a rich New Yorker then, or a midwestern pioneer. She read to discover how not to be Charlotte, how to escape the prison of her own mind, how to expand, and experience.

Thus has reading wound in with living, each a complement to the other. Charlotte knows herself to ride upon a great sea of words, of language, of stories and situations and information, of knowledge, some of which she can summon up, much of which is half lost, but is in there somewhere, and has had an effect on who she is and how she thinks. She is as much a product of what she has read as of the way in which she has lived; she is like millions of others built by books, for whom books are an essential foodstuff, who could starve without.

So, this morning, Charlotte settles herself on Rose's sofa, after breakfast, and opens *The House of Mirth*, which is part of a deliberate program to revisit books that have been influential for her in the past, and see if they still taste the same. But after five minutes or so her attention starts to stray; she is looking out of the window, not at the book, staring at Gerry's meticulously clipped garden hedge while her thoughts drift, unfocused—she simply sits there, and realizes suddenly that half an hour has passed. She reads a few pages, relapses once more, is gazing at the hedge, at a white butterfly dancing along it, at a plane forging across the sky above.

The morning is half gone. She gets up, crutches it to the kitchen, makes a cup of coffee. This will not do, she thinks. I cannot spend the next few weeks in a trance. If reading is to fail me thus, then something else must be found.

She cannot do useful things around the house, because of the crutches, and anyway Rose would not hear of it. She cannot get out and about. Today is her adult literacy class, where she is not. The class floats into her head, person by person. There is Lesley, who is in her forties, had some debilitating illness in childhood, missed much schooling, emerged unable to read, and has somehow got by ever since with subterfuge and the help of her family. There are the Bangladeshi mother and daughter, who cannot read or write in their own language, let alone English, but are now triumphantly mastering whole sentences. There is Dan, in his late fifties, a builder and heaven alone knows how *he* has got by, but he has, by dint of a compendious memory and a wife who does the office work; Dan has been propelled to the class by becoming a grandfather, he would like to be able to read to the kids, and this of all motives has Charlotte fervently at his side, wishing that there was more scope for one-on-one attention. There is seventy-year-old Liz, who has been bullied into coming by her daughter but doesn't actually give a hang whether she learns to read or not, she's got along all right without all her life, hasn't she? Yes, it's a nuisance sometimes in the shops, but you can always ask someone. There is eighteen-year-old Paul, who also missed much schooling, was labeled dyslexic, but is not, he just needs patient coaching. There is the girl who is half Somali, half English, born here, and quite why she has had so little school is a mystery; thereby hangs a tale, no doubt, but she is making headway at last, a confident finger rushing from word to word. There is Anton, a newcomer, a soft-spoken man, central European of some kind—Charlotte hasn't gathered from where—his spoken English good but some block where reading is concerned. That is why he is on an adult literacy course, rather than English-as-a-foreign-language; reading is the problem, not speech.

Teaching people how to read is a far cry from teaching teenagers how to appreciate reading. Sometimes, Charlotte tries to see the words in the way that the members of the class must see them—black marks: shapes, lines, a baffling code that has to be cracked. She compares the mysterious eloquence of a page of Arabic or Japanese, to which one is blind. The members of her class move around shut off from the cacophony of advertising, the instruction of road signs, the information of newspaper headlines. They are in the world, but not entirely of it. Their inability to read is crippling; a failure to respond to literature is merely a restriction.

Charlotte drinks her coffee and considers. She is now focused. And the idea comes to her. She cannot get to the adult literacy class, but why should a member not come to her? Someone for whom extra coaching would be a godsend.

She makes a phone call to Marsha, the class coordinator. Marsha is delighted to hear from her, wants to know how she is doing, when they can hope to see her again. Charlotte is one of the most valued members of Marsha's team. Her innate skills as a communicator work just as well on getting people able to read as on the exegesis of *Pride and Prejudice* or the *Ode to Immortality*. Charlotte is a born teacher, that's all there is to it. "We need you back," says Marsha.

"Look," says Charlotte. "I'm wondering if . . ."

Marsha ponders. This is a touch irregular, but she doesn't see why not. The class is full to bursting, there are several people for whom some extra teaching would make all the difference. She ponders further. Then she makes a suggestion. What about Anton?

Charlotte is surprised. She had imagined the Bangladeshis, or maybe Dan.

But Marsha is pressing Anton. The thing is, she explains, that he is clearly highly intelligent, but for some reason he is not making progress. He is frustrated, he is somewhat out on a limb in the class— reserved, diffident, much more sophisticated; he could benefit greatly from some personal attention.

"Right," says Charlotte. "Let's have Anton then."

She makes a successful foray to the garden gate, her spirits lifted. Now she has a purpose, something to do, she can be useful.

Henry does not have anything to do. Or rather, he does not have that essential something. He has not identified a way of reestablishing his name, grabbing the attention of academia—no, of the cognoscenti generally. Restlessly, he sifts through his papers, in the service of the memoirs, in order to keep busy; all those files and boxes, in which are interred reputations, disputes, scholarly scandals. Could it be that the answer lies here?

He finds it on a Thursday morning, at around ten-thirty. He tips out the contents of an unpromising-looking wallet file without a label, and flicks through the pile of papers. Letters. Letters that have never been sorted and filed. Letters from a while ago, from way back; he is looking at the late 1960s here, when he was not yet forty, the rising star of academia, the clever young man who knew everyone, whom everyone wanted to know. He picks up a letter with House of Commons heading, glances at the signature. Ah. John Bradshaw—Labour elder statesman cultivated by Henry and who had taken Henry up, got him into that think tank, wined and dined him and fed him tidbits of political gossip.

Henry reads the letter, which is a quick note proposing a lunch and throwing out some digs at Harold Wilson, with whom Bradshaw is currently on bad terms. Not of great interest. Here's another—what's this one about?

Bradshaw is long dead. Henry has not much thought of him in years. He had quite forgotten he had those letters. He reads the second letter, with growing attention. What's this? Bradshaw is pushing an issue he wants taken up by the policy unit, and is talking about Hall, a fellow minister. "Hall agrees entirely about this—incidentally (strictest confidentiality here) he admitted to me that he's dead worried because he's been having an affair with Lydia Purkis. Of all people! Is trying to break it off—all very painful, deeply fond of her etc. Silly ass! My god, if the press get hold of this . . . Sleeping with the enemy and so forth, they'd go to town on it. We have to see they don't."

Henry had forgotten all about this choice nugget, buried here. Lydia Purkis was the wife of a Tory grandee, hence the shame of it—crossing party lines—though to be caught sleeping with anyone's wife, enemy or not, would be a resignation matter, probably, for a cabinet minister. But this never was. The press never did get on to it, the whole thing was whisked under the carpet, and all concerned are now dead.

Well, well. Henry sits with the letter in front of him, his mind ticking. A suppressed scandal, but the names are still familiar—there could still be an interest. Suppose . . . It occurs to Henry that there is a nice contrast here with misdemeanor in eighteenth-century high society—politicians, royalty—and the way in which it was lampooned by the pamphleteers and the cartoonists. Gillray, Rowlandson, Hogarth. Exposure was an art form; today it is the heavy hammer of the gutter press. This particular scandal never reached the red tops, but if it had the headlines would have screamed.

Henry has it. The idea. The answer.

An article for one of the broadsheet Sundays. An article ostensibly contrasting the eighteenth century's way of outing the misbehavior of the great and the good as opposed to the practices of today. A scholarly piece, which would cite instances from both periods, but which would slip in—quite offhand, as it were—this intriguing instance of a scandal that got away: ". . . a letter in my possession." Furthermore, this will be a trail for the memoirs—a hint of further interesting revelations.

Now—how to handle this?

Anton arrives for his first session a couple of days later. Charlotte had barely registered him, a new arrival to the class. She is struck now by his rather formal manners, his courtesy. She installs him in Rose's sitting-room, one afternoon (he can only do afternoons, apparently, he has a morning job), but he leaps anxiously to his feet when she gets up to look for paper, or put the kettle on for tea. Rose has gone to Brent Cross on a shopping expedition, so they will not be in the way. Charlotte now takes in Anton's appearance—a man pushing fifty, perhaps, neatly dressed in gray trousers, white open-necked shirt, black leather jacket. A lean body, long face, and notable eyes. He has these large, dark brown eyes that to Charlotte are interestingly foreign; these are not homely English eyes, they are eyes from elsewhere, central European eyes, eyes with forests in them, and Ruritanian castles, and music by Janáček or Bartók.

Anton can speak pretty good English, he understands well, but he has this great difficulty with reading the language. There is some mysterious block between English in the ear or on the tongue and English on the page.

He spreads his hands, a gesture of defeat, taps his head. "I am so stupid. It is here—but in the books I cannot see it."

Anton must be able to read. He explains: "If I read, I get good job. Without read—job, yes. With read—job I can like."

Anton is working on a building site, but he has none of the building trade skills. He is not a plumber, or an electrician, or a carpenter, he tells Charlotte. "I wish," he adds with a smile—that beguiling, apologetic smile.

So what is he, what has he been, when he was at home, Charlotte wonders, and why is he here? And Anton knows that she wonders. He was—is—an accountant, he tells her. But there are no jobs where he lives. He has tried other places, with no luck, he was jobless for months. And then came the EU membership, and the possibility of work outside the country. Work here, in the UK.

Anton's English was learned not at school but from contact with visiting English-speaking colleagues. He felt confident that he could manage, once here; he had not reckoned with this reading problem.

Anton is concerned about Charlotte's injury, and shakes his head angrily when he hears the reason for it. "That is terrible," he says. "A lady like you."

An old lady, he means. Charlotte smiles. "A soft target, I suppose. They prefer not to take on the young and fit."

Anton looks puzzled. She translates herself. "Soft target—something easy to . . . to hit."

He sighs. "English is so . . . so many ways to say. But my language like that also." A wry smile—and Charlotte glimpses the easy fluency in another tongue, the ability to say exactly what he means, but now he is floored, fettered by this lack of language, made to seem child-like, stupid.

"Your English is not so bad at all," she says. "And it will get better all the time, the longer you are here."

She has made tea; this is an acclimatization moment; she wants to get to know him better. "So how long have you been here?"

Anton has been in England for six weeks. He is staying in a house in south London that is an enclave of his compatriots; mattresses on floors, communal meals. Those who land a decent job move out to a bed-sit or a flat-share. Some are seasonal only, trying to earn enough in a short time to fund some long-term plan back home: the deposit on a house, the wedding. Anton is older than most; "I am uncle," he says, smiling. Literally so, in one case; a nephew of his is here, doing waiter work. "He read well. He have English from school. He try to teach me, but no good. So I look for the class."

Something more emerges. There is something else, in the crevices of what he says, or rather, of what he does not exactly say. He has no family; no children, and his wife has left. Charlotte senses someone whose world is all awry. At one point he shrugs: "I come to England because . . . because it not matter where I am. Perhaps I can start new." Then he becomes embarrassed; he is here to be taught, not to unload his personal problems. He takes a hasty gulp of his tea, tells Charlotte that he is now quite a tea addict: "Before, always coffee. I learn tea on the building site and now I like. But this tea is different?"

"Earl Grey," says Charlotte. "No builder would touch it."

"It is good," says Anton. "I shall buy."

They set to work. They study words in isolation—nouns, verbs, pronouns, adjectives, connective words. They move on to a few simple sentences: the day is fine, I go to the shop, what is the time? Anton struggles, intense in concentration. He sits on the sofa alongside Charlotte, staring at fragments of language, at sequences of language, frowning, pursing his lips, breaking into a smile when he has triumphed over a word, a clump of words. Charlotte has met many adult literacy students, but she has seldom come across one more determined, more fervently applied to the problem. He does not find it easy; he can be stumped by some new combination of letters. "Chair," he cries angrily. "Chair, chair, chair." "I sit on the chair."

They take a break, and some fresh Earl Grey. Anton picks up the book on the coffee table, Charlotte's book, and tries to read the title. "The. The house. The house of . . ."

"Good," says Charlotte.

Anton scowls.

"Mirth," says Charlotte. "*The House of Mirth*. That's a hard word. It means . . . laughter."

"What is it—the book?"

"It's a novel—a nineteenth-century novel by an American writer. Edith Wharton. Set in New York. I enjoy her work very much—I'm reading this for—oh, for the third or fourth time."

Anton picks up the book, opens it, turns over the pages, tries to read a line, sighs with frustration.

He is a reader, he tells Charlotte, he reads a lot of fiction, he likes crime fiction, he has read P. D. James in translation ("This is English writer, yes?"), but he is eclectic in his tastes, he has enjoyed John Updike and Ian McEwan. He reads home-grown, he reads in translation. "I like story," he says. "I read for story."

Of course, thinks Charlotte. Many of us read for that. Most of us, even. That is how children learn to read, why they do so. You reach them through stories, you lure them on with story.

And here is Anton having to plod on with The day is fine, I go to the shop, thinks Charlotte. And she experiences the first faint smolder of an idea.

But the afternoon has rushed by. Far more than the statutory hour has passed, and here now is the sound of the front door. Rose is back. Oh, dear.

Rose comes in, slung about with carrier bags. She looks frazzled. An afternoon at the Brent Cross shopping mall would annihilate anyone.

Anton leaps to his feet. Charlotte apologizes. "We've finished. Anton is just going. I forgot the time. This is Anton, Rose. My daughter Rose."

Anton holds out a formal hand, which Rose takes, a touch awkward.

"Thank you for I come to your house," he says.

"That's all right," says Rose. "Don't feel you must rush off. I'm desperate for a cup of tea, that's all."

She moves toward the kitchen, but Charlotte waves the teapot. "This is still hot. Just get a cup. Don't go, Anton. I want to give you some work for next week."

Rose returns, sinks into an armchair with the reviving tea.

Charlotte sorts out some homework for Anton. He is greedy for it. "Some more," he says. He lays a hand on *The House of Mirth*. "Perhaps in the end I read this." He looks toward the well-stocked bookcase in Rose's sitting-room, and then at her. "You have many books. You like to read?"

"Well, yes," says Rose. "Of course. I mean, I could hardly not, with my parents being what they were."

Anton looks confused, and Charlotte has to explain that both she and her husband were teachers of English literature. Anton has clearly been assuming that adult literacy instruction was her trade. He is much impressed. "Ah," he says. "Ah. I did not understand." He gets up. "May I look?" he asks Rose, and goes over to the bookcase. Rose watches him, interested. She glances at Charlotte, eyebrows raised.

Anton is studying the shelves. He pulls out a book. "This name I know. I have read translation. R . . . rut . . . Ree . . . Ree . . ."

"Ruth Rendell," says Rose.

He looks at Charlotte in satisfaction. "Nearly I read that. I see the name and I know I have seen before."

Rose says, "It must be so frustrating—because you speak English well."

Charlotte explains to her that Anton is an accountant; once he can read and write English with confidence he can aim for an appropriate job.

"With your mother I learn," says Anton. "Better than the class. I learn better." He beams.

"And it's good for Mum to be able to do something," says Rose briskly. "She was bored to tears."

Sidelined, Charlotte inclines her head gracefully.

Rose seems well disposed toward Anton. She asks where he is living. He describes the compatriot enclave, amusingly. "We live like student. They eat out of tins and I am cross—the nasty uncle. I am too old for this. Soon I must find a bed-sit."

More emerges of his circumstances. He has an eighty-year-old mother to whom he sends money. He would like to send her some clothes—everything is so much better here, she would be delighted. "But it is difficult. I look in the shops and I do not know what size, what is good."

Half an hour or more has passed in talk. Rose has apparently recovered from Brent Cross. Then Anton gathers up his things, his homework books stashed carefully away in a rucksack. He thanks Charlotte warmly, turns to Rose. "And thank you for your nice house." He goes.

Rose carries the tea tray through to the kitchen. Charlotte follows her, saying, "Sorry about that. We overran. I'd meant him to be gone before you got back."

Rose says, "He seems a nice guy." A pause. "Amazing eyes."

So she too saw the forests, thinks Charlotte. The castles. That elsewhere.

It was on the fourteenth of April that Charlotte Rainsford was mugged. Seven lives have been derailed—nine if we include the Dalton girls, who do not yet realize that their parents are on the brink of separation. Charlotte, Rose and Gerry are thrust into unaccustomed proximity; Charlotte is frustrated and restless. Henry Peters—his lordship—has been chagrined and humiliated and is desperate to reestablish himself. Stella Dalton is taking five different kinds of medication, phoning her sister twice daily, and instructing a solicitor. Jeremy Dalton is writing placatory letters to Stella, nervously inspecting his accounts, and trying to sell an eighteenth-century overmantel for an exorbitant sum. Marion Clark is soothing Jeremy while wondering if in fact this relationship is really going anywhere; she is meeting George Harrington for lunch next week—a potential business partner looks suddenly more interesting than a romantic fling. She too has been preoccupied by her accounts.

Thus have various lives collided, the human version of a motorway shunt, and the rogue white van that slammed on the brakes is miles away now, impervious, offstage, enjoying a fry-up at the next services. Just as our mugger does not come into this story, not now, anyway—job done, damage complete, he (or she) is now superfluous.

CHAPTER FOUR

S tella Dalton is distraught, she is in a state of nervous prostration—
her sister fears for her mental stability—but she is also curiously
focused. Deep within, she is experiencing an unusual calm, a
strange sense of acceptance and of purpose. Now that it has happened,
the catastrophe that she has always expected, and she knows its nature,
she can grab hold of the lifebelt and swim for shore. Jeremy has
betrayed her, he is a liar and an adulterer; but the girls are not under
a car, the house is still standing. In between bouts of tears, hysterical
tirades to her sister, raids on that phalanx of pills, she is almost steady.
She can look the thing in the eye—divorce—and while it is scary,
unthinkable, taboo, it is also her own initiative, something she has set
in train all by herself, albeit powered by the inevitable—what else
could she do, after what has happened?

And she is bolstered now by Mr. Newsome. Paul Newsome. He sits
behind his desk, in his cool quiet office with its filing cabinets and its
glass-fronted bookcases, and nods sympathetically. He has the most
eloquent nod. When he talks, what he says is cool and quiet and practical; he makes everything sound sensible and routine and normal.
Paul Newsome was recommended by a friend of a friend of Stella's
sister, who had had a beast of a husband who tried to take her to the
cleaners and Paul Newsome sorted everything out quite brilliantly. So
Stella made that initial fraught and nervous phone call and he couldn't

have been nicer, and now here she is in that office, time after time, and really he is becoming her lifeline, the shoulder on which she leans.

Paul Newsome is not one of those divorce lawyers whose first move is to urge some counseling, a visit to Relate, a cooling-off period. He is an old hand and he is in this business for a living. Divorce is divorce. When one comes along you buckle to and do your job which is to get as much as possible for your client. Occasionally, you hit the jackpot when there is a cash-heavy couple; more usually you're engaged in a tug of war over a three-bedroom semi and a bite off some not very impressive salary. *Dalton v. Dalton* looks on the face of it much like that: excitable wife, half-million-quid house, child maintenance, guy who runs a reclamation business and there will no doubt be a problem getting any sort of income estimate out of him. There you go; another day, another divorce. Another slice of bread and butter; dab of jam if you're lucky.

That may be Paul Newsome's interior view, but in person he comes across quite differently. Stella finds him understanding and supportive, in every way. He never makes overt criticism of Jeremy, but you know that he thinks Jeremy is a rat. It is clear that he has the girls' interest very much in mind. It is equally clear that he is aware of what Stella is going through, and will do all that he can to make this wretched divorce process (oh, that word . . .) as smooth as possible, with Stella left as well cushioned as is her right.

Stella realizes that she should have married someone like Paul Newsome. Jeremy has always been a bit flaky—his precarious way of earning them a living, his tendency to do wild, risky things, like the restoration workshop that was to be a productive sideline and came unstuck because the so-called restoration expert was a fly-by-night immigrant, and the ruined manor house for which he paid far too much and then couldn't sell on. Way back, at the start, Stella had thought all that rather glamorous and unconventional, when her friends were setting up with guys in the city or in industry. And Jeremy had seemed so positive, someone you could rely on, the supportive partner that Stella desperately needed. He had been so insistent, too; he had shown up and noticed her in a big way, and wouldn't take no for an answer. Not that she had said no. And he is very charming and good-looking, Jeremy, all her girlfriends said so. Have other women been saying so, for years, to Jeremy himself? Has he swept up others in the way that he swept her up? This Marion Clark woman—is she just the latest of a series?

Stella knows that she is needy. She is only too conscious of her own erratic personality, this wretched tendency to flip, those times when she just cannot hold herself together, when she seems to have no control over what she is saying or doing. Gill says she has been like that right from when she was small, their mother couldn't do a thing with her sometimes, and aunts and grannies used to mutter about tantrums and spoiled, but of course it wasn't like that at all, she couldn't help it, can't help it. There's something wrong. Gill has always said this, Gill has been there for her all along. Gill found the analyst person when Stella was in such a terrible state a few years ago, not that that solved much—Stella didn't really like him, you never felt that he was on your side, that he *sympathized*, he was always so detached and dispassionate, with his questions, and then just sitting there while you talked, not even a nod, unlike Paul Newsome.

She'd rather have had Paul Newsome as an analyst, but of course he is a solicitor, which is another matter entirely. But he is being awfully good for Stella's morale, whatever. He keeps her informed as to how things are going. They aren't going very far at the moment, which he says is usual, at the start. Apparently Jeremy refuses to instruct a solicitor himself. He replies to Paul Newsome's letters by saying that he doesn't want a divorce anyway, and he wishes only to talk to Stella and sort things out. When Paul writes to say that his client declines to enter into discussion Jeremy fires back a shirty letter accusing him of coming between man and wife, or words to that effect. Paul reports this to Stella, with an expression of pained regret. The word "unreasonable" is heard, and Stella feels vindicated. Paul Newsome has never met Jeremy but he is clearly alive to what he is like, his refusal to face facts, his elusive quality which has been shown up in this horrid infidelity. Stella no longer feels so alone; she has someone alongside in this awful traumatic time.

———

Jeremy thought he had a buyer for the overmantel—a couple who seemed dead keen, coming back tomorrow with their architect, and then never another word from them. Not that five thousand quid would have dealt with the financial problems, but it would have helped, and would have made him feel he was getting something done. He has had to put the plans for the customer reception area and the parking bay on hold, but the bank is still breathing down his neck. It is too bad, just when he thought he was all systems go with the marvelous new site and a doubling of his stock and potential turnover. He is having to work all hours, because the guy he is employing to help out at the warehouse and be there when Jeremy is off in pursuit of new items is proving somewhat inadequate. Admittedly he is cheap—an amiable but dopey young Irishman prepared to do it for the minimum wage. Maybe one should have aimed higher and paid more, but all expenditure has to be pruned back at the moment.

Jeremy lies awake at night doing sums in his head, and composing letters to the shit of a lawyer whom Stella has hired. He is not lying in Marion's arms as often as he would like because she seems to be rather distracted these days and often pleads weariness. She too is hit by the economic downturn, she explains; she does not have the bank on her back—yet—but she is concerned about the dearth of customers and commissions and is having to think about possible diversification. Oh, she is still very sweet and solicitous about all the business with Stella—as she should be, Jeremy sometimes thinks, after all it was her text message that triggered the whole thing—but the initial zest seems absent from their relationship, just when he could most do with it. He's still not sure where it would be going, in the long-term, and he is desperate to sort things out with Stella, but he does need Marion, so calm and reassuring.

Jeremy does not want a divorce, period. No way. It simply is not necessary. Yes, he has committed adultery—that silly, biblical word—and he was stupid to have admitted as much, but he had felt that honesty was the best move, he hadn't wanted to lie and then get further embroiled later on. He had known that Stella would throw a wobbly, but hadn't reckoned with this terminal reaction. That bloody sister has egged her on, no doubt, and now there is Stella's solicitor, demanding that Jeremy produce one of his own so that the pair of them can go hammer and tongs and ratchet up their fees—nice little earner if you can get it.

Well, he's not playing. He is not agreeing to be divorced. Can Stella divorce him one-sided, if he's just lying there with all four paws in the air? What he needs is to be able to *get* to Stella, talk to her, make her see that this has all got out of hand, that he's sorry, sorry, that she's being taken for a ride by that bloodsucking solicitor, that her sister is a conniving bitch. But he can't get near Stella. Her phone is always on answer, his letters are ignored, if he gets the girls on their mobiles they are just embarrassed and monosyllabic. He has been allowed back to the house once to collect some clothes and other stuff; Stella was not there, and a note required him to leave the keys on the hall table.

Jeremy thinks himself pretty well equipped to ride out circumstances. He is a natural optimist. When something tiresome turns up he doesn't allow himself to get panic-stricken; there's always a way out. Confront the situation and you can usually sort it. That double-dealing Pole was a shock, leaving him high and dry with the restoration project, but he had managed to pull the plug on it without too much loss—reneging on the rental for the workshop meant he'd better steer clear of that guy in Clapham, but who needs to frequent Clapham? It had been a bit of a shock to find that he couldn't get any takers for Bickston Manor, when he had stripped it of the Jacobean staircase and all the other recyclable features; he had thought there were always people who wanted a nicely gutted subject to re-create from scratch. The place was pretty well a ruin when he'd snapped it up; obviously the thing was to strip it down properly, give someone the chance of a tabula rasa. People are so unimaginative. In the end he had to settle for a ridiculous amount from that demolition company—outrageous when you think of the opportunity lost, but there you go. And the staircase didn't fetch as much as he'd hoped. The bank had started snarling somewhat at that point, but Jeremy hadn't let them get him down; he'd talked up various potential deals—very potential in some cases—and stayed confident, and sure enough within weeks he'd had a marvelous stroke of luck with an amazing junk yard in Somerset, dotty old fellow who didn't know what he was sitting on. Jeremy bought the lot for some folding money and a few pints in the local pub. Whole stack of de Morgan tiles, covered in mud under a pile of sacking, fantastic wrought iron gates, a treasure trove. The old fellow had pretty well lost his marbles—high time he wound up the business, he was doing him a favor.

That's the trick—to stay cool when things look nasty and with a bit of luck you win through. But this time he's got the jitters. The threat of divorce terrifies him—it's so climactic, so final. He doesn't want to lose Stella, he's *fond* of Stella, however trying she can be at times. He doesn't want to lose that familiar, reassuring base—the house, the girls. Divorce would be bad for the girls, no question. And bad for him, definitely, from what he's heard about it. Apparently everything you've got between you gets split in half, no matter who's been paying for what, so Stella would get half the house and half his measly pension money and half of the cars and half the new Bang & Olufsen TV and half of the ride-on mower—despite the fact that it's he who has been paying for the mortgage and pretty much everything else. That's the way it is now, he's heard, in which case it's amazing that the divorce rate has been going up, you'd think most men would hang in there for all they were worth, unless of course it was one of those marriages in which the wife is doing nicely, in which case it's the guy who is going to profit. Is that how they reckon the system is fair?

It wouldn't be fair in this case, which is why Jeremy has to put up a furious resistance, fight off that solicitor, persist in trying to get through to Stella. Divorce would be ruin, not to put too fine a point on it. The bank chasing him is bad enough, but the bank plus divorce would clean him out. He might as well jack in the business, and set up as a house clearance firm with a van and a sleazy flat over a garage.

Marion's lunch with George Harrington took place at a restaurant she knew to be pretty swank. Certainly the prices were that—she had a good look down the menu while he was attending to a call on his mobile, for which he was full of apologies: "Wretched things. Remember when one could be genuinely unavailable?"

She has checked out George Harrington, so far as possible. His financial organization was not known to her but is, she now sees, a bank—one of the smaller and more recherché banks. Like Barings, maybe—but that came to grief, didn't it? So George Harrington, even if in a minor way, is one of those who have brought the world to its financial knees. He is an architect of the recession, to be reviled, and strictly speaking one should not be breaking bread with him. In fact George Harrington should not be breaking bread himself, let alone Brittany scallops with a bean, shallot and parmesan cream sauce or tian of smoked chicken with wasabi mayonnaise and pancetta crisps, but here he is, in a suit that Marion's shrewd eye knows to be the best, evidently in good spirits, and with the maître d' bowing and scraping.

And, it turned out over the crispy pork shoulder, celeriac puree, wild mushroom and poached egg and the grilled John Dory fillets, Niçoise salad, banana salsa and mandarin and elderflower foam, he is still buying property for renovation. Is he oblivious to the economic downturn, or foolhardy, or does he know something others do not know, including the Chancellor of the Exchequer who has warned this very morning that there will be no green shoots for many months to come? None of these, it seems. George Harrington is being perfectly logical; the market has almost certainly bottomed out ("Excuse me— such an inelegant term") in which case this is the expedient thing to do. There are golden opportunities around for property investment, if you are equipped to take advantage, which George evidently is. For Marion, the word "bonus" floated between them, only to be batted away as an indelicate introduction; after all, who was she to question this man's circumstances—a potential business partner whose personal arrangements were no concern of hers?

The lunch proceeded most agreeably. George Harrington's latest purchase was a flat in Hampstead: "Lovely job—old building newly converted, bags of room, prime location, sort of place that gets snapped up by foreign executives here for a year or two. How would you kit out a property like that?"

Marion asked a few quick questions, offered a selection of ideas—modernist, traditional, or a take on her own signature style. She suggested that he visit her showroom to get an idea of what she did; George whipped out a diary.

Eventually, over coffee, some terms were proposed, which Marion found eminently acceptable, though not without a tweak or two of her own—always be businesslike, never let people think they can roll you over. George listened and nodded: "Absolutely . . . I appreciate that . . ." He pushed his cup aside: "Well, I think we've got a deal—Marion, if I may. Such a relief it'll be, to forget about curtains and kitchen fittings. Give my secretary a ring, to arrange yourself an inspection visit, and we've fixed a date for me to see your own place."

The flat was in the final stages of conversion, apparently, and not much more than an empty shell, which is just what Marion liked. She would use her own subcontractors for the various installations. It only remained for George to decide on what style he felt would most appeal to some American fund manager or German diplomat. The final sum for the spend would be agreed when George had made his decision. Marion's own commission would nicely stem her looming cash-flow problem; she reflected on this with satisfaction as she washed her hands in the restaurant's luxuriant Ladies, which had some choice effects, she noted—neat, those light fittings, where do they come from? She was unable to enter a room without assessing it and was tiresomely aware of this.

When she rejoined George he was busy once more on his mobile but quickly put it away: "I can't wait to see what you do with the flat. I don't think minimalist, for Hampstead, do you? Countrified but smart, maybe? Anyway, we can discuss and then I shall leave it to you. I'm off to my place in Greece for a week but after that let's talk."

They parted outside the restaurant. Marion saw him flag down a taxi. She walked to the bus stop, thinking about money. She was parsimonious about taxis these days, and about other things, indeed. No holiday this year; no new clothes except essentials. But money is such an elusive concept. It serves up something concrete—the taxi, the cashmere sweater, the week in Corfu—but is also an absence, vanished behind the figures on a screen, the columns on a page, the immense piles and pages of figures that have announced a global crisis and ravaged millions of lives. George Harrington comes from the world of figures; he presumably thinks differently about money. It is not, for him, the taxi or the new pair of shoes, though it has presumably provided these, along with the place in Greece and the flat in Hampstead and the Clerkenwell studio apartment and the penthouse by the Thames—the property portfolio that is his hobby, it seems, and that he sees as a foray into creativity. It has delivered all this, but serious money, for him, is that evanescent stuff at which he stares on his screen, and to which he responds in a way that is quite mysterious to Marion. She understands figures—oh yes, quite well enough to run a small business without, so far, going bust, but she realizes that this is a far cry from the relationship that George Harrington has, and others like him. She has a vague idea of what is being done—money is being moved around, all the time, second by second, great invisible intangible mountains of the stuff, and these strange notional movements drive the world's economies and, when they go awry, can rock individual lives.

She took the bus back, spending a notional amount from her Oyster card, stopped off at the corner shop, where she handed over real cash, and arrived home. No prospective clients had phoned or e-mailed. The woman for whom she was currently doing a small job had left a message disliking all the curtain samples that Marion had provided. Marion thought with relish of George Harrington, who would presumably give her a brief and leave her to it. Women clients were always the worst; sometimes she thought she hated women.

There was also a message from Jeremy, a touch reproachful, saying hadn't she had his text, or was her mobile on the blink? She had indeed had his text, on the bus, and had not replied. He wanted to come around this evening; Marion had been planning soup and a salad in front of the telly. If Jeremy came she would feel she had to cook a proper meal, and the evening of privacy and relaxation would be gone.

When you prefer soup and the telly to a few hours with your lover there is something not quite right. Marion confronted this truth, while wondering what to say to Jeremy. Yes, so far as she was concerned the affair had lost its panache. She still liked him, still enjoyed his company, sex was indeed most welcome; but an element of take it or leave it had crept in. She was growing more than a little tired of hearing about his struggle to access the tiresome wife, and the aggressive letters from the solicitor. And where his financial headaches were concerned she felt entitled to point out that her own were just as bad, except that for the most part she did not. In Marion's family it had been considered bad form to talk about money. Admittedly they hadn't much had to worry about it, if ever. Her mother thought you just took it out of the bank, when needed. She had never really got it into her head that Marion's business was such, that Marion earned a living; she saw it as "such fun for Marion, so clever of her."

A smidgeon of this attitude had perhaps rubbed off onto Marion. Certainly, she found too much discussion of financial problems both tedious and rather ill-mannered. She did not want to hear much more about Jeremy's skirmishes with the bank, amusing as he could sometimes be. And she definitely did not want to get drawn further into his despondent analysis of what divorce would mean, how he would be ruined, effectively, left with half a house and half a car and half this and half that, and he was not making any attempt to be amusing about this, no way.

She felt that she was being sucked into things. The implication was that it was after all partly her fault. For heaven's sake! Jeremy is grown up; he knew what he was doing. The wife is of course being impossible, but that is nothing to do with Marion. People are answerable for their own wives; Jeremy presumably knew Stella's potential for combustion. No, Marion is not going to be drawn into some situation in which she is allied with Jeremy against the manic Stella. Jeremy is on his own where his wife is concerned. Marion will listen with sympathy, offer advice maybe, when appropriate, but that is all.

So she hesitated over how to deal with his message. Eventually she called him, still hesitating, and her resistance was immediately undermined by the fervor of his response: "*There* you are. Thank goodness. I've been *needing* you."

He had had a foul day. A delivery of new stock had arrived with a prized mirror cracked right across. The woman who was going to take that marble fireplace had rung to say she'd changed her mind. Another letter from Stella's solicitor.

"So I've been dreaming of you—thinking, please, please can I see her this evening. Can I?"

This is the original Jeremy, the initial Jeremy who was so beguiling and refreshing. He can surface still, putting Marion back at square one, when she walked into the warehouse that morning.

"All right," she said. "Yes, that would be nice."

CHAPTER FIVE

C harlotte's nights are not good. Sometimes her hip hurts, sometimes her back; there is no such thing as a comfortable position, and when she has to go to the bathroom she is afraid of
waking Rose and Gerry. At home, she would probably go downstairs
and make a cup of tea; she longs for the release of home. She falls
heavily asleep in the early morning, often, and then she dreams—
vivid, surreal dreams in which one scene segues into another like the
scenes in *Alice*—and Carroll must of course have been inspired by the
inconstant landscape of dreams, Charlotte has always been sure of
that. In these dreams, she is not the Charlotte of today but another,
younger Charlotte, and sometimes Rose is there, often a child once
more, and always Tom is present, not always as himself, exactly, but
simply as a shadowy companion figure who is, she knows, Tom. This
morning, she and he are in the house they had in Edgbaston, when
both were teaching there, looking out of the window, and all around
there is water—water has crept over the road, the garden, is lapping
round the walls. And as they observe this a rowing boat appears,
manned not by people but by two dogs (very *Alice*). Neither she
nor the shadow Tom are surprised by this, but she is wondering if all
this water will have affected the electricity. And then the scene melts
into another, in which she is with her old university tutor, who is
going to drive her somewhere in a little motorized caravan, equipped

with cooker and sink and folding beds; this time, Charlotte *is* surprised.

Then she wakes, is confused, as on each of these mornings. Where is she? Oh, Rose's house.

You slide, in old age, into a state of perpetual diffidence, of unspoken apology. You walk more slowly than normal people, you are obliged to say "what?" too often, others have to give up their seat on the bus to you, on train journeys you must ask for help with your absurdly small and light case. There is a void somewhere in your head into which tip the most familiar names; President Obama went into it yesterday, for all of five minutes, along with her over the road at home who has just sent a get-well card from "Sue," but what on earth is her other name? You can use a computer, just about, and cope with a mobile, but with such slow deliberation that the watching young are wincing.

When you were young yourself you were appropriately nice to old people, gave up your seat and so forth, but you never really thought about them. They were another species, their experience was unimaginable, and in any case it was irrelevant; you were not going there, or at least not for so long that there was no need to consider it.

Nowadays, you eye the young and remember—oh yes, just—how it was. How it was to have smooth skin and a supple body, to be able to bend and squat and lift and run for a bus and skip down the stairs. To have this long unknowable future, in which lurked heaven knows what, and it is the mystery that is so alluring. Your own future is also unknowable, except that you can make a few shrewd guesses, and it is not particularly alluring.

You are on the edge of things now, clinging on to life's outer rim. You have this comet trail of your own lived life, sparks from which arrive in the head all the time, whether you want them or not—life has been lived but it is all still going on, in the mind, for better and for worse. But don't imagine that anyone else wants to know about it; this narrative is personal, and mind you remember that. Even Rose can take only so much of that holiday we had at Mevagissey, and the birthday party when you dropped the cake. It is strange that for so many years your life ran parallel with hers, but she knows little of how yours was—and, indeed, her child's eye view is opaque to you. What did she see and hear?

She saw you and Tom, presumably, and that you were happy together. She must have seen and heard affection, compatibility and consideration. Oh, the occasional spat, of course, this was marriage, and the best of marriages meet rough water from time to time. But she saw unity, a unity that is quite rare, Charlotte has come to realize, observing and hearing over a lifetime. How lucky we were, she thinks, how lucky ever to have met, to have been able to link up and sail ahead together, until that malign little cell began to form and grow, destroying him, and everything.

So Rose saw . . . happiness. Charlotte is not quite sure that she sees happiness here, in Rose's house. She does not see unhappiness, oh no. What she seems to see is an equable coexistence; nobody shouts, nobody slams out of the house, there are no disturbing silences. There are conversational exchanges of an anodyne nature; there are brief discussions about domestic requirements or arrangements. Rose reports e-mails or phone calls from one or other of the children. She does not much speak of how her time has been, with his lordship; nor does Gerry, of his day at work.

Here are two people who live equably together, and maybe that is as much as anyone can ask. Charlotte is embarrassed to be a witness to this, to be thinking about it. She has never actually lived with Rose and Gerry before, close as she has been to them. And she is aware that these thoughts are prompted because she knows that this marriage is not like her own; it is colorless, by comparison, it lacks the zest, the give and take, the hours of discussion and debate, the hand on the knee, the arm round the shoulder, the silent codes of amusement and of horror. The laughter.

She would have wished this for Rose. But then, she does not know what it is that Rose and Gerry have. We only think that we know the lives of others. So, she tells herself, mind your own business and leave Rose to hers, it is bad enough that she has you foisted on her like this, not that she would use that word or even think it. And this is for a finite period only, eventually Charlotte will be crutch-free, able-bodied or thereabouts, she can go home and resume normal living. As can Rose and Gerry.

These thoughts arrive on a bad day. Pain is in residence. Charlotte is a pain expert, or maybe connoisseur is a better term. She can rate pain on a scale of one to ten, as required in hospital, even slipping in a half on occasion. "Six and a half this morning," and the nurse's pen falters—the charts do not allow for this. But when you have lived for years with pain you are nicely tuned to that extra notch up or down. More than that, she is familiar with the way in which pain chases around the body, popping up where it should not be. Referred pain, this is called, a sly escape from the root site of the problem. Indeed— but Charlotte sees it also as pain's malign capacity to mutate, to advance and retreat, to behave like some bodily parasite with its own agenda, gnawing away when it feels like it, going into deceptive hibernation only to spring back grinning just when you thought the going was good.

Today her back is howling. This should not be. If anything has a right to howl it is her hip, her broken and mended hip. But the hip is quiescent, and pain has sneaked into the back, which is because the fall, it seems, badly strained the sacroileac joint, thus exacerbating Charlotte's long-term back condition, which has had her hampered and in frequent anguish for a decade. So pain has seized the opportunity, has danced into her spine—and into the backside and down the legs—and has shoved the hip aside for the moment. Tomorrow all may be otherwise; hip may snarl, back may be in remission—pain's agenda is unpredictable, perverse, defiant. For the moment, she has two options: endure, or take one of the painkillers that may or may not kill but will make her drowsy and play havoc with the gut. She decides on endurance; Anton is coming this afternoon, which will at least be a distraction. She can cock a snook at pain. Half a snook.

Anton arrives late, breathless with apology. He had had to stay longer at work, then wait for a bus. Charlotte had been concerned about having to have the lessons in the afternoons, thus occupying Rose's sitting-room, but this apparently did not bother Rose: "Look, I've always got things I need to do—I don't sit around in there anyway, and it's only for an hour." So today she could be heard in the kitchen busy at something, while Charlotte and Anton settled to the lesson.

Charlotte had decided to put her idea into operation. They spent some time on the standard work, going through the words and sentences, and then Charlotte produced a book.

"This," she said, "is a story. You like stories, as do I. I think you are tired of 'This is our house,' and 'What is the time?'"

Anton studied the cover of the book. Charlotte had him attempt the title. Eventually, he achieved it: *Where the Wild Things Are.*

He looked at Charlotte. "I think this is a book for children?"

"Indeed it is. An interesting one. You'll see. Let's go." She turned to the first page.

Anton read, with hesitations, false attempts, and prompts, the adventures of Max and his wolf suit.

They reached, at last, the end.

Anton laughed. He turned back the pages, looked right through the book again. "This is a clever book. A clever story. It is about how the child feels. How he is angry and cannot stop his angry. He cannot . . . control. This is the wild things. And then he find that he can control. And his supper is still hot." He laughed again. "Very clever." He turned back and looked once more at the text, running his finger beneath words.

Charlotte grinned. "More fun than what we've been doing."

Rose came in. "Tea? Or am I interrupting too soon?" Her eye fell on the book. "Oh. Sendak."

"Next week," said Charlotte, *"How Tom Beat Captain Najork and His Hired Sportsmen."*

"Isn't this rather unorthodox, Mum?"

"Possibly. Anton isn't complaining."

"I am like child," said Anton cheerfully. "Child learn when he is interested. When he want to know what come next in the story. Nothing come next with 'I go to the shop' and 'This is our house.'"

Rose put down the tea tray, sat, poured out. "It's Earl Grey, Anton. Mum said you liked it."

"I like and I have—buyed."

"Bought," said Charlotte.

"Bought. And I send to my mother, so she can be English. Soon I try to find English clothes for her."

Rose frowned.

"But clothes I see in the shops are for girls," Anton continued.

"Quite," said Charlotte. "I have the same problem. The senior citizen is disregarded by the fashion industry."

Rose broke in. "I know a place that does sensible stuff for the older lady. If you like I'll take you there sometime, Anton."

Anton stared at her. The forest eyes. The lakes. "That is kind. That is very kind."

"You've never taken *me* there," said Charlotte.

"It's where I got you that jacket for Christmas."

"Oh."

Rose went to the kitchen and returned with a plate of scones: "I've just made these." Charlotte was impressed; Rose was not given to baking. Anton ate two, with relish. They sat over tea and scones, the exercise books and Sendak laid aside. Anton talked of his mother, of her bad knee—Charlotte grimaced in sympathy—of his desire to move her from a flat to a bungalow, if possible: "She likes to have a garden." Further fragments of his circumstances emerged: he himself lived in a city apartment—"For a time now, since my wife go. Before, there was a house in the country"—he had worked with an accountancy firm until made redundant last year –"Not just me—many, many—they have no work for us." Rose and Anton discovered a shared taste for walking. This was something that Rose and Gerry had in common; their holidays usually consisted of a hike along Offa's Dyke or the Pennine Way. Anton described week-long excursions with two men friends, camping beside lakes, amid forests. Of course, thought Charlotte, seeing these reflected, he still carries them about him, somehow, that whiff of elsewhere, making the Pennine Way look homely.

"Perhaps one day I walk in England," he said. "When I have a job, and holidays."

Charlotte suggested Richmond Park, to be going on with, one Sunday. Rose fetched a London map, and showed him how to get there. She brought out photos from her own walking holidays and showed him pieces of the Lake District, of the Black Mountains. He pored over these, intently: "These are places I would like very much." He pulled a face. "It is a pity I see only Stratford and Tottenham." He was working at the moment on a vast building site in Tottenham. "Everyone from central Europe, Eastern Europe. If you shout 'Anton,' five–six people answer." He laughed. "Shift work—that is why I am mornings."

Charlotte noted Anton's crisp blue shirt, his hair that she could see had been freshly washed. He comes off the building site, and cleans up for his sessions here, she thought. Of course—an office is his natural habitat, not a building site. He has had to grit his teeth and adapt. She tried to imagine Gerry on a building site, in sagging jeans and a dirty vest top, heaving a barrow. I don't think so. Or Tom? Possibly, possibly. If the economy had gone pear-shaped, if history had run differently. Tom could have changed color, if he had had to—become someone else, survived.

"My mum is quite nutty," said Rose to her best friend Sarah. "She's teaching this man out of children's books—the one who comes to the house for adult literacy."

"How's she getting on? The hip?"

"So-so. Actually, it works—he's reading. Sort of."

They had met for a quick lunch—Rose after her morning with Henry, Sarah in her break from the hospital where she worked as secretary to a consultant. Rose and Sarah had been at college together, had proceeded through life in parallel, sharing complaints and anxieties about husbands, children, their own feelings—close in a way that women can be. Today Sarah was worried about a daughter distraught after the collapse of a relationship. She was not much interested in adult literacy.

"The thing is, he wasn't up to her in any case. No way."

"They never are," said Rose. "Lucy has gone through several wet lettuces, in my view."

"Did we?" said Sarah.

They laugh.

"Or did we marry them? Perish the thought."

This might not be a laughing matter. Grievances concerning husbands have been exchanged from time to time—lightly, not to be taken too seriously. But recorded, all the same.

"Of course not," said Rose. "The wet lettuces are a learning curve. Tell your Julie that."

"Oh, I do. I do." Sarah sighed. "And my man is being difficult," she continued. This was a reference to the consultant. "He wants our database entirely revised. How's his lordship?" She was amused by Charlotte's term for Henry and always used it.

"We have never risen to a database," said Rose. "Or sunk. But I have a feeling he's up to something. There's a lot of writing going on, and chuckling: 'I think this may set the cat among the pigeons, Rose.'"

"At least he's a character. Mr. Summers is colorless, I have to say. Super doctor, perfectly nice, but zero personality—except when he's got a bee in his bonnet about databases."

"I could do with less personality, on occasion. And perfectly nice sounds to die for."

"But you've hung in there—what?—fifteen years?"

Rose sighed. "So I have. Well, it suits me, I suppose. The easy option, my mum thinks—though she's tactful enough never to say."

"Ah, your mum. Now there's a personality, and I mean that as a compliment. A mind of her own."

"You can say that again."

"Come on—as mothers go, you struck lucky."

"Hmm . . ." Actually, Rose was inclined to agree. When you looked around, considered other possibilities. Not, of course, that any alternative is ever conceivable, when it comes to parentage. You have what you have, they are from whence you have sprung, and had you not, then you would not be who you are, so that is that. Occasionally, Rose looked in the mirror and saw a flicker of her mother, a brief flash of her father—something about the eyes, the set of the mouth.

She said goodbye to Sarah, and left for home, still thinking about parentage. Her own children were rather rudely defiant of descent, refuting any physical resemblance ("I mean, I'm not being rude, Mum, but I just can't see that either of us looks like either of you"), and heading for determinedly different activities (James a fledgling banker, Lucy reading chemistry at college). You wait, she told them—as she stopped off at the supermarket for a few things, and that Irish bread that Charlotte liked—you wait.

She felt nowadays these painful twinges of compunction where her mother was concerned. Not just on account of the hip, but the whole business of age, of what has happened to her, what happens, the way in which a person is pushed into another incarnation, becomes a different version of themselves. Her old mother was still herself, but she was diminished in some way, had lost emphasis, was not the figure of Rose's childhood and youth, and Rose felt in some irrational way guilty.

Her father had been spared that, dying in middle age. Rose could not imagine him old—no, no. In her head, he was forever the vigorous, charismatic figure of her childhood—alive with opinions and proposals, cheerful, fun. He and Charlotte were lodged together there, sometimes arguing, often laughing, the immutable unit. Except that of course the unit had not been immutable, and now there was this other, solitary mother. Carrying on. "Your mother will carry on," people had said. Well, of course. What else?

Rose knew that Charlotte found it agonizing to have to live with her and Gerry, and knew why—that it was not just that she wanted to be in her own house, but that she felt intrusive, superfluous. Rose was occasionally woken in the night by Charlotte's stealthy forays to the bathroom, and experienced simultaneous irritation and pity.

I know what she feels, Rose thought, and she knows that I know. No point even in discussing it. And then there were those companionable moments—rubbishing a TV program, talking about James or Lucy. Providing tea and scones for this Anton.

That shop, she thought. Things for his mother. Why not? Next week, maybe.

Anton sometimes thought of his own mother, when he was with Charlotte: the two women were much of an age. But that was all they had in common; his mother was anxious, dependent—widowhood had thrust her into a childlike neediness. His sister and brother ministered, tirelessly. While the English woman, he sensed, was relatively robust when not felled by this accident—and with a productive working life behind her. His own mother had behind her the long, troubled, deprived past of their country—a lifetime of making the best of things, scrimping and scrounging, doing menial jobs when any were offered. She had been a school dinner lady, she had cooked in a cheap restaurant. Now, she sat in her two-room flat, day in, day out—waiting for her children to come, for Anton to phone, which he did, each week, at a set time.

For Anton, his experience with Charlotte and Rose was an oasis in his present wasteland of an existence. He relished his visits to the house. He was not depressed or despairing—by no means. He was a man equipped with a certain natural optimism which had seen him through difficult times before now, and he had made the decision to try his luck abroad with determination: things could not be much worse where he was—chances were, they might be better over there. The time of despair was under his belt now, the bleak months after she walked out, when the plug was pulled on fourteen years of marriage, just like that.

The building site was an education, he told himself. Now you know what it is like to work with your hands and your back, not your head. To do what most men do all the time, the world over. His body ached, protested, reminded him that it was not made for this. In the evenings, in the crowded, fetid household of younger men, he made a joke of it, stoically. Besides, he did not want to find himself laid off. This is not forever—he told himself that also. This is just a tiresome induction period, until I can get going here. Until I have enough of a grip on the language to offer myself for a real job. Until I can read it better.

Language blazed at him—all day, every day. It challenged him from the sides of buses, in the Tube, from newspapers. On the radio, the television, in the street. He looked and listened, trying to follow. He snatched what he could—Ah! that I understand, this I can get. Swathes of it escaped him, chattering away into oblivion. And parallel to this perverse, obstructive language ran the words in his own head, the easy, fluent eloquence of his own tongue. Into which he fell back in the evenings, in the grumbling, joshing company of the young. When in a foreign country, he thought, you are behind a fence, or in a cell—everything is going on around you but you are not quite part of it. You open your mouth and you sound like a child; you know that you are someone else, but you cannot explain it.

With the teacher and her daughter he did sometimes feel that his real self could emerge. He had been at first amused by Charlotte's recourse to children's books, but now saw that this was enterprising and effective. He took the books back with him and pored over the texts, hiding them from his nephew and the other young men. He read about talking rabbits and tigers that came to tea, with satisfaction. He remembered learning to read as a child, discovering story.

He talked of this to Charlotte, when next they met. Tried to talk of it, hobbled as always by the search for the right word. He had been thinking about story—how it works.

"Story go always forward—this happen, then this. That is what we want. We want to know how it happen, what comes next. How one thing make happen another."

"Exactly," said Charlotte. "Narrative. But a contrivance—a clever contrivance, if successful."

"Con . . . trivance?"

"Made up. Invented."

"Yes, yes. And that is why we enjoy. Because it is not like our life—the way we live, which is . . ."—he frowned—". . . very much accident. You get job. Your wife go. You lose job. You are knock down by bus, perhaps."

"You get mugged," said Charlotte. "You break your hip."

Anton frowned further, then smiled. "And so I am here, like this, in your daughter house, because of that."

"We have a word for it—an odd one. Happenstance."

"And it is story," said Anton. "But not like story in book. It is . . . no one can control."

"Anarchy. Contingency."

"Sorry?"

"No—*I'm* sorry. The unruly world in which we have to live. One's unreliable progress. Are you religious, Anton?"

He spread his hands, shook his head.

"Me neither. It's said to be a consolation. Or a crutch." She tapped hers.

"My mother, yes. She go out now only for the church."

"I rather envy her. I tried, way back, but faith eluded me. There was no way I could believe."

"And in the Bible," said Anton thoughtfully. "There are many stories."

"Indeed. The good Samaritan. The loaves and the fishes. But stories with a message. All very well, but people can be put off by messages. The form needs to get more sophisticated."

"When I was a boy," said Anton, "I liked very much . . . how do you say? . . . stories about princes and princesses and giants and magic things."

"Fairy stories, we say. Not that fairies much come into them. Messages, again."

"The poor person always come out good in the end?"

"Exactly."

"Which is not what happen in the world."

"Quite so. But we love to think it might."

Anton smiled. "In fairy story, the poor workers on the building site all find bag of gold, and the rich developer man is eat up by the giant."

"Instead of which, the rich bankers let all their gold melt away, or so we understand, so there is nothing to pay the poor workers and no work anyway."

He laughed. "But gold is not all good. There was the king who wished everything he touch turn to gold, and then he could not eat or drink."

"Ooh . . ." said Charlotte. "We're into mythology now. Midas."

"From school, I remember this story. But that is message too. You must not want too much."

"Yes. Greed. But you're right. Messages die hard. The modern novel has tried to shed them, though I suppose they creep in here and there."

"And children books have, sometimes."

"Absolutely. Although not, I think, in this week's study. Our new text is about a pig and a spider, Anton. Actually, we are moving up the age range. This is for people of around eight or nine. Or seventy-six. Or . . . ?"

"Forty-five," said Anton.

"And the spider has my name, Charlotte. So I have always identified. Right—let's get going. Have a try."

"'Where's . . . Papa . . . going . . . with . . . that . . . axe?'" read Anton . . .

An hour later, they were still immersed. For Anton, the building site had receded entirely, along with his evening world of food out of tins and desultory chatter. He was exhilarated by a growing mastery of the words on the page, charmed by this simple, beguiling tale.

"'No, I . . . only . . . distribute . . . pigs . . . to . . . early . . . risers,' Early risers—what is this?"

"People who get up early," said Charlotte. "We'll have to stop—here's Rose with the tea."

Rose picked up the book. "Oh—I used to love this. So did Lucy and James."

"Listen," said Anton. "'Fern . . . was . . . up . . . at . . . daylight . . . trying . . . to . . . rid . . . the . . . world . . . of . . .'"

"Injustice." Charlotte beamed. "Huge progress."

"Great!" said Rose. She held out a plate. "It's chocolate brownies today. And Earl Grey, of course." She smiled at Anton.

He sat thinking that he could imagine a time when he would begin to feel at home in this country. When it could cease to be so imperme-able, so tacitly hostile, so eternally other. When he could buy a news-paper and read it, laugh at the jokes on a TV program. Some of his younger compatriots already did this. But how long will this take? he wondered. And how long will I stay?

"Your mother and I have been talking about story," he told Rose. "Stories."

"Oh, well—she's the expert. Her subject."

"And I am thinking—everything has to be story. On the TV—advertisements are little story, often. I watch, because these I can understand, sometimes."

"I used to like the one about the girl who walks out on her man but takes the car," said Rose. "A year or two ago. Car advert, of course. Maybe you should have had a career in writing ads, Mum, and we'd all be rich."

"Oh, I could never make up stories. Only talk about them."

"When I was a small boy," said Anton, "I make up stories very much, and I am in them. I have big adventure—I am very brave."

"Oh, I did that too." Rose smiled. "I was amazingly beautiful, and pursued by rock stars. Duran Duran."

"Really? Who?" said Charlotte.

"Exactly. You didn't know about my inner life. And you wouldn't have known who Duran Duran were."

"It's sad you cannot do that when you are—grown," said Anton. "You have just your own story, that you live. That you cannot choose."

Rose held out the plate. "Have the last brownie, Anton. And I don't know about that—I'm doing some choosing right now. I'm going to propose to Gerry—no, tell Gerry—that we must have a new bath-room installed."

"That is small choosing," said Anton. "I mean—big things that happen."

"Well, you chose to come here—to England," said Rose.

"Yes. But I did not choose to lose my job. At home."

"All right. I take your point. Sometimes we choose. And some big things too. You choose who you marry."

"I think my wife choose me," said Anton. "I was very—shy. When young man. And later unfortunately she choose not me any more."

There was a pause. "Well, I'll tell you what," said Rose. "Why don't I take you for a whole choosing opportunity next week? Shopping opportunity, that is. Things for your mother."

Later, in the Tube, on the way back to the communal house, Anton opened *Charlotte's Web*. He sat there in the shuddering, hurtling London netherworld, his lips moving as he traveled from word to word, from line to line. Occasionally he copied a word into his notebook, for further inquiry. Sometimes he skipped a word, eager to move ahead— pushed it aside to deal with another time. He rattled through the darkness, reading.

CHAPTER SIX

Henry Peters, too, was reading.

"Scandal, gossip and innuendo received majestic treatment in the Augustan Age. Some of the most elegant art of the eighteenth century addresses itself to the perceived weaknesses and transgressions of aristocrats, royalty and politicians. Think of the style, the wit, the delighted savagery of Gillray, of Hogarth, of Rowlandson. Cartoons, broadsheets and flyers enabled the public of the day to savor the goings-on of the great and the good by way of raucous humor . . ."

Henry had always enjoyed reading his own work—appreciating a turn of phrase, an appropriate word. He sat at his desk with the handwritten sheets spread out in front of him; the first draft was just about done, ready for Rose to type up, and then he would get down to the final tweaking and polishing before sending it off to one of the Sundays.

He read on. More about eighteenth-century circulars and broadsheets, with quotes. A Gillray would be nice as illustration—note to the features editor on that, and a suggested choice. References to some scandals of the day. Move on to a comparison with contemporary style—the crude sledge-hammer operation of the gutter press, the dogged nature of investigative journalism, its sobriety, the absence of any élan. And then the tidbit to make the point that even in the day of investigative journalism things slip through the net—potential political dramas. For herein lies the crux of the whole piece—the nugget of information, in what is almost a throw-away aside, that will be the whole reason that the features editor will light upon this otherwise unprovocative article: "A letter in my possession serves up a nice instance of a choice item thus undetected . . ."

"This should set the cat among the pigeons, Rose. To the Features Editor of *The Sunday Times,* please, with the covering letter from me—handwritten, I don't know the man, but a personal note always looks well."

But *The Sunday Times* was not receptive. Nor was the rejection letter in any way personal. Henry was annoyed—offended, indeed. "One does wonder if it landed on the right desk. Well, *The Sunday Telegraph* may well have been a better choice in any case."

The Telegraph was equally swift to make clear its lack of interest, as was *The Observer.* Henry was now tight-lipped, wounded rather than outraged. "The fact of the matter is, Rose, that these people don't know one's name—one's reputation. I've mentioned the forthcoming memoirs each time, so you would think . . . Or are they so young that they've never heard of Harold Wilson's government?" A mirthless laugh.

Rose had come to dread the sight of those long white envelopes. She shook her head and tutted.

Henry picked up the sheets of paper and put them into a drawer in his desk. "Thank you for your efforts, Rose. We shall have to put this down to experience. One will need to think very carefully when settling on a publisher for the memoirs—some firm with senior, knowledgeable editors. Coffee, Rose, could you?"

She went through to the kitchen and put the kettle on. Oh dear. Poor old boy. She felt a frisson of pity, and was surprised at herself.

Henry reviewed the situation. Evidently a thirty-year-old political scandal that got away was of no concern—at least not in the eyes of the sort of Johnny-come-lately who ran newspapers today. Time was, journalists were more astute. All right, so that was not the way to attract a bit of attention, restore one's name.

He thought again about a scholarly article. Something not neces-sarily of generous length, but shrewd, succinct, throwing new light on a neglected part of the eighteenth century.

On what aspect?

He thought. He did some desultory reading. He got out old notes. And, somewhere far away and untouchable, the eighteenth century sneered at him.

No. One's best work in that area is over and done with—better to face up to that. Archival work is for younger men.

That evening Henry switched on the television. Apart from the news, there were hardly any programs that he watched, except for a furtive interest in costume drama, but he had become mildly addicted to the current series on medieval monarchs. A personable young his-torian addressed the camera with fiery enthusiasm, scrambled up castle ramparts, strode over the sites of battlefields. Henry could have done without the interludes of enacted coronations, feasts and jousts, and retained a slightly patrician disdain about the whole thing—he had never been able to see the attraction of medieval studies, merely a warm-up to the time when history really gets off the ground—but nevertheless he found himself watching with interest. This young chap was quite compelling, if somewhat unscholarly in appearance (though the credits listed him as Fellow of a prestigious Cambridge college).

When the program was over, Henry poured himself another glass of claret, and reflected. Television programs are watched by millions of people—even programs about history. Books about history are read by thousands—or not even that, in many cases. Television is of course for the masses, but a program of this kind is for the more discerning elements of the masses. Henry has seen other such programs, in which other loquacious younger academics held forth; he had watched with a certain detachment—populist stuff, not to be taken seriously.

On the other hand . . . Could one be wrong about this? Long ago, Henry had himself appeared on television. But that was back when it was acceptable for an academic simply to address the camera, at length. A kind of filmed lecture. He seemed to remember that portraits of

Walpole and George II had been shown at some point, but there had been no nonsense about striding around the landscape, or people in fancy dress. Once that kind of program was defunct, Henry had dismissed the medium, insofar as serious discussion of history was concerned. Now, he found himself reconsidering. Is it not an obligation on the scholar to transmit to the widest possible audience? To enlighten as many as possible, to invite even the uninformed to consider the past, to listen to history? The more Henry thought, the more he revised his former contempt for this medium. Books and articles can address the few; a privileged number have access to the lecture and the seminar. But in a democratic society something further is required, and television has supplied this need; one had been misguided not to have realized this before, not to have made oneself available.

Well, it was not too late. By no means. Indeed, thought Henry, the fact that he was *not* some young sprog in jeans and a sweater could be a positive asset. Age would lend gravitas, authority. He would not be doing the scrambling around hillsides and sprinting up ramparts, but ramparts were a dead duck by the eighteenth century, anyway; no—a wander round Blenheim, maybe, and a stroll through the grounds of Rousham, talking about the picturesque. And then of course a session in the Soane Museum, discussing the Hogarths. One would have to try to veto those dramatized sequences that were apparently de rigueur— all too easy to imagine the kind of vulgarities that would be dreamed up when it came to dramatizing a bit of Hogarth or Gillray. No, the style would be elegant, restrained, purposeful—the object, to inform and entertain. Back to Reithian principles, in fact, which seemed so often forgotten in the present climate of broadcasting. One had of course known Reith quite well, way back.

When Rose arrived the next morning Henry was busy making notes. "Ah, Rose. Something for you to type up later—some memoranda about a new project. I'm planning to make a television series— half a dozen one-hour programs, I envisage, on aspects of the eighteenth century. One has vastly underestimated television, I've come to realize. Time to put that right, eh?"

She hadn't seen him in such a good mood for a while. She tried to assume an expression of polite enthusiasm. He hasn't got a clue, she thought. Well, nor have I, but I've a pretty good idea that you don't just decide to make a TV series and bingo! you're off. Even if you're his lordship.

"I must admit that this is not a world in which I have many contacts," said Henry. "None, indeed. One has not paid much attention to broadcasting lately. But it's presumably just a question of having a word with some key people. Oh—and Rose, I've been trying to get hold of my niece but there's always that maddening voice saying she's not available. Could you persist, and ask her if she'll come to lunch on Saturday?"

Marion was finding the Harrington project a shot in the arm. The agreed budget was generous, she had a free hand, on the whole, within a general brief of "traditional, nothing too recherché but a few interesting surprises would not go amiss." In other words, do what you like, but don't frighten the horses. The flat was spacious, flooded with light from high windows, plenty of room for a dining-room as well as a lavish kitchen, two en suite bedrooms, huge sitting-room. The ultimate place for a picky foreign financier or diplomat.

She wandered around amid the dust and rubble—the plumbing and electrics were going in, to her specification, and some supervision was needed. She was having to spend quite a lot of time here. Clipboard in hand, she made notes about possible color combinations, thumbed through sheafs of Farrow & Ball, broke off to have a word with the electrician. Her mobile rang and she glanced at the screen: Uncle Henry, yet again—he would have to wait.

As would Jeremy. A missed call from him also. The Jeremy situation was a problem—though in many ways a self-inflicted one, as Marion realized. Did she want to carry on with this affair, or not? No sooner had she decided that no, she really must pull out, she must explain that honestly things weren't going anywhere, and didn't he agree, than she would find herself susceptible once more to that charm, that absence of guile, that rather touching vulnerability. And they would be back in the little French bistro they so liked, and back in bed.

Marion knew that she was pretty self-sufficient, and was proud of this. Her marriage had been troubled, and eventually a burden; it was a relief to have laid it to rest, a while ago now. She had never been looking for a repeat performance. Occasional passing relationships were quite fun, and she had never wanted children. Sooner or later, she would have to make the position clear to Jeremy, but sooner kept becoming later, and after all there was no harm in coasting along like this for a while, and the man was in such a stew about the tedious Stella and his money worries.

Her own, she felt, were on hold for the moment, thanks to George Harrington, and the flat. He had made a payment up front for the first few weeks which would tide her over nicely, and he would be topping up on a regular basis. No other client of any significance had turned up—recession still biting away, it would seem—but she need not feel too bothered about this just yet.

The electrician was offering a mug of tea. He and the plumber had established squatters' rights, where essentials were concerned. Both were Poles—brothers—and had come into Marion's life when she realized that their quotes far undercut the firm with which she had previously worked. Both were amazingly quick to latch on to the latest requirements by way of uplighters and wet rooms. Their English was minimal, and consisted mainly of trade terms: polyfilla, halogen light, power shower, double socket. Their seventeen-year-old nephew, raised and schooled in Ealing, acted as interpreter. "If you have any trouble with them," he told Marion during the briefing visit, "just call me—here's my mobile number." She had asked him if he planned to go into the building trade himself. He had smiled; no, the idea was a career in the City, finance of some kind.

She sat on a box of tiles in a shaft of sunlight, drinking the tea and enjoying a moment of relaxation. One scuttled too much, had been scuttling for years, catering for the whims of rich people. For Marion's mother, who had never worked, a busy day meant a trip to the hair-dresser and lunch with a friend. And Marion would not have wanted to live like *that*, but even so, a bit more pure leisure would not come amiss. That was the trouble with running your own business—there were no office hours, you never really knocked off. You found your-self going over accounts after supper; you spent weekends sourcing stuff. Oh, you did it because it was what you enjoyed doing, but you were seldom able to shed the whole thing, forget about it. A business has to be driven, serviced, and if you are the sole driver and server it has you in a stranglehold. And no business, no income; no home, no food on the table.

So a moment in the sun with a mug of tea was to be relished. She would make no phone calls, no further notes, simply sit for a while and consider whether she could splurge on a new spring outfit, given this bit of money in the bank.

And then her mobile rang. Uncle Henry's Rose this time. Damn. She'd have to take the call. "Yes, Rose?"

"Half a dozen programs, I think," said Henry. "The overall title prob-ably *The Augustan Age*—quite simple. But each of them homing in on a different aspect."

Marion took another—small—mouthful of Corrie's cottage pie. "Yes, I see." Except that I don't. Uncle Henry as Simon Schama? I don't think so.

"One will use all the prime sites, of course. Or locations—isn't that the term? Blenheim, Chatsworth, Dr. Johnson's house. A fascinating prospect. I will allow you to take me to a good tailor for a new suit—one must dress the part." He laughed indulgently.

"The thing is," said Marion, "I just wonder if . . ."

"I see it as thematic rather than chronological. Though one will of course try to get across the momentum of the century. An entire program on industrial developments—much as one rather dislikes the north of this country. But the canals would make a nice setting—one could be filmed talking from a narrow boat."

"I'm just a bit doubtful as to how . . ."

"So where you come in, my dear, is to sort out some key person I should be getting in touch with. I'm not particularly *au fait* with that world, and you have so many contacts all over the place, don't you? You are always telling me about your prominent clients."

Marion stared across the table at him. Challenged, it would seem. Hoist with one's own petard, is that it? Trust Uncle Henry to put you on the spot when it suits him.

"Well . . . actually, I'm not at all sure that I . . ."

"Someone well established in the BBC, or the other outfit—whatever it's called." He waved a deprecating hand. "One of those in charge of program making. I wondered initially about going straight to the top chap at the BBC, the . . . the . . ."

"Director-General, I think."

"Quite. Find out who he is and put the proposal to him—but, on second thought, it makes more sense to deal with the people who're going to actually *do* the program, don't you think? So—who do you suggest?"

"I don't . . ." she began. But I do, she thought. I've known for the last two minutes that I do.

Henry pounced on the hesitation.

"Yes?"

All right. It's not going to come to anything, in any case, and all it means is that I look a bit of an idiot, unleashing Uncle Henry with this fantasy.

"Well, there is someone I did some work for a couple of years ago who does BBC documentary programs, I understood."

"Ah. Senior figure?"

"Very, I think."

"Excellent. What's his name?"

"Her."

"Oh. Really?" Henry had never quite got used to women in top positions, even after Mrs. Thatcher.

"Delia Canning," said Marion wearily. "I'll look up her details and phone them through to Rose."

She had done up a Chelsea flat for Delia Canning; all cutting-edge sophistication, she remembered. Delia Canning will think Uncle Henry a figure out of the Ark. Sorry, Delia—but you're a smooth operator and will get him off your back in a trice.

"Good girl," purred Henry. "I knew you'd come up with the answer. Let's ring for Corrie—I think she's made us one of her jam rolls."

Jeremy left Marion another text: "Hope uncle lunch not too trying. Tonight? Please, please." There was a couple hovering around the new stained glass panels; their second visit, and he needed to chat them up a bit more, point out that Edwardian stained glass butterflies are the ultimate, you can hardly ever lay hands on them. Those panels had only come in a day or two ago, and were not yet priced; he slapped on another hundred quid as he crossed the warehouse to engage the couple.

Marion was being a bit iffy these days which was really boring of her, just when he needed all the support he could get. Mind, he had never assumed that this was forever, but he must have someone, and now was not the time to be looking around for greener grass, with the solicitor and the bank on his back. There had often been someone, over the last few years—a necessity, with Stella the way she was—but most had been passing fancies, and he'd felt Marion to be a tad more serious—more than a tad, really. So he needed her, he must keep her onside, at least until . . . well, he had no idea until what, or when.

The solicitor's letters crashed through the door of his flat once a week. God, how he had come to dislike that flat; he had never planned on *living* there, it was just to be his London pad, convenient for the warehouse, convenient for—well, some personal independence. Instead of which it was apparently now his *home*—an abuse of the term. Home was the dear old Surrey farmhouse, with all its attractive things—Stella could do a place up nicely, you had to hand her that— and supper ready when he got in at night, and the girls all welcoming and amusing, and Stella affectionate and attentive and not in one of her states.

The solicitor's letters received cursory treatment. Jeremy would skim through the demands, then write a petulant and noncommittal response, the subtext of which was a further plea to Stella for direct contact: "Kindly convey to my wife . . ."

And not only did the bank refuse to consider a further business loan but they were getting shirty about the payments on the previous one. Well, stuff them. Jeremy had been fending off banks for the last twenty years and he knew how to do it. So far, anyway. Something would turn up—he'd find some gem and make a killing, or at least a small stash. He'd sort the bank out, one way or another. Eventually, surely, Stella would see sense and sack that bloody man and life would get back to normal, or as normal as it had ever been—one had never *wanted* a bog standard, nine-to-five existence.

Jeremy had never believed in planning life. It's nerds who plan and structure—the sort of people who go for the sort of job interview that says: "Where do you see yourself in five years' time?" And of course they see themselves as a few rungs up the ladder, smug. Boring, boring. Far more interesting to take what comes, make what you can of it, veer off course if that looks like a good idea. Way back, he'd gone to university, to please his parents, but was soon tearing his hair out at the tedium of lectures and seminars; as for exams—forget it. He dropped out, or rather, slid off, and eventually admitted to his parents that actually he was going great guns with a market stall in the small town near the university campus; soap and cosmetics and stuff that you bought cheap in bulk and then sold for twice as much—magic! A guy in a pub told him how to do it and after a couple of weeks he was hooked. But he got tired of that in time, and then the mirror gave him a better idea—the old mirror he picked out of a skip and sold to his landlady for a fiver.

Skips did him proud for a couple of years. It's amazing what you find. One person's rubbish is exactly what someone else has been wanting. All that's needed is the middle man—the man with the van, and the yard on the outskirts of town: Jeremy. His granny died—bless her—and left him ten grand, so there was the van sorted and the down payment on the yard. He called it Jeremy's Place—big quirky painted sign alongside the main road, and an ad in the local paper every week. He teamed up with a guy who was good at restoring furniture—the table with a leg missing, the chest that just needed a coat of paint—and who could help heave the lengths of wood. They had timber by the ton—spewed out of one house by builders, snapped up from Jeremy by some more impecunious do-it-yourself home owner. He was a conduit—through him, those with too much subsidized those who did not have enough, and in the process provided Jeremy with some cash.

He discovered that his own personality was an asset. People expect a junk yard to be run by some dubious character in a greasy T-shirt. Not by Jeremy, with his nice public school voice (Mummy and Daddy paid a wad for that) and his manners and his jokes and his helpfulness: "I'll drop it over to you in the van—no problem."

And so it all began. Jeremy's Place is a long while back—he outgrew it, saw possibilities that were far more enticing, more productive. And had learned by then that the golden rule is never to plan. Something will turn up—dear old Granny chose a most tactful moment to kick the bucket, Jeremy did that nifty deal with the people demolishing a hotel—one thing enables another, if you seize the moment.

He'd had to get himself better informed. Once you're into the more fancy stuff you need to be able to talk it up, to know your Georgian from your Victorian. Actually, he'd come to enjoy that. Book work in the service of exams had been punitive; book work in the interests of commerce was at first stimulating and then rewarding in itself. He found that he liked to find out, to check, to look up; he acquired quite a library on furniture, ceramics, stained glass, metalwork. When something remarkable came his way he would recognize it.

He did. From time to time there was a windfall—the lovely Spode piece in a box of rubbish, the murky old screen that when cleaned up turned out to be an early eighteenth-century treasure. He found out how to dispose of such things—where to get a decent price. Good fun—negotiating with the big boys, the pukka antique specialists, who thought they could take a novice for a ride, and then found they couldn't.

The pleasure of this game, for Jeremy, was its unpredictability. All right, you never knew from one month to the next what you'd be pulling in, but except for the occasional crisis period there had always been enough, and every now and then a positive surplus. In crisis periods you crossed your fingers, kept cool, and told Stella to stop fussing; in a surplus situation you moved Stella and the kids into a better house, bought a nice car, or took a business risk on Bickston Manor—and yes, that went off the rails but we all make mistakes.

Follow your nose, that's the recipe for an interesting life. What's the point of plotting and planning anyway? You might die tomorrow. That was Stella's problem—one of Stella's problems: she was always in a stew about what might happen and what can you do to stop it? You can't. What you do is go with the flow, see where it takes you, spot the next possibility. One thing throws up another—that's the charm of it.

The couple eyeing the stained glass panels were bothered by the price. At least the guy was. When he wandered off to look at doors and brass fittings Jeremy went to work on the girl for a bit and soon had her seeing she just must snap up the glass before someone else did. He saw the pair of them out to their car, all smiles and no pressure. They'd be back.

There were only a few other people around, and the Irishman was on hand. Jeremy went into the office for a quick coffee and a look at his messages. Nothing from Marion. In an hour or so he'd try her again. Meanwhile, time for another wave at Stella—she never replied but he kept at it: "Tell your horrid man to stop wasting paper. I want to talk. Love you—even if you don't believe it."

Stella deleted Jeremy's text. How typically thoughtless of him to send texts, given that treacherous little message that had triggered all of this. In any case, Paul Newsome had advised her not to reply to anything—letters, e-mails, texts, whatever. Responses from her might compromise future negotiations: "That is what I am for, Stella—the buffer between you." They were on first name terms now, though he always spoke hers with a certain formality. It was she who had said, "Oh, I can't go on calling you Mr. Newsome."

Her sister said divorce took absolutely ages. The friend for whom Paul Newsome had done so well had been at it for a couple of years. Gill said there was absolutely no point in rushing things, you had to make sure that there was the best possible arrangement for yourself and the children. Actually, there seemed to be no alternative to delay, in any case, since apparently it was impossible to get going properly until Jeremy saw fit to serve up a solicitor of his own: "Your husband's intransigence—perverse intransigence, if I may say—has us somewhat stymied at the moment."

Gill was saying that it could well be that subconsciously Stella had been wanting a divorce for a long time. After all, he hadn't been exactly the ideal husband, had he? Of course, Gill has never liked Jeremy and made that clear long ago. Actually Gill doesn't really like men in general. Stella had sometimes felt that if you were as determinedly unmarried as Gill then you couldn't have much of an idea what it is like to be in a marriage. Gill ran dog training courses, was a churchwarden, and had a staunch circle of women friends whose lives also centered around dogs. Stella had once wondered if she might be gay, which would have somehow made her more—well, emotionally normal. But no, apparently not. Gill didn't want or need anyone, just dogs. She was eight years older than Stella, had bossed her around when they were children, and then after their mother died young she had become Stella's support and lifeline, which suited them both. Stella would reach for Gill whenever she felt things were getting too much for her, and if Gill thought Stella was heading for one of her nervous crises she would drop everything and come over, at which point Jeremy would leave home until she had withdrawn once more.

Gill said Stella was basically unstable—not her fault, quite possibly something genetic, they'd had an aunt who was like that too—and what she needed was lots of support in her tricky times, and people who understood that she shouldn't be upset. Some breeds of dog have that tendency, and it's just a question of management. Gill knew a therapist who said that of course family circumstances are crucial in a case like Stella's, her husband must be aware of his role; whenever Gill referred to this she would raise her eyebrows and sigh. They both knew what she meant. Gill had a vast acquaintance; she drew on many people for expertise, from the latest in supplementary medication to counseling at one remove, and of course for the provision of a top divorce lawyer. Both Gill and Stella were grateful for Paul Newsome; Gill had wondered about coming along with Stella for some of her sessions with him, but somehow he hadn't seemed very keen.

Paul Newsome was going to cost a bit. Mercifully Stella had the money her parents had left her, which was in shares and building societies, safely tucked away. Gill had always been firm that Stella must never let Jeremy get at it, and thank goodness. In fact Jeremy didn't even know about it.

At the moment, Stella couldn't work out how much she was missing Jeremy, or what she felt about missing him forever. She was too angry with him to feel anything but resentment; the intimate sign-off from that Marion woman was seared into her brain: ". . . love you." The last thing she wanted was to see him, to hear the excuses, the protestations, the promises. She just wanted him out of sight and, while not out of mind because that was impossible, out of the house and out of her daily life. So long as he was not there, and silent because she refused to listen, she could try to stay calm and resolute—and really, she was surprised at how level-headed she had been since she had decided that it was divorce, and that was that. She had had no real crisis days, few shaky ones, she wasn't taking the pills, or not many. Each time she went to see Paul Newsome she felt—empowered, yes, that was the word. This was the first time in her life that she had taken a big strong decision, all on her own. Oh, life was all decisions—but paltry decisions, like where to go for the summer holiday, and what to get the girls for Christmas. This time, she had redirected her entire life, she had taken control, she had not allowed an event to floor her, but had made it the occasion for a radical move. In the twenty years of her marriage, it had always been Jeremy who directed things—by being either broke, so it was worry, worry, or having a windfall, so it was let's move house again. Now it was her turn.

CHAPTER SEVEN

On Saturdays, Gerry did maintenance work. He tinkered with the car, washed and polished it. He replaced washers on taps, and sometimes interfered with domestic appliances, to Rose's annoyance, because he thought they were making a funny noise. When he ran out of this kind of job, he retired to his shed at the end of the garden, and could be heard sawing and planing; for the last year or so he had been making a table. Charlotte sometimes felt that Gerry had taken the wrong road in life; he was not an engineer or a carpenter but a local council official. He presided over an office; his daily routine was paperwork and meetings. Saturdays seemed to be some kind of gesture, a statement about his further capabilities. It was not that he felt himself to be by nature an artisan—not that at all, Gerry was extremely conscious of status. More that he needed to demonstrate manual efficiency, the ability to get things fixed. Perhaps in local government nothing ever did get satisfactorily fixed.

Charlotte had always been aware of Gerry's Saturdays, but now that she was living with him and Rose she saw them in close-up: Gerry's special Saturday garb—the old trousers that didn't matter, the sweater with the oil stain; his tool bag with each implement filed in its proper place; his pursed expression as he dismantled a hairdryer that wouldn't work.

"You don't mend hairdryers," said Rose. "You get another one.

Fifteen quid or thereabouts. But never mind." She was in the kitchen, out of earshot, dressed to go out, and Charlotte knew where she was going.

Gerry was a man of routine. Of course. Most people have rituals—Charlotte was aware of having accumulated a fistful, in old age—but his were more remorseless than most. He let the cat out at precisely seven-thirty in the morning; he laid his briefcase and the car keys on the hall table before going up to bed; he had a cooked breakfast on alternate days; he marked promising television programs in the *Radio Times* over his first cup of coffee on Saturday morning. He was disturbed by any disruption from the norm. Charlotte knew her presence in his house to be a disruption, and appreciated that he was making the best of things. He went out of his way to find some common ground for a conversation; and was forever opening doors for her and offering chairs. The hairdryer was hers; she had produced it with quiet satisfaction, knowing that Gerry would pounce.

"Keep him happy for hours," said Rose, inspecting herself in the kitchen mirror.

She went through to the sitting-room, where Gerry was happy with the hairdryer. Charlotte, washing up some lunch things (she was allowed now to do a few small domestic tasks), could hear their exchange.

"I'm off out," said Rose.

He grunted, evidently absorbed. As an afterthought: "Going to the supermarket?"

"No. I'm doing good Samaritan stuff. Mum's reading pupil. You know—I told you."

Another grunt. The hairdryer required his full attention.

Rose paused in the hall. "Bye Mum." The front door slammed.

Charlotte dried her hands and went to offer Gerry a cup of coffee. She could do very short distances now without the crutches—a triumph.

Gerry declined the coffee. He was looking put out. "I'm afraid this thing has defeated me. I think the heating element has packed up, in which case there's nothing one can do."

"Don't worry. Many thanks for trying."

"I was sure I could do it. I don't like to be defeated."

"And by a mere hairdryer," said Charlotte. "Pesky thing. Let me get rid of it for you." His afternoon was blemished, she saw; this challenge should have lasted for far longer. She thought of her Tom, who never so much as changed a lightbulb. Their houses had disintegrated around them, smirking as pipes leaked and gutters sagged.

She sat down, stowing the hairdryer away in her bag. "Please note, Gerry, no crutches. I can do ten yards now. Fifteen with a following wind. No time at all, and you'll be shot of me. You and Rose have been saints. Are being."

"Our pleasure." Stiffly. Gerry doesn't do emotion. And he is embarrassed.

Charlotte rattled on, to cover the moment. "Being derailed like this is a slap in the face. And having to impose myself on you adds insult to injury." Dear, dear—cliché upon cliché. "Anyway, not for much longer. I get more agile by the day."

Then he surprised her. "If something like that happened to me I would be far less resilient. I know it. Go to pieces, I dare say."

It struck her that nothing much ever had happened to Gerry. Nothing adverse. An impacted wisdom tooth, she remembered. A trivial car accident, provoking a dispute with the insurance company.

"Probably not, Gerry. We all tend to . . ." No, no—not rise to the occasion, or take it on the chin. ". . . well, we accept, in a rather odd way. There being no alternative."

He inclined his head, which meant he didn't agree. "I have always found the unexpected extremely hard to take."

"I know," said Charlotte, surprising herself now.

He looked at her, and she saw a vulnerability that did not often show. Gerry had features that were a touch severe, a habitual slight frown. The eyes, now, spoke of something else.

He shook his head. "One is reminded. When . . ." He waved a hand in her direction—indicating, she took it, her ravaged hip.

"Yes," she said. "You've been lucky. Rose too, thanks be."

She wondered if he was perhaps someone who feared death, for whom the idea of death lurked always at the edge of the mind. She did not; she was afraid of the run up to death, not the thing itself.

She thought: I hardly know Gerry, after all this time. Only the surface of him—the Saturdays, the likes and dislikes.

"Lucky . . ." he said. Considering the word, it would seem. "It doesn't feel so much lucky as—normal. Straightforward. It's the other things that are . . . I don't know . . ."

"Violations?" Charlotte suggested. The mugger. The broken hip.

He nodded. "And, as you say, I've been spared. We have. So I doubt any capacity to cope if . . ." A dry laugh.

"You could surprise yourself," she told him. "People do."

"I hope you're right."

She sensed that the chink he had opened was about to close. "You can feel challenged as much as violated. Though at my age one is less keen on challenges. When young I rather enjoyed them. Tom positively sought them, of course."

"Yes, I remember. I used to feel he stuck his neck out. And envied him for being able to do so."

"Oh. Did you?" Well, well. Goodness me.

"I don't mean to be rude."

"I know you don't."

"The time he chose to move to that school."

She nodded. Gerry was referring to an inner city school at which Tom had taken over, considering that with drive and skill he could rescue it from its "sink school" performance. He had succeeded.

"I admired Tom," said Gerry. "He wouldn't have known that."

"No, I don't think he did." If only you had shown it. Told him, even. Tom thought you—well, a pretty buttoned-up sort of person. But you wouldn't have known that.

"I used to feel that perhaps Tom didn't think much of me." The dry laugh again.

"Oh . . . Oh, no. You shouldn't think that."

"We could do with a few chaps like Tom where I work. Unfortunately local government doesn't much attract them."

It just gets people like me. The unspoken coda hung between them, and Charlotte winced.

Gerry stood up. "Well, I must go out to the car. Oil change needed. Nothing I can do for you?"

She shook her head. He went. She heard him crunch down the gravel of the garden path, out to where the car waited, groomed and maintained to perfection. She felt grateful to the hairdryer, for having enabled this glimpse of a Gerry she had not known.

Rose removed her coat, took the green jacket off the hanger and shrugged it on. She adjusted the shoulders, did up the buttons. "You're sure she's about my size?"

"A little smaller," said Anton. "Not much. Perhaps a little more short, too."

"What about the color? Does she like green?"

"I think."

Rose put the garment back. "Actually I don't care for it—it feels a bit stiff, the material." She wandered along the rail, took down a thick soft gray knitted jacket. "Ah. This is a possibility." She put it on. "Nice. My mum would wear this. In fact so would I."

"Gray is not always for old lady?"

"Not necessarily. We might look for a bright scarf to go with it, if we settle on this. What do you think?"

Anton spread his hands. They had already ransacked the shop, the assistants observing Rose with respect. They knew a fastidious shopper when they saw one.

"If you like I am sure it is good. And I like. On you it is very nice."

Rose showed him the price ticket. "Is that OK? It's not cheap—but it's good value."

"That is fine."

The deal was done, the jacket wrapped in tissue and put in a large shiny bag with the designer's logo. Anton patted it: "I will send her this too. She will like for her shopping."

Outside, Rose paused. "We need a scarf, but there isn't anywhere around here, really. A Marks & Spencer would do nicely, but none handy."

"But there is Starbucks," said Anton. "I could buy you coffee. For thank you. Please?"

They settled in Starbucks, with a small cappuccino for Rose, a Chocolate Cream Frappuccino for Anton. "I am like small boy with this," he said. "I must try."

"You could go for broke and have an apple and cinnamon muffin as well."

"Broke?"

"Oh, sorry . . ." She explained, adding, "The thing is, I forget there are expressions you don't know, because actually your English is good."

"But that is fine," he said. "That way I learn. On the building site I say now to the site manager, 'I go for broke and move all these bricks.' But I think the apple and cinnamon muffin is . . . too much."

"A bridge too far," said Rose. "There's another one for you."

"Ah. So I say to the site manager, 'You tell me to do all this today is a bridge too far.' Good. On the site I most learn bad language. I can say bad words now in four–five language. My mother would be—not pleased at all." He smiled. "She does not like the building site, but I tell her it is just for a short time, until I am a big man in accountancy firm." He went on, more soberly: "Until I read well."

"Which you soon will. Mum says you're making terrific progress."

"Then it is her good teaching."

"It must be very odd to have to—go back to school, at your age." She added, embarrassed, "Our age."

"It is not difficult. Perhaps there is always something in our head that is ready to learn. And I remember when I was boy, how you are—hungry—to learn things."

"When my son was five he knew the names of all the dinosaurs," said Rose. "You know—prehistoric creatures. *Tyrannosaurus rex* and stegosaurus . . . Strings of names."

"What is *his* name?"

"James. And my daughter is Lucy."

"I have no child," he said. "My wife did not want." Then, seeing her expression: "You should not feel sorry. It is a long time ago now. I am—accepting."

There was a small silence. "And now," Anton said cheerfully, "I have house full of child—children. My nephew and his friends. Last night I am very father and I tell them—we clean this place up. There is much . . . much not want to."

"Grumbling," said Rose. "I can imagine."

"Live like student is fine if you are age of student. But I am not. So I get brush and bucket and soap and thing and I am like manager on the site."

"What happened?"

"They grumble. Then they do it. And I have to buy beer for everyone. Very expensive cleaning—for me."

They both laughed.

"You have to set up a rota," said Rose. "Turn and turn about. That's what we did, when I was in a student flat at my university."

"But girls are different. They like to be clean. Young men are . . . horrible."

"Oh, I know. I remember James. And now he's a banker in a sharp suit and expensive shirts."

"He is banker? He is one of the people who make the credit crisis?"

"No," said Rose. "He's only a baby banker. More like the office boy, though he'd have you think otherwise."

"And you? You work for a history man, your mother say. History man—is that right?"

"It's historian. But I like history man."

"He is old man, she say. Important old man."

"He'd like important. Though he was, I suppose." She told him about Henry. "Right now, he's trying to get into television—to make programs. He hasn't a hope, I imagine."

"I like to watch programs like that. Where you learn something. But my nephew and his friends—not. So we have argument and I do not win."

"Sounds like family life," said Rose. "At least when your children leave home you get hold of the remote control. What does your nephew do? Before coming here, I mean?"

"He work in a bar. Is not bad job but pay very little and he want to get married. So he come here for a year to have money for wedding and to start home. He is a nice boy—and the others—but I would like place by myself. Soon I look for a room somewhere."

"The building site . . ." Rose began, diffidently "It must be well, tough, doing work like that when you aren't used to it."

"Oh, often I am please with myself. Look! I have lift this, and move that, like I am a real worker! I have work hands now"—he opened them on the table and she saw calloused blisters—"but I hope is not for too long. I would like nice clean office again."

"It won't be," she said. Suddenly anxious for him, and determined.

"All the time I try new reading. Look." He pulled a book out of his rucksack. *Walking London*, she saw. He opened it at random: "'Enter the . . . dome, yes? . . . to your right, and use the foot tunnel to cross the . . . river . . . to Green . . . Greenwik.'"

"Grenidge," said Rose. "Place-names are impossible. But it's nice there, and you go under the river through this tunnel, like it says. So have you been doing these walks?"

"A little bit. On Sunday. And I like to try to read the book, and look at the pictures."

"Gerry and I used to walk in London. My husband. Way back." Not for ages now, she thought. Never, now. Why not? "There's a fantastic walk along the river." She flipped over the pages of the book. "Yes, look—here it is. Kew and Richmond." He leaned forward, following her finger on the map. "Or there's the City churches, that's interesting."

He was intent, listening to her. "St. Paul's . . ." she said. "And you must see Hampton Court. And even just the parks . . . St. James's is my favorite—the lake, the ducks." Some kind of possibility seemed to smoke up from the book, from what she said, from her warmth, from his attention. She put the book down, picked up her cup, drained it. "Well, yes," she said. "Yes, you must . . . see more."

"I would like."

"Perhaps . . ." she began. Then, briskly, "How is the Chocolate Cream Frappuccino?"

He pulled a face. "Too sweet. I cannot finish. I have learn a lesson—not to think like small boy."

"Have an espresso," she advised. "To cancel it. Actually, I could use one too."

She watched him while he was at the counter. She wondered if everyone had that very dark thick hair, where he came from. She heard him give the order, thought of his daily struggle with language, but in his head was that alien fluency—his other world. Once, he turned, and their eyes met in the mirror on the wall; he smiled.

"*Two* coffees," she said, when he was back. "I don't usually live it up like this."

"This is special day. For me," he added. "For my mother, soon—when she have her coat."

Rose thought: for me too, in a funny way. I'm enjoying myself, for some reason.

"When I was young," she said, "wine bars were the place to be seen, to hang out with your friends."

He looked at her. "And you are still young. Grown-up child—children—does not make old. And *I* am young." He laughed. "I tell myself this when I come to England. I am young enough so I make new life. But then I find I am not young enough for live like student and eat out of tins."

"I don't *feel* young," she said. "But I see what you mean. I am, by comparison. We are. Old is—different. My mum. Forty-something is just—older."

"And is good time. Young is . . ." He scowled. ". . . problem, problem. I have not girl. I am stupid, I have spot on my face."

"It's one's hair, with girls. I thought about my hair about half of every day."

"So now we are young still but better sort of young. We do not mind about spot or hair. We have learn to enjoy."

Well, yes, she thought. Even in a Starbucks on a Saturday afternoon. Surprise, surprise.

"On the building site," he said, "I enjoy now the tea break. You wait for—you watch time. Then—whew! Sit down. Talk. Learn more bad word in Kosovo. Play cards. Read newspaper—try to read newspaper. What are you enjoying?"

She pondered. What? "Oh . . . Weekend mornings, getting up later, tea in bed. Lucy coming back from college, chattering non-stop." Pause. Thought—no, impulse. "Actually, weather. I enjoy weather. Wind. Rain, even. Sun, like now, this spring. I sort of love weather— lots of it." Goodness, I've never said that to anyone before. "Good thing I'm not living in California. Always the same there, they say."

"For me, things that grow. On the building site, we are growing only cigarette ends and crisp packets. But on my way I look into gardens. English gardens are—beautiful. All flowers, all different. Some names I learn." He smiled. "Your flower. Your name. Rose."

She had never cared for it, name-wise. Miranda, she had wanted to be, aged eight. Coming from him, it sounded suddenly fresh, new. Rose. With his accent. A different name. She liked it.

He told her his grandparents had been farmers. "So I remember their growing. The growing and the . . . cutting."

"Harvesting."

"Yes. So perhaps from that I get to like. But my father come to the city when young man, so no more farm. But perhaps inside me is person who want to grow things, who remember the . . . the earth. Never mind. When I am accountant again I grow numbers." A wry smile.

The clientele of the coffee bar changed, and changed again. That noisy group of girls left; a courting couple came, and snogged in a corner; two young mothers traded babies, were replaced by a father restraining a toddler. Rose and Anton did not much notice any of them, somehow. Midafternoon became late afternoon. He had told her about those visits to the grandparents' farm when he was a child, about his father's death when still quite young, about his dislike of rock music ("My nephew and the boys, all the time—I try not to hear"); about his love of opera. She had talked of Lucy and James (but not too much . . .), of Henry and his idiosyncrasies; she agreed about rock music, but confessed to a lacuna where opera was concerned. They found that both liked to do crosswords; Anton produced a dog-eared book of these in his own language and Rose stared in fascination at the mysterious network of the one he had just completed. She reached in her bag for the *Guardian:* "Here—let's have a go. One across: 'Study of handwriting.' Ten letters."

After a few minutes he was laughing and shaking his head. "No, no—this is a bridge too far."

She glanced at her watch. "Heavens! It's past five. I must go." She began to put on her coat, to gather her things. "I do hope your mother will approve of the jacket."

"I know that she will. And thank you."

"But . . ." Rose hesitated. "It really does need a scarf to go with it."

"You think?"

"I do think."

There was a little silence, against the splutter of the coffee machine, a baby's wail. "Next Saturday, maybe?" she said. "There's a Marks and Spencer not far from where we live. Would you like to meet up?"

"I would like," he said. "I would like very much."

Charlotte made a pot of tea at five. Gerry came in from his shed, had a cup, read the paper. Charlotte said, "I'd have thought Rose would be back by now."

"Mmn. Got held up, I suppose."

Run over, thought Charlotte. Knocked down by one of those manic cyclists. It dies hard, maternal anxiety. In fact, it doesn't die at all. A life sentence. Well, one wouldn't wish otherwise. All the same, where is she?

When at last Rose appeared Charlotte experienced that comfortable rush of relief. "I'll make some more tea. This pot's cold."

"No thanks, Mum. I'm fine."

"Successful shopping?"

"Yes. Nice gray jacket."

"How was Anton?"

"Fine."

Not run over, not picked off by a cyclist, but something on her mind. One always knows. Oh well—whatever, she's not saying. She never does, does she?

Gerry came in from the garden. "That new clematis doesn't look very happy to me. Where did you get it?"

Rose stared at him.

"The clematis. That new one."

"Oh," she said. "Oh—Clockhouse garden center, I think."

"And I'm afraid your mother's hairdryer was too much for me. Heating element gone."

"A bridge too far," said Rose.

Charlotte eyed her. And you're not quite with us, are you? What's wrong? Has his lordship been playing up? This TV nonsense? Rose made it into a joke, but one's heard what he can be like when he gets obsessive about something.

Gerry picked up the cat, which had been winding round his legs. He was attached to the cat, and she to him, in an ostentatious way; others could feel relegated. "She's off her food. Didn't touch her lunch. Should you take her to the vet?"

"No," said Rose. "She's dramatizing as usual. The place seems to be falling apart, in my absence. Clematis, hairdryer, cat." She sat down, and opened the *Guardian* at the crossword. Half done, Charlotte saw.

Gerry took the cat through to the kitchen; he could be heard urging her to try some milk.

Charlotte said, "Maybe what his lordship needs is diversion. Take his mind off this television idea. A cruise. He could afford it."

Rose frowned. "Mmn? 'Cause of unexpected mechanical problem'—seven letters. This is supposed to be the *quick* one—my mind's a blank today."

"Gremlin," said Charlotte. "Get him a Swan Hellenic brochure—tempt him."

"Henry? Oh, he's very chirpy. He's seeing someone this week.

Some woman. 'Rather influential in that world, I gather.'" Rose put on her Henry voice, laughed, returned to the crossword.

Gerry came back. "She won't touch milk, either."

"Try champagne," said Rose. "We must have a bottle of Krug around somewhere."

CHAPTER EIGHT

"An hour," said Delia Canning. "A single feature. Docudrama, maybe. I can promise nothing. We'll have to think."

"No, no," said Henry. "Six parts, I envisage. A series."

They were in her office, where supplicants were normally at a disadvantage. He was not, it seemed. His loud, plummy tones filled the room. His capacious form filled her office chair; she hadn't seen a tweed suit like that in decades. Her grandfather had had one, for church on Sundays.

She shook her head. "Out of the question, I'm afraid."

Small, sharp-featured woman. Trousers and a shirt; one would have thought something more formal, for a person in a top job here, or so one understood. He felt wrong-footed, having to negotiate like this with a young woman. She hadn't yet got the hang of what he had in mind. He elaborated: ". . . the essence of the Augustan age—the politics, the art, the architecture—one would look at science and industry, of course, plenty of visual opportunity there, your people would be able to work out the . . . locations . . . Ironbridge, that sort of thing . . . I wouldn't be averse to the occasional period costume, I gather it's expected these days, but not too much—enlightenment would be the idea, enlighten and inform the viewer, enlightenment the appropriate word for the eighteenth century, don't you agree?"

Unbelievable. You didn't come across people like this today, at least she didn't. She eyed him. A certain awful appeal, there was no getting away from it.

"So six parts seems about right. The structure to be a matter for discussion between us, as I said in my letter." He beamed, expansive now—into his stride. He had decided that she was looking more as though she followed what he was proposing.

Almost a parody. You'd have to have him wearing a waistcoat and watch-chain, and that suit, or something similar. The voice, the pronunciation, the mannerisms. It could work. Could it? Hmn.

"Just conceivably," said Delia Canning. "We might consider a single program. As I say, possibly. I can't promise, at this stage." She rose, she smiled—a smile that those alert to the surface codes of her trade would have interpreted as meaning absolutely nothing.

Henry was not alert. He decided she was really quite an intelligent young woman after all. "I'm so glad you're keen on the idea. Let me know when you'd like to talk again. Next time, you must lunch with me at my club."

When he had gone, she stared again at his proposal—no, his letter, his self-important letter which would have been dismissed had not the mention of Marion Clark's name caught Delia's eye, and Marion Clark had done such a good job on the flat, and Delia felt she couldn't bat Marion Clark's uncle aside out of hand, this Lord Whatsit. She had her secretary check him out; it seemed that he was indeed—or had been—a well-known academic. Suppose I'll have to see him, she had thought. Academics are two a penny, but never mind. Waste of half an hour, that's all.

A certain awful appeal. The voice, the manner, everything. You'd be sticking your neck out a mile, putting him on. People would love him or hate him. A provocation. Risky—oh, yes. But just might be a winner.

Take a chance? Yes? No?

"So one's name still counts," Henry told Marion. "She seems to favor a single program, for some reason."

I don't believe this, thought Marion. Delia Canning? Uncle Henry? No, no. "Are you sure?"

"I still prefer six. I dare say she'll change her mind."

"You did actually *see* Delia Canning, Uncle Henry?"

"Of course I saw her. Pleasant young woman. A most useful introduction, my dear."

"I do wonder . . ." Marion began, and then broke off, "I'll have to go, Uncle Henry. I'm at this flat I'm doing and the bathroom people have arrived."

The bathroom was coming in over budget, which was tiresome. George Harrington had taken against her original specification, and a whole lot of instructions had arrived from his secretary involving a suite that Marion spent an entire weekend sourcing. He had visited some friends, apparently, and been taken with their installation. Marion never seemed to speak to Harrington himself these days; he was always in a meeting or out of contact, and the secretary acted as intermediary. This first tranche of money would soon be exhausted, but apart from this glitch over the bathroom Marion was not too concerned; the Poles were performing excellently, and she was confident that the job would finish on time.

Not that she had much else in view. Recession still biting, it would seem. A few inquiries, which petered out as soon as she came up with an estimate. Bedroom makeovers were going on hold until next year; she imagined trophy wives all over Chelsea pouting in frustration.

Marion did not often like her clients. If women, they usually had too much money and too much leisure and a paucity of taste. There was a certain satisfaction to be had in steering them away from their wilder excesses, and persuading them to discover some unsuspected residue of style. Quite often, she could deliver a finished room that caused her little or no offense and that the client really really loved, much to their surprise since they had thought they wanted something entirely different.

She had liked Delia Canning. Partly because she was a working woman, earned her money, and had no more leisure than Marion herself. There had been mutual respect. Delia had been brisk, businesslike, knew what she wanted, and none of it caused Marion any distress. A bit sleek and neutral, perhaps, but not a job of which she could feel ashamed.

Uncle Henry was fantasizing, of course. Must be. No way could Delia Canning take a shine to Uncle Henry; she was from another planet. Maybe he had seen some sidekick, thought it was her. Had misunderstood.

The bath was not going to fit. Six inches too long. Would throw the whole bathroom design out of kilter. Damn. What to do?

"A pilot," Henry told Rose. He read from the letter in front of him: "'. . . no commitment at this stage, of course.'" He chuckled. "That's a formality, I imagine. A pilot is apparently a sort of . . ." he waved a hand vaguely ". . . a sort of trial run. They film me, talking."

"Oh," said Rose, whose mind was elsewhere.

"Rather amusing, it should be. One will have to decide on a theme. Walpole, possibly—stick to one's particular field at this stage."

Rose surfaced. He was on about this television thing, it would seem.

"They want to do it, then?"

"Of course," said Henry. "Just a question of sorting out the details now. Let's write to Miss Canning, Ms. Canning, that is—we must observe the conventions. 'Dear Ms. Canning, I am delighted . . .'"

Good grief, thought Rose. His lordship on the telly. Some mistake, surely?

"She must be out of her mind." Marion told Jeremy. "Even *thinking* of it. Uncle Henry! I thought at first he was making it all up. Not that she'll go through with it, once she sees him in action."

Jeremy has never been much interested in Uncle Henry. He is not now. He has his own matter of the moment.

"The bloody solicitor's behind it, of course," he told Marion "Or her sister. Or both. Stella knows I can't afford it, haven't got the dosh. Christ, I'm paying the mortgage, aren't I?"

Money was required, apparently. Maintenance. A considerable sum of maintenance. Jeremy was to pay up, in monthly installments.

"I'm maintaining already till I'm blue in the face. I paid the house insurance last week, and now she's claiming they need a new boiler, all through Paul fucking Newsome—sorry, darling. 'My client instructs me to tell you that . . .' It's a stickup. They've got her drugged to the eyeballs, no doubt—I know Stella when she's on the pills, zombie isn't in it—and she'll be signing up to anything. If only I could *talk* to her."

Marion sighed. Here we go. They were in a Turkish restaurant that they hadn't tried before. Here I am, she thought, discussing with my lover how he can be reconciled with his wife. And I'm not sure about this lamb kofta—rather too spicy. She pushed it aside.

Jeremy put down his knife and fork, reached out and took her hand in both of his.

"I adore you," he said. "No, don't look at me like that—I know what you're thinking—I adore you, and you're such an angel to put up with me, and you're keeping me sane through this slough of despond, and I agree with you about the lamb kofta—I'm not finishing it either. We'll go back to the French bistro next time."

She laughed. You had to. This was always happening. She'd be deciding that really, she had to end it sooner rather than later, and maybe sooner . . . And then he'd cut the ground from under her feet.

"There," said Jeremy. "No more lamb kofta, and no more Paul sodding Newsome either, or Stella. I promise you won't hear another word. But listen to this . . ."

He had been up north. This amazing Victorian place. Heard about it on the grapevine—got in and sweet-talked the developers just as they were gutting it for a country house hotel. Some fantastic stuff, this paneling . . .

He exuded enthusiasm and energy once more. The lamb kofta was removed; baklava arrived, and was seriously good. She had forgotten her irritation, was enjoying herself; later rather than sooner, no need to rush into anything.

"Some general reflections on the historical process," Henry told Rose. "My ideas on the wayward nature of the past—why things happen as they do. Rather nice for a taster, don't you think, to open the series?"

Rose nodded. Whatever.

"So if you would just type it up. No—let me read it to you first. The piece is after all designed to be spoken. To camera—that is the term, I think." He cleared his throat, addressed Rose in a resounding tone, with stagy pauses for effect. "I myself have a soft spot for what is known as the Cleopatra's nose theory of history—the proposal that had the nose of Cleopatra been an inch longer the fortunes of Rome would have been different. A *reductio ad absurdam*, perhaps, but a reference to random causality that makes a lot of sense when we think about the erratic sequence of events that we call history. And we find that we home in on the catalysts—the intervention of those seminal figures who will direct events. Caesar himself. Charlemagne. Napoleon. Hitler. If this man or that—no, this person or that—had not existed, how differently could things have turned out? Focus upon a smaller canvas—England in the eighteenth century, or, indeed, any other century—and we find again that it is personalities that direct events, the human hand that steers the course of time. The ebb and flow of power; the machinations of politics. A decision is made in one place, and far away a thousand will die. There is an analogy, I understand, with a process that interests the physicists—chaos theory. The proposition that apparently random phenomena have underlying order—a very small perturbation can make things happen differently from the way they would have happened if the small disturbance had not been there. A butterfly in the Amazon forest flaps its wings and provokes a tornado in Texas." Henry inclined his head and smiled. "A rather nice image, don't you think?" But he was not addressing Rose now; he spoke to a camera, to a vast invisible audience, watching enthralled from their sofas. "Mind, I find the physics hard to follow—I'll admit that—but I'm intrigued to apply the theory to the historical process. This happens, and triggers that, which leads to something unexpected. But what, indeed, can be expected at all? We can only apply the wisdoms of hindsight—for once the cliché is appropriate."

Henry dismissed the camera, the nation's sofas. He returned to Rose, benignly inquiring, "How does that sound?"

Loud, thought Rose. I'd have been turning the volume down.

But Henry was not really seeking comment. "Quite a telling little introduction, I feel. We'll send it to Ms. Canning as the script for the pilot. So two copies, please, Rose—one for her and one for the file."

One had impressed, it would seem. That young woman had recognized the impact of age and experience. The weight, if you like. As opposed to young chaps scrambling up hillsides.

Henry had felt at a disadvantage with Delia Canning and had had to summon up all resources to overcome this. He had felt old, actually. He did not normally feel old. Old was of course a condition, and a condition from which one suffered, but the dignified and expedient thing was to dismiss it, as far as possible. It was annoying to find one-self getting out of breath on even a mild slope (hillsides out of the question); the digestion was more unreliable than in the past. Worst was this fearful and betraying tendency to lose entirely some name—names so familiar that they were second nature. The Elder and the Younger Pitt, for heaven's sake. Well, a lesson had been learned, there. But one had no need to go climbing hills, and going easy on Corrie's cream and brandy trifle was perhaps a possibility. Those occasional twinges in the chest were to be ignored. Henry had always been impa-tient with people who fussed over their health; they were the ones who kicked the bucket first, by and large.

Senior citizen was the term now, apparently. Smacked of the French Revolution—*citoyen*. Who dreamed up such expressions?

Some civil service apparatchik. *Citoyen* Gladstone, *citoyen* Bismarck, *citoyen* Churchill—plenty of senior citizens directing the course of history. In early societies the elders were respected and consulted, for good reason. The cult of youth is an entirely modern phenomenon, and a tedious one at that.

In his own youth, Henry had made sure to cultivate the elders; you never know who might give you a leg up. Always wise to see to it that the right people know who you are. In due course, comparable young had come knocking on his door, and Henry had rather liked that; a little circle of clever young men was an appropriate attribute for a scholar of substance. These had rather fallen away nowadays, though a few still kept up, especially when they were applying for some post and wanted a fresh reference. One had one's uses. But the young as such were really out of sight now, so far as Henry was concerned, except of course the ubiquitous young, yowling out of radios and hurtling along pavements on their bikes, doing their best to run Henry down. Today's young needed to be put in their place, not made into a cult. Bring back mandatory apprenticeship; there was something to be said for child labor.

"No," said Delia Canning.

Henry laid the script down on his desk, adjusted the phone. Had he misheard?

"*No?*"

"None of it, I'm afraid. It's—well—wordy. Not the sort of thing."

Henry blinked. Wordy?

"You wouldn't be doing yourself justice," said Delia. "We need something much more immediate. One of our young researchers here is going to draft a script, and then he'll go over it with you before they film. You'll like him—he's got a history background. Did history at—um—Manchester, I think. You'll hear from me when I've seen the pilot. Bye now."

Henry put down the phone. *Wordy?* The cheek of it. But one will have to play along with them, if this thing is to go ahead.

Marion had had to redesign the bathroom entirely. Much time. Indeed, this flat was gobbling up time. Just as well that she didn't have other commissions on the go. The Poles were delightful and hardworking but did require maximum supervision. There could be misunderstandings, linguistic confusions; the nephew had to be sent for more than once. He treated his uncles with kindly tolerance as wayward children who could not help their deficiencies. "They do a really good job," he told Marion. "It's just a nuisance they can't get their heads around the language." His own speech was pure London.

"How did you come to be brought up here?"

He smiled. "Oh, my dad came here to do a computer course when he was twenty, and never went back. He'd rather seen that IT was the place to be, even back then."

She enjoyed the company of the Poles, which was cheery and undemanding. They sang and whistled, and plied her with mugs of tea or coffee. They talked much to each other. Could have been saying anything: "Persnickety bitch—fussing over every light fitting." Probably not.

Actually, the flat was the biggest job she had done for some time. It was the garden floor of a big old building in a prime part of Hampstead; in the flat above, the halogen lights and the wood floors were already in. Range Rovers and BMWs stood outside. In the local eateries, expensively clad young women whiled away time over coffee at an hour when most people of that age are working; in the High Street, it was easier to buy designer gear than a loaf of bread. The place smoked affluence. What did the Poles think of this? Nothing much, perhaps; it blew work their way, and that was all they cared about. And me too, thought Marion. Who am I to complain? I depend on people who have money to spare. That said, I prefer the Poles to the glossy girls in Carluccio's and Maison Blanc. And I can't afford a little item from Hobbs to lift the spirits so I am not even going to look.

Marion's clients were way out of her league, financially. She did not feel particularly envious or resentful, merely a bit impatient with all that spending power. It did not seem to make them extra happy; most of the trophy wives appeared either edgy or vaguely mutinous. Presumably the status itself required staying power: you could be traded in at any moment.

She wondered if George Harrington had a wife. If so, she had never featured. Marion would have liked to have a further word with him about the bathroom, but the secretary said he was abroad and unavailable for a week or two. The fact was that his volte-face over the chosen suite had set Marion back considerably in terms of time; she thought of mentioning this, and decided not to. There might be further commissions coming from that direction; best to appear flexible and accommodating.

He was unusual, as a client. Most of her clients arrived through word of mouth recommendation, not because she happened to sit next to them at a lunch. Fortuitous, you could call him. Usually, one satisfied client had brought in another; the Web site helped, no doubt, and a couple of years ago she had had a stroke of luck with a feature in a Sunday newspaper magazine—that led to a period that was quite frenetic. She had even taken on an assistant for a while.

No call for that now, so be thankful for the fortuitous George Harrington, and indeed for Uncle Henry and that trip to Manchester, tiresome as it had seemed at the time. Why was it that one had had to stand in for Rose? Oh, something to do with her mother—some accident. Well, it had turned out providential in a way—at least there was work to be going on with.

These thoughts prompted a sudden warmth toward Uncle Henry. Standing in the sunny window of the Hampstead flat, with the Poles hammering and singing behind her, Marion took out her phone. "Uncle Henry? Just thought I'd check in, see how you are . . . Oh, you've done it, this pilot. How did it go?"

He had imagined some appropriate setting—maybe they would be taking him to the Soane Museum, somewhere like that. In the event, there had been a curt call from someone who was very much an underling to say that they would be coming along to his house tomorrow, to film there. "A quiet room," said the underling. "That's all they'll need."

"Coffee, I suppose," he told Rose. "Four of them, I gather. And we'd better tidy my desk."

"Flowers," said Rose.

"*Flowers?*"

"Cheer the place up a bit." She went to the local florist and came back with a bespoke bouquet in golds, creams and russets (thirty quid—he wasn't going to like that). Henry was astonished. Lansdale Gardens was not normally graced with flowers. Rose arranged them in a vase on the small table beside his big armchair. The room still looked very brown, but she could think of no further remedy.

They arrived, and immediately set about moving all the furniture. Henry protested: "No, no—the desk is never over by the window." The woman who was evidently in charge took Rose aside: "Could you sort of get him out of the way until we've finished setting up?" Rose lured Henry upstairs with the proposal that actually a lighter tie would be more effective than the one he was wearing.

Henry felt sidelined, in his own house. Everything was in the wrong place, his study was full of people, once again he found himself confronted with a commanding young woman. This one was tall and fair as opposed to Delia Canning's small and dark, but clearly they came from the same stable.

"If you could just sit here, beside the desk. Lovely." The flowers were now on the desk, where piles of papers should be. A light shone in his eyes. A camera pointed at him. A young man stepped forward with a sheet of paper. Very young man—he looked to Henry about sixteen, but Henry would concede that his judgment could be faulty, where age was concerned.

"Here's the text I've roughed out for you. Do feel free to depart from it." Henry beamed. Quite a nice boy, possibly. "Just cast your eye over it before they get going. See if you feel it will do."

Henry read. He was to speak in general terms on the eighteenth century. Age of transition, of innovation, of political intrigue. A somewhat alien style—short, sharp sentences. Actually, not much in it to which he could take exception. Well grounded. One might, though, slip in a few observations of one's own. A word or two about—um, Walpole. (A moment of panic—another name had teetered at the edge of the black hole.)

He beckoned to the boy. "I can't quarrel with this. Quite well put. I may well depart, at points, as you suggest . . . um, I didn't catch your name?"

"Mark."

"Mark. I can see you've read up a bit on the eighteenth century, Mark."

The boy was all charm, a touch self-deprecating. "Well, not really. Actually, I've just finished my Ph.D.—on the Scottish Enlightenment."

Henry looked at him in alarm. "Really? How interesting. Not my field, of course. I'm a politics man. Well now, do you think they're ready to get going?"

The next twenty minutes were purgatory. The light shone, the camera stared, Henry spoke. He spoke sitting, he spoke standing. He spoke with and without Mark's paper prompt, whose crisp sentences should have been easy enough to remember, but somehow were not. He experimented with delivery, and found himself stumbling. He who had been renowned for his lecture theater fluency. At last it was over. "OK," said the young woman. "That'll do. Lovely."

"One is out of practice," said Henry stiffly.

"Not to worry. In fact, hesitations can be rather effective."

"More natural," said Mark.

Up to a point, thought Henry. Except that hesitation was bloody nearly full stop. He thought of that unshaven young fellow in jeans, declaiming while shinning up some Welsh mountain. Not quite as simple as one had imagined, this.

The room was put back to rights. More coffee was had, with polite conversational exchange. Mark asked what Henry was working on at the moment. "Oh, some ideas on electoral patronage," said Henry evasively.

They went. Henry sank into the armchair. "Rose . . . I rather think I'll have a glass of claret. Could you be an angel?"

CHAPTER NINE

"No," said Charlotte. "There is absolutely no need. Minicab there and back. Helpful driver. On arrival, I can demonstrate my crutch abilities."

Charlotte was to go to the hospital for a checkup. Rose frowned: "Why couldn't they have given you an *afternoon* appointment. Then I could come—no problem."

"Clinic is mornings, I suppose . . . I shall be fine. Think of it as the first step to independence."

In fact, independence seemed still a distant utopia. Charlotte had had a near fall, though she was not going to mention this; she felt weak and unsteady, at moments. And pain forever growled, of course.

"I'm going to tell Henry I need to . . ."

"*No.*"

Interesting, thought Charlotte. Role reversal. Now I am the one to be pigheaded, obstinate. I know how she feels.

Rose, like her mother in the past, capitulated in the face of determination. "All right, then." A little exasperated shake of the head. "I'll sort out a minicab."

And interesting also the shifts in negotiation, mother versus daughter, over time; the ebb and flow of power—no, not power exactly—the way in which authority tips from one to the other. When she was a child, you were the fount of wisdom, of instruction. In old age, you have stepped to one side, it is you who look for sustenance. Trying not to, silently complaining, aghast. How has this come about?

But grateful. Bear with me, she tells Rose (silently). I am only doing what you once did—trying to stake out my own ground, establish myself. I will go to the hospital alone to show that I can. To look time in the eye.

So that is settled. And, meanwhile, days progress. Rose goes to work, Gerry goes to work, Charlotte exists. At least, that is what it feels like. Before the mugger's intervention, daily life was considerably more than mere existence; it sparkled with event—things seen and heard, conversational exchanges, going somewhere, doing something, news and views and stimulus. Not so, now. Oh, but that is not true. There is conversation with Rose and Gerry, there is news, there are views. But there are tracts of solitude, with only pain nudging its presence.

Charlotte found that her reading had undergone a seismic shift. She read now purely for distraction. She had had to scupper the plan to revisit familiar territory: *The House of Mirth* became hard going—goodness, surely not?; *Howard's End* had no appeal whatsoever. As for *Paradise Lost*—forget it. But distraction took curious forms. High voltage thrillers did not work at all—but then, she had never much cared for crime. P. G. Wodehouse did the trick, but Rose's shelves could only throw up two titles, quickly devoured. She read Gerry's *Telegraph* from end to end, surprised to find herself visiting the arcane suburbs of Business and Sport, and it was a nice diversion to quarrel with the letter writers, and most of the columnists. Rose often brought back a *Guardian*, and Charlotte fell into that with relief. To know about the world beyond her own present discomfort was somehow deeply important, an antidote to self-absorption. Everything going on regardless, the helter-skelter of the historical process, and in the grand scheme of things you yourself are neither here nor there.

But while still here, hanging in, you wish to perform satisfactorily, and it annoyed Charlotte that the reading habits of a lifetime seemed to be compromised. She was not bolstered by books in the way that she always had been; they were no longer that essential solace, retreat, support system. She thought that she could identify the problem: angst. When everything is wrong—you are in the wrong place, and your body has betrayed you—then malfunction is total. The mind too is out of order.

The malfunctioning mind seemed to require light nourishment only, and of a curious kind—things that would never normally attract her attention. On a foray to the corner shop—essential crutch practice—she bought *Good Housekeeping*, and read with superficial interest about the age-defying tricks that really work and the secrets of stylish living. No—diversion, not interest. And there was the constant need for reassurance—the need to reach out and touch the world, to make sure it was all still going on, and that even if you were not normal yourself, everything else was. When Rose and Gerry were out, she had the radio on most of the time. The news, on the hour, every hour: ah, attention has shifted to Zimbabwe, to Brussels, to some home-grown political spat; there is a new disaster, a new crisis, someone else is grabbing the microphone.

Charlotte winces at the disasters. People picking their way through floods, on the other side of the globe; a dead soldier, someone's son; children with stick limbs and swollen bellies. To have sampled distress yourself—in a minor, Western, cushioned way—is to become more sensitive to the distress of others. She flinches. What have I got to complain about?

Gerry was concerned about the cat, which continued to be off its food. Malingering, said Rose, dismissive.

The cat exchange took place at breakfast, on the day that Charlotte was to go to the hospital for her checkup. Rose was writing down the number of the minicab firm for her, in case it was late or did not turn up. Cats were not on her agenda.

"And you will have your mobile on you?"

Charlotte nodded. "Of course."

Gerry had gone to fetch his raincoat. He came back, with briefcase, kitted out for the office. He hoped that the hospital would go well, to Charlotte; he laid a hand on Rose's shoulder. "My choir night. Early supper?"

Charlotte was not quite as calm about the hospital trip as she pretended. It would be the first time that she had been farther than a few yards from Rose's house; the move felt both adventurous and daunting. She was ready half an hour before the minicab was due, and then stood in the window waiting for it. A few minutes before the due time, she realized that she had not thought to look out some reading matter—there was bound to be a long wait, one knew hospital clinics all too well.

She looked around the room—have to find something quickly—the car would be here any moment. Gerry had taken his *Telegraph* with him. There was a small pile of books on the coffee table—current reading matter. Rose had the new Jane Gardam from the library, and a paperback Carol Shields, both of which Charlotte had read. And there was *The Da Vinci Code*. This had been sitting there for a while, ignored by Rose; Gerry had acquired it at a station, before a train journey. Whether or not he had read it was not known.

Outside a car hooted. Charlotte grabbed *The Da Vinci Code*, and hopped toward the front door.

The journey was seamless, the driver entirely helpful, escorting her right to the doors of the hospital. During the journey, Charlotte had established that he was from Eritrea, and that minicab driving was for him a secondary occupation that funded his main concern, which was the compilation of the first dictionary that would give three-way reference between English and the two main languages spoken in Eritrea. This conversation had been prompted by Charlotte's having noticed that he had a copy of Samuel Johnson's *Rasselas* lying on the passenger seat. She had not been able to resist remarking on this, to which he had replied that his interest in Johnson stemmed from the *Dictionary*, being himself a dictionary man. All this quite took Charlotte's mind off the business of the day, and confirmed the impression she had had before now—that some of the most interesting people in London are plowing the city in minicabs.

The waiting-room for her clinic was full, as she had anticipated. The lame, the halt, the terminally bored. Charlotte settled herself down and took out *The Da Vinci Code*. She noted that few others had a book. People read magazines—their own, or the dog-eared ones supplied by the hospital—or they simply sat, staring at each other, or into space. One girl was immersed in a paperback with candy pink raised lettering on the cover. An elderly man had a battered hardback library book. She wanted to know what it was but could not see—unforgivable inquisitiveness, but the habit of a lifetime.

A few pages of *The Da Vinci Code*, and she knew that she could go no further with this. Moreover, she felt that her reading matter nailed her: the woman beside her had glanced at the book before Charlotte opened it, and given her a complicit smile and nod. I am seen as a *Da Vinci Code* person, thought Charlotte. Well, there would be a certain affectation in being someone who sat in a hospital waiting-room reading Dostoevsky.

Time passed. For some, the call came; for most, it did not. The waiting-room thinned out—a little. Those whose tolerance threshold was low made inquiries at the reception desk, and reported that the consultant was running late, the level of delay being unspecified. A certain camaraderie sprang up. The woman next to Charlotte was one of those whose hour came; rising, she said benignly to Charlotte, "At least you'll get time to enjoy your book."

Her other neighbor was restlessly impatient. She visited the reception desk several times, and came back shaking her head: "Is no good, wait so much. I have job this afternoon." She was Turkish Cypriot, it emerged, and had broken her wrist tripping over her grandson's toy fire engine. Complications had set in and there was talk of surgery, she told Charlotte. She patted her bag: "So I have here present for the doctor."

Charlotte registered surprise.

The woman opened her bag, furtively, and revealed a bottle of Famous Grouse whisky. "I give to the doctor, and then he arrange I have surgery soon, not wait to go on the list."

"Actually," said Charlotte, "I don't think it works like that."

The woman smiled sweetly. "Oh yes, I think so."

It seemed to Charlotte that the plot stemmed from a certain innocence rather than guile. She made no further comment, and they exchanged medical experiences until the woman was called. She emerged from the consulting room after a relatively short space of time; Charlotte longed to know if she still had the whisky.

By the time her own turn came she was so accustomed to the wait that a summons came as a surprise—an intrusion, almost. The consultant was not the person who had done the surgery. Of course not. The National Health Service likes to make sure that you achieve as wide an acquaintance as possible among its operatives.

He thought she was doing pretty well. Mobility not bad. Pain unfortunately is always a hazard. It will improve. Patience is essential therapy, I'm afraid, with an injury of this kind.

Pleasant man. At how many old women with bashed-up hips has he beamed in that reassuring way? Charlotte began to struggle to her feet, dropping her bag in the process. The doctor hurried round his desk to help her, picking up the bag, and *The Da Vinci Code*, which had fallen out.

"Ah," he said, handing it to her. "Isn't that a terrific read!"

What could one do but nod? Smile.

Anton was reading *The Finn Family Moomintroll*—in the Tube, back at the flat in the evenings. He had given up concealing what he read, and amiably endured merciless ribbing from his nephew and the other young men. All that mattered, to him, was that his mastery of the language improved by leaps and bounds. At his last session with Charlotte she had been astonished.

He laughed. "You see! That is because I must know how the story goes."

"We'll have you on *Pride and Prejudice* by the end of the month," said Charlotte.

This increasing facility, this breakthrough, reminded him of childhood, of that extraordinary realization that all those black marks on a page could speak, that they were words, language, that they related to what came out of people's mouths, out of his own mouth. This time round, the black marks of another language began at last to make sense, to leap from obscurity, to tell a story. It was as though you broke into a new world, were handed a passport to another country. He rode through the city staring at language; advertisements had begun to shout to him, newspapers to inform.

He was anxious to demonstrate his progress to Rose, when they met up for the purchase of the scarf for his mother. He bought a *Guardian;* solution of the crossword was beyond him, but he could have a stab at the clues, and show her.

He sometimes felt, these days, a sort of exhilaration, and was surprised. Each day on the building site felled him, physically; each evening was spent recovering, but at the same time he could have these periods of uplift, of pleasure, of well-being. They came and went. But when they came, he knew that they signaled a development of some kind. Glimpses of a future. They told him that perhaps he could have a life in this place. A new and different life. That perhaps he could be happy.

He had known happiness. Much happiness. He was a person with a natural capacity for joy, and just for contentment. And then his marriage had turned sour, he had known that his wife no longer loved him. When, in time, she went, he entered a long period of emptiness, of moving from day to day without any expectation, any enjoyment. He was living, but hardly noticed life. He worked, ate and slept—or did not sleep—and there seemed no point to it. And then he lost his job, could not find another, and that, in some strange way, was the prompt, the kick-start. You have to do something, he told himself. Act.

And so here he was. Laboring and recuperating. Reading children's books. Sniffing the air, perhaps.

Gerry liked to sing. He was a founding member of the local choir. To Charlotte, this was always an unexpected aspect of Gerry; he was not otherwise given to collaborative pursuits, and he was never heard to sing at home—in the bath, or while planing away at that table in his shed—but he had apparently a good tenor voice. He would thus disappear for the evening once a fortnight, and twice a year Charlotte and

Rose would hear a *Messiah* or a *Requiem* in the big Victorian church a few miles away. Charlotte—and perhaps Rose also—would observe with slight surprise that familiar face lined up amid strangers, singing. It seems such an assertive, expressive, uncharacteristic thing for Gerry to do. But he did, and one respected him for it. The passion and exuberance of sacred choral music seemed so alien to Gerry's personality; perhaps that was the whole point. Whatever, it was clear that the choir was important to Gerry, and that he enjoyed it.

So, on choir nights, Rose served an early meal, and Gerry would vanish, in noticeably good spirits. They were rehearsing *Elijah* at the moment; Charlotte had inquired.

She was relieved to be done with the hospital visit, and glad now to have time with Rose, once Gerry had left.

"The consultant was most encouraging. I do feel I can soon get back home."

Rose eyed her. "Told you to abandon the crutches, did he?"

"Well, no, but . . ."

"I rest my case," said Rose.

"You've had your hair cut. Infirmity has made me so self-absorbed I've only just noticed. Nice. Youthful."

"Aha . . ." Rose glanced in the kitchen mirror. "That was the general idea, I suppose."

"Tell me," said Charlotte. "Has Gerry always sung?"

"Intermittently. When there was something to sing with. Why?"

"Just wondered."

"I know," said Rose. "It seems a bit un-Gerry. Fine. We all need to act out of character in some way. Maybe I should take up athletics."

"I don't think so. Sport was never your strong point."

"Exactly. Needlework, then. But I don't deviate, do I? Entirely predictable."

Charlotte considered her. What is this? And edge to her. Something up? Or down? "On the contrary, you're confusing me right now."

Rose laughed. "Far as I'm concerned, Gerry's choir is essential therapy. Gets him out and about. Company. He never was a pub man, was he?"

"You used to walk a lot, you and Gerry."

"Mmn. We seem to have given that up."

There was a silence. Charlotte thought about the mutation of relationships, the shifts and balances. Sometimes Tom had needed her; at others, he could drift away. Mostly they were close; sometimes they quarreled. Alone, you most miss that abiding interaction, the to and fro of it.

"Pity," said Rose. "I could do with some exercise. I'm getting fat." She became distant, reflective. Thinking, it would seem.

"Not fat. Just . . . more rounded."

"Delicately put," said Rose, suddenly brisk. "Actually, middle-aged spread. Mid-life. Crisis time. I'd better be careful, hadn't I?" She reached for the paper. "Absolutely zilch on the telly tonight. There's nothing for it but a good book. By the way, I saw you had *The Da Vinci Code* in your bag, Mum. How are you getting on with it?"

"Suppose we weren't who we are," said Rose to her friend Sarah, "Who would we want to be? We haven't had children—so we haven't spent all that time and energy. Maybe we don't have husbands. What are we doing?"

Sarah looked at her watch. "Fifteen minutes left of my lunch hour probably isn't enough to deal with that. And what's this, anyway? You're the one who said she never wanted a career."

"This may not be about careers. And that was before I'd not had one."

"If it's not about careers, what is it about?"

"Accidents, I suppose," said Rose. "The things that didn't happen. Alternatives."

"Ah. Then I blossomed in the under-tens ballet class, instead of being completely duff, and I've been a prima ballerina, and am now a national treasure. You?"

"That *is* a career. Or are you calling it talent?"

"All right, then. You can have a talent, if you like."

"No, I think I'm interested in alternatives. But I can't think of one.

Is that lack of imagination? Or is it that once you are what you are you can't conceive of anything else?"

"Oh, come on," said Sarah. "You got a job with a film mogul instead of his lordship, and now you're in Hollywood, and you're married to Hugh Grant. Sorry Gerry."

"No, thanks. I don't like Hugh Grant. And I wouldn't like the California climate—the weather's always the same."

Sarah sighed. "Then I'm afraid you're stuck with Enfield." She glanced at her watch. "I told you we'd run out of time—I've got to pick up some milk on the way back." She got up. "Tuesday again next week?"

"Unless I've left for California," said Rose.

Rose and Anton were in Hyde Park; a scarf had been bought—in Selfridges, eventually. Rose had decided that the local Marks & Spencer would not come up to scratch, and had proposed meeting in Oxford Street. Now, they walked—on a late spring afternoon, when sun and shadow chased over the grass, the trees were in leaf, when things start afresh.

"This is a good place," said Anton. "It is where the city can . . . breathe."

"Actually, I hardly ever come here. I haven't walked here for years. I'd forgotten how much space there is."

"And all for buy the scarf. So it is a good scarf—it bring us here."

"I'll confess," said Rose. "When I suggested Oxford Street I thought too—I bet Anton's never seen the park."

"Ah," he smiled. "But it is still the scarf that bring us. When I see my mother wear it I shall remember." He was looking round, intently. "So many dogs. English people are very proud of dogs. You have a dog?"

"No, we're cat people. At least, my husband is."

"Big dog, small dog. And then dog chase other dog, like over there, and that woman think the big dog will hurt her small dog, and she is shouting at the man . . ."

"Whoops! Stand-off between dog owners. Ah—he's grabbed it." They laughed.

"And now he talk to her," said Anton. "Perhaps they make friend."

"And live happily ever after. Like in fairy stories."

"I hope. Perhaps. But perhaps it is just he ask where she get her nice little dog, he want one like that."

"Let's stay with the fairy story," said Rose. "Shall we sit down for a minute?"

They found an unoccupied bench. "And so many people who run," said Anton. "If people are not take dog out, they run. We are only people here do nothing."

"We are recovering from a shopping experience. At least, you are. Men hate shopping."

He nodded. "And you are be kind to foreigner."

She thought about this. Is that what I'm doing? Not quite what it feels like, actually.

"I learn these new words," said Anton. "Foreigner. Migrant. Asylum seeker. But I am not an asylum seeker, I am economic migrant. I learn this from the radio. Economic migrant is better than asylum seeker." A wry smile. "Asylum seeker is big problem. Economic migrant is perhaps good thing for UK—pick fruit, and work on building site."

"And be an accountant," said Rose.

"I think you are . . . you look always for what will be good."

"Optimistic. As opposed to pessimistic. I'm not sure that I am. There's realistic, too. What is likely, what is possible."

"More words. I like optimistic and pessimistic. And I say now to the site manager—'Please be more realistic.'"

"Does he have a short fuse?"

Anton turned to her, perplexed. She laughed. "Does he get angry quickly, that means. Another expression for you. Like . . . like when you light a fuse and it burns and then—bang."

"Oh—yes, yes. I see. A short fuse. That is good. No, he is man who is always the same. Do this. Do that. Always same voice . . . same way of talk. When he fire someone, it is just, you go, not come back, thank you, goodbye. Short fuse is more interesting, perhaps."

Dark clouds had rolled across. A few drops of rain spattered.

"Ah," said Anton. "We have found for you some weather. You like weather, I remember."

"This is weather that could be a nuisance. But I think there's a café place in that direction—or there was when I was last here."

They got up, walked fast. "Yes," she said. "There it is."

Anton said, "Not Starbucks."

"No. But we shouldn't get set in our ways."

He laughed, touched her arm for an instant. "Set in our ways. No. But I like now Starbucks."

Me too, she thought. Never used to, particularly.

Over coffee, they watched falling rain, joggers, the dogs.

"I know that kind of dog is German Shepherd," said Anton. "They have on the building site. Guard dog. Not nice. What is that—with leg like . . . like very small chair leg?"

"Dachshund," said Rose, laughing.

"And that over there? Sniff, sniff all the time."

"Some sort of spaniel."

"Spaniel. There—now I learn two kind of dog. And that—small white dog?"

"Terrier, I think. Probably Jack Russell terrier. This is the most *useless* information, Anton—breeds of dog."

"Is any knowing—*useless*?" he said. "It all go in there," he tapped his head. "Perhaps one day useful."

"I suppose so," said Rose. "I'm not at all interested in dogs but I've somehow picked up which dog is what."

"And so we have talk about kind of dog. This is not useful but it gives names to this place, for me. What is that tree?"

"Oh, goodness . . . Lime, I think. Those over there are easy— willows. I'm not great on trees."

"And it is bad I make you a teacher. No more names. Enough. But when you are . . . foreigner . . . you are all the time look for things to know. I must know what is this, I must know what is that. Like a child." He smiled.

"Yes, I've felt like that on holiday abroad. In Greece, once. Help! What does that sign say!"

"So you understand." Another smile.

"Except," she said. "That for you it's not a holiday. It's . . . serious. I think you're very . . . determined. Brave," she added, after a moment.

"Brave?" He was surprised.

"You make me feel I've had a very easy life."

"I make you uncomfortable? I am sorry."

"No, *no*. Just—sort of apologetic. I'm the one who is sorry."

Anton threw up his hands. "We are going for a nice walk, and now we are saying sorry, sorry. What has happen?"

He was laughing. Rose also.

"Ridiculous," she said. "And it *is* a nice walk, and the rain's stopping. We should go on. You haven't seen the Round Pond yet."

"Last week I walked by the river. Like you told me. I take the book and the map, I walk far, far. It was good."

"Oh. It must have been. I wish . . ."

They were standing now, about to set off again. "I wish . . ." She hesitated.

"You wish?"

"I wish I'd been there too. Maybe . . . Maybe next time we could do a London walk together."

"I hope perhaps you say that," said Anton. "I have hope very much."

CHAPTER TEN

Henry has misgivings about the filming. He has never been a man prone to misgivings and the experience bothers him. He needs to put an end to it. He needs to hear from Delia Canning. He needs to hear that contrary to the misgivings, his performance was admirable, and the program—programs, preferably—will go ahead.

"Letter to Ms. Canning," he says to Rose. Then, frowning, "No, on second thought, I think you should make a phone call. Letters sit around, get put aside. Phone call to Ms. Canning, saying that you are Lord Peters's PA, and that Lord P. would rather like to hear what developments Ms. Canning has in mind for the program. The series. Polite but insistent—that is the tone."

Rose makes the phone call, while Henry listens, drumming his fingers. Needless to say, she does not reach Delia Canning. PA speaks unto PA. Stalemate.

Rose makes Charlotte and Gerry laugh with her Henry voice and then with her Delia Canning PA voice, which is sweetly fluting: "I'm *so* sorry but I'm afraid Delia can't take your call. Of *course* I'll see she gets the message right away."

"Poor old boy. He's right out of his league with these people. I'm actually sorry for him."

Charlotte enjoys seeing Rose in this jokey frame of mind. Indeed, Rose seems in high spirits at the moment, which is further relief for Charlotte because it makes her feel that her continuing presence can't be too irksome. And it will end, she tells herself, though right now repatriation to her own home looks a rather distant prospect. There has been a glitch. She slipped while pottering in the kitchen, and gave her hip a knock—nothing too drastic but enough to have her hobbling once more, with pain triumphantly nudging in. There! says Rose's expression: so you think you could manage back on your own?

With time on her hands—too much time—Charlotte is much given to reflection. She reflects upon the past, she reflects—with irritation—upon the present. The past is not gone, but is now that abiding ballast without which she would capsize. She visits constantly, in appreciative recognition of that moment, this place, those people. Her head is full of what was said—what Tom said, what Rose said, in a different incarnation, young Rose, child Rose. Marvelous, she thinks, the way in which it all goes on still, not lost, surging up unsummoned, indestructible. Until I go.

The present is less inviting, as material for reflection. The present is a matter of nagging concerns, of hour-to-hour negotiations. Should she or should she not take a painkiller? Check again that date for the next clinic appointment. Will Rose be cross if she suggests doing something useful, such as a bit of ironing? When, when will she be able to go home? And then, like sudden bursts of sunlight, there arrive, as ever, those glad moments: the silver sliver of a new moon against the evening sky, lilac—snuffed as she shuffles to the gate, the sound of the girl next door practicing the piano.

And Anton presenting her with a bunch of creamy tulips: "For thank you, because now I read. Nearly I read." And it is true; Anton's reading has progressed apace. No wonder he was cheerful, flourishing his tulips.

Anton has little time for reflection. You do not do much reflecting when engaged in heavy manual labor, and when not working he cannot spare the time; he needs to read, to sleep, to pay attention. The climate of the flat is certainly not conducive to reflection: television, card games, beer, banter. Nevertheless, there are crevices each day into which he finds himself retreating for moments, for a minute or two; he is surprised by satisfaction, by a sense of possibilities. It was right to come here; soon I shall read this language well enough to offer myself for a real job; and see—it is spring, nearly summer, feel the sunshine.

The past, for Anton, is indeed ballast, but a freight that he does not particularly wish to investigate. When his former wife surfaces, he tells her to go away—polite but firm. Childhood and youth are welcome, but he doesn't have time to dwell there. Family and friends deserve a wave, a nod, he is glad of them, he values them, but he cannot spare them too much attention at the moment.

This moment. This now. This present which begins to feel less alien, which begins to feel like a place he can inhabit, where he can spread himself, take charge of his life perhaps, cease to be driven by circumstance.

He sits composing a text message, during the lunch break on the site: Thank you for yours. I have look . . . looked . . . on the map for Richmond Park, and in the book. Yes, I think very good for a walk.

"Unsatisfactory," says Henry to Marion. "One wants to know where one is with this project. Ah, here's Corrie with the pudding. Trifle today—excellent. A small helping, Corrie—well, not too small."

Marion eyes the trifle. "Gorgeous—but just a bit for me, Corrie, please. So many of these things come to nothing, you know, Uncle Henry."

"Really? Not a world I'm familiar with, of course, but I do feel one could contribute." Henry digs into the trifle, appreciatively. "I've rather revised my views about popular performance. It has its place, I feel, these days. We need to give ordinary people access to superior discourse."

Oh, gawd . . . thinks Marion. Please, Uncle Henry.

"I look forward to making my ideas more . . . generally approach-able."

"People-friendly," says Marion, gritting her teeth.

Henry beams. "Is that the term? You are always wonderfully up-to-date, my dear. Anyway, it is very tiresome to be held up in this way. Not to hear when we get started. Ah, well," He lays the subject to rest. "So how are your own affairs going?"

If Marion were to give a meaningful report, she would say that affair Jeremy is going but that she occasionally wonders if it should not be gone, while affair Hampstead flat is beginning to give her a certain amount of grief. The restructuring of the bathroom was a wobble, but now a couple of other things have come in well over budget, and there begins to be a cash-flow problem. She has had to become more press-ing with George Harrington's secretary.

"I really do need to have a word with him."

"I've passed on your messages. I'm sure he'll be back to you very soon. He's got New York, and then L.A. It's just rather a busy time."

Well, we're all busy, thinks Marion with irritation. This must not go on. As it is, she is having to hold back on paying suppliers, which is something she does not like to do—never has done. She has prided her-self on efficient business management. Even though she had never seen herself as a businesswoman, when she embarked on a career in interior design. Creativity, that was the point. Using your skills with color, your imagination, your talent for serendipitous discovery. The business aspect was a bit of a shock, but nothing that she couldn't cope with, and cope with pretty well. She is good at figures, she is good at budgeting, she has learned how to gauge costs and a reasonable profit margin.

Her mother had been proud of her but also slightly shocked. She herself had grown up in a world where girls did not bother their pretty little heads with money—the dying days of that world, admittedly, but the family was somewhat retarded. Bolstered by inherited funds, business ventures would have been inconceivable, Trade. And now here was Marion, dealing with cash in, cash out. Her mother had concentrated on the products and determinedly ignored the seamy side: "Such lovely curtains and things, so clever with her ideas."

Cross with George Harrington, Marion is glad of the Poles, who are always cheerful, who work away, who, it would seem, never worry. Never grumble. Who have adapted to circumstances.

Could be a lesson to some, she thinks, putting down the phone after an extended wail from Jeremy.

Rose says, "I've said I'll take Anton to Richmond Park for a walk next weekend."

It is breakfast time. Saturday breakfast. Charlotte looks at her: "Oh—well, I'm sure he'll appreciate that."

Gerry is going through the *Radio Times*, marking programs.

Rose says, staring over his head, out of the window, "Do you fancy coming, Gerry?"

He makes a mark, then another. "Who? Oh—him. No, no—I need to change the washer on that tap upstairs."

Rose continues to gaze out of the window. Birds have burst into song, and oh! Look at the cherry!

Jeremy has seen Stella. That is to say, he has seen Stella but has been unable to speak to her. He has something to wail about, he feels. He was within an ace of being eyeball to eyeball with Stella, when he would have been able to put his case, to talk to her reasonably and sensibly, perhaps to persuade her to dump the odious solicitor, and enter into personal negotiations. All this was within his grasp, and was then whisked away.

He had driven to the surgery where Stella worked, knowing the time when she was likely to leave. He had seen her car, had parked his own as unobtrusively as possible, and waited in the shelter of a nearby gateway. At last she came out of the surgery. He stepped forward, and met her on the path from the door. When she saw him, her hand flew to her mouth.

"Stella," he said. "Stella . . . Darling, I must talk to you."

She stood there. The hand came down. She hesitated. She was about to speak.

And then the surgery door was flung open. Someone called "Stella—you've forgotten your shopping." Some idiot was waving a carrier bag, came toward them. Stella turned, took the bag, looked again at Jeremy, and the moment of hesitation was gone. She swept past him, ran to her car. He heard the door slam, the engine start.

That was that. Fuming, he drove back to London. Should he have pursued her to the house, tried to confront her there? No, she was in crisis mode, once she had fled. There had been that one instant—hand falling away from her mouth, what was she going to say?—and it has been lost.

He poured out all to Marion, who seemed not entirely receptive.

Stella rushes into the house. In the kitchen, she reaches for her pills, takes two, puts the kettle on. Tea. She is desperate for tea, with sugar. When you are in shock you crave for tea, she has read.

Mug in hand, she sinks down onto the sofa, picks up the phone, calls her sister.

"... *normal*. The thing was that it didn't seem odd, to see him there. I mean, he sometimes used to come and pick me up from the surgery. I just thought 'Oh, there's Jeremy . . . ,' and I was sort of *pleased*. I was going to start *talking*, and then . . ."

"Well, thank goodness you didn't," says Gill. "Tell Paul Newsome."

"Tell Paul Newsome?"

"Of course. Jeremy is out of order. Completely out of order. No contact, that's the rule. While the divorce is proceeding."

"Oh," says Stella. "Yes, I see."

". . . desist from approaching my client . . . maintenance claim remains unresolved . . . must inform you that . . . must warn you that . . . shall be obliged to . . ."

Jeremy bins the solicitor's letter.

———

Sometimes Jeremy cannot remember how the hell all this began. How and why did his life fall apart? Oh yes, the wretched text from Marion. What on earth was it about? Nothing much. She couldn't meet up, for some reason. Something to do with that uncle of hers. What the devil has her uncle got to do with Jeremy? Why should he be persecuted by a solicitor because of someone he doesn't even know? It is so wrong.

Stella sees Marion as a scarlet woman. Marion, in her mind's eye, is tall, dark, sleek, ruthlessly seductive, she wears skin-tight dresses with plunging necklines and is wreathed in expensive perfume. Stella would be surprised by the real Marion, who is of medium height, a bit plump, has fine, fair hair, and is personable but no siren.

Actually, Stella does not much think of Marion, who is indeed the reason for all this but has become somehow irrelevant. It is Jeremy who is at issue, not the rather evanescent scarlet woman. It is Jeremy's betrayal that matters; with whom he was betraying is somehow not especially important. When her mind is churning away, and she has to reach for the pills, or for her sister, or for Paul Newsome, it is thoughts of Jeremy that prompt a new outburst of distress. She is trying to concentrate entirely on the divorce process now, and she does indeed feel much more in control, much aware that for the first time she has made a firm decision, that she is running things. But these insidious thoughts of Jeremy will keep sneaking in. And when he suddenly appeared like that she was thrown, quite thrown. Well, momentarily thrown.

Henry has rather lost sight of the original spur toward television fame. That dire occasion in Manchester has faded from his mind—mercifully. He has forgotten all that soliciting of newspaper editors. His old enemy's acolyte still occasionally smirks at the edge of his vision, but the full horror of that day's humiliation has subsided, tactfully, into a for once obliging black hole. When Marion referred to the trip, he could not remember why she had been with him. Oh, something to do with Rose's mother.

And still Delia Canning does not call, or write. Most inconvenient. It is not that one's diary is so very full, but one wants to be able to plan ahead. Most of all, Henry wants to get going on his scripts. That young fellow—what was his name?—was all very well, didn't do a bad job, but the real thing will need professional polish. The common touch will be required, of course—the nation's sofas are not an audience of cognoscenti—but Henry fancies that he will be able to pull that out of the hat. So come along, Ms. Canning.

"Well?" says Delia Canning.

Colleagues are silent.

Someone says, "Wow!"

"Interesting?" says Delia. "Or not?"

There is further silence.

Someone else says, "Actually—this may sound barmy—but I rather like him."

"He does compel. In a sort of awful way."

"Huge risk."

"We could have egg on our faces."

"How old *is* he?"

"A throwback? Or a new departure?"

"He'd *have* to wear that suit."

"The voice . . ."

"You couldn't *invent* him."

"The delivery . . ."

"So . . . ?" says Delia Canning.

Marion is vaguely sorry for Stella, but finds her pathetic. She feels no guilt, where Stella is concerned. All right, she has been having an affair with Stella's husband but she had—has—no intention of appropriating him, and all this is a storm in a teacup, frankly. Stella should know Jeremy well enough to be able to rise above this. Marion does not think that Jeremy is a philanderer, but neither does she flatter herself that she is his first and only aberration. Stella should have the measure of Jeremy by now, and recognize that if she wants him she has got him anyway, for better or for worse.

If she doesn't want him and so it would appear, with all this rattling of solicitors, then it is Jeremy who has to face up to things.

Just leave me out of it, thinks Marion. I have my own problems.

One of the Poles has sprained an ankle and can only work at half strength.

George Harrington is said to be in China.

Marion had not realized that banks charge such punitive rates for an overdraft.

"Not that one was in any doubt," says Henry. "But it is good to have confirmation. Filming in a couple of weeks' time, apparently. It might amuse you to come along and watch, Rose. Oh, and I think perhaps my tweed suit should go to the cleaners before then, if you would. Actually, more than just watch, I think it would be advisable to have you there as PA—check that I have the script, that sort of thing. We don't want any hitches. The script is not yet in its final form, of course. I am working on the draft. Walpole, I propose—a definitive consideration of the man. So back to the drawing board."

"What on earth can they be thinking of?" says Rose. "Out of their minds. They won't know what's hit them. People will be asking for their license money back."

Charlotte observes that television history programs are in any case a minority taste. Perhaps the minority will take to Henry.

Rose snorts. "Whatever—he's being insufferable. PA duty, and get my suit cleaned, and type up this draft, and then next day print it off again with three words changed. He's driving me up the wall."

"Never mind," says Charlotte. "It's Thursday. The weekend's coming up."

And it is, it is. Rose looks at the weekend, at Saturday, and it gleams.

For Anton too the weekend shines out. Weekends are always a blessed oasis, but this one has a special quality. He realizes that he is looking forward to something, that he is experiencing anticipation for the first time in months—in many, many months. He looks at his life with detachment, and thinks that it is a poor sort of life that has not known expectation, the pleasure of savoring ahead. So enjoy it while you have it, he tells himself.

CHAPTER ELEVEN

Henry too is in a state of anticipation. He anticipates with complacency; this filming—which will (he anticipates)—reveal an unexploited talent for popular communication. Occasionally, he practices in front of the mirror in the hall (Rose has caught him at it, and has retreated to her office with a smile); the expansive gesture, he is after, the humorous lift of the eyebrows, the smile that will draw in the viewers, show that one is sharing, not patronizing. Yes, that's it. Sharing one's scholarship, one's breadth of vision.

He is keen to get going, but there is now a silence, where Delia Canning's outfit is concerned. That brief call from the boy—what's his name? Mark—to say that the project would go ahead, and now nothing. This is tiresome, but he can get on with polishing and amending his script, working on some ideas for further programs.

Henry is pleased with the script, when eventually it is groomed to his satisfaction; a lively presentation of Walpole as man and as politician, with some entertaining digressions—other personalities of the age, the intricacies of eighteenth-century political life.

"Very nice, I think, Rose. I fancy this is going to come across rather well. Send it to Ms. Canning, would you? Maybe that will get them going—we need a date for filming."

With the script off his hands, Henry is at a loose end. He decides to go through old lecture notes in search of inspiration for future programs, comfortably confident that they will decide on a series, in the end.

Henry's papers are not in good order. They consist of many files and boxes, inadequately labeled. There is no reliable retrieval system, and in order to find anything he has to do much tipping out of the contents of any file or box onto his desk, to see what exactly we have here.

What we have, he realizes—what we have collectively—is a most confusing paper trail of his own life. Letters, notes of his reading, notes for his lectures—a whole lot of arbitrary evidence as to who this person was and what he did. Henry is in fact capable of a degree of detachment about himself, and he views this accumulation with some interest. He finds himself picking out seminal moments, names, themes. He finds himself thinking that things could have gone otherwise. The clever young man with his starred first class degree could have headed for the civil service rather than academia—one might have ended up a Whitehall mandarin. Or politics?

And what about this? He has come across a letter from Lorna Mace, pushed into a file of ancient lecture notes, along with other unsorted old correspondence. Lorna Mace was a colleague with whom he had had briefly what would nowadays be called a relationship, though Henry is not aware of that use of the term. He thinks of Lorna Mace— or rather, seldom does think of her—as a young woman he once (twice, actually—maybe thrice) bedded, in appropriate eighteenth-century language. Henry's sex drive is low; back in his youth he had a couple of mild sexual experiences, of which Lorna was one. In the course of these he discovered that so far as sex was concerned he could take it or leave it, and since then, on the whole, he has left it. But the sight of Lorna Mace's letter prompts a sudden vision of what might have been, had his ardor been greater, had she been more pressing herself. One might have married. One might have had children.

Henry's capacity for detachment stops short of imaginative flight. This glimpse of an alternative life is there for an instant, and immediately rejected. He has no regrets—in that direction or any other. He is who he is, has done what he has done, and is satisfied. Just occasionally he finds himself bewildered by other people's wilder excesses, which are frequently triggered by sex or parenthood, it seems, those areas mysterious to him—and is relieved to have been spared all that.

Henry glances at the letter from Lorna Mace, does not bother to read it, remembers for an instant brown eyes, a habit of pushing her glasses up with one finger, and the frankly dismaying sight of pink undergarments tumbled upon a chair. No, no. He does not wonder what became of her—she is off his radar now, in perpetuity. Except that she lies here in one of his files.

The betraying nature of evidence. Henry does think for a few moments of this; an investigator who knew nothing of him might assume from this piece of paper that Lorna Mace was of significance in Henry's life. The problem that faces the historical researcher: what weight should be given to any single piece of evidence?

Indeed. Henry picks up Lorna Mace's letter again, tears it across and drops it into the wastepaper basket. One's biographer . . .

But the point of this trawl was to ferret out something that would inspire the second—third, fourth—of these programs. The close scholarship of the past is to be the springboard for future popular fame. What about that stuff one did once on the South Sea Bubble? Where is that? Financial speculation is much in the news these days.

He finds the right box. Ah, yes—promising. Dear me, how assiduous one was. Reams of notes, references. Henry reads, skims, reads. Hard to distill all this into a handful of succinct comments; there is quite a challenge here. But he is up for it, in his present state of heightened endeavor, of youthful ability.

A week or so later he has a nice draft of a script on the South Sea Bubble. To be filmed in the City, maybe? Ironic—all those soaring twentieth-century buildings. And then one morning the boy rings up. Rose takes calls in her office and brings the phone to Henry if appropriate.

"It's Mark from Ms. Canning's office."

"Ah, yes, yes. I'll take that." Henry settles himself more comfortably. "Good morning, good morning. Now, how are the plans? You've had my script, of course?"

Yes, but no.

"*No?*" says Henry, incredulous.

Not Walpole, it seems. Delia Canning and her team are not interested in Robert Walpole. They are interested in issues. Eighteenth-century issues. Issues of crime and poverty. This is to be the theme of the program. The idea will be to evoke the atmosphere of eighteenth-century London, the apposition of wealth and penury. The teeming stews.

Henry has never paid much scholarly attention to the stews. Not his field. He is silenced.

"Hogarth . . ." the boy is saying.

Hogarth. Of course. They were bound to rope in Hogarth.

"People in fancy dress?" Henry inquires, wearily.

"Actually, no," says the boy—the hint of a smile in his voice. "Sound effects, more, I think . . ."

Henry interrupts. "Ah. *The Beggar's Opera?*"

"Well, no—not that that isn't quite a nice idea. Atmospheric effects, against clever shots of the Hogarths, and contemporary prints, London as it was then, that sort of thing. Though I believe reenactment is not entirely ruled out at this stage."

Henry grunts.

"There was a thought that possibly you yourself . . . An idea that perhaps a sequence in costume—ironic, you see—the presenter himself becoming part of the past."

"*Me . . .* in *costume.*"

"Well, maybe not," says the boy hastily. "Just a vague idea, I think. As I say, nothing's absolutely firmed up yet, just the general approach. The theme and the treatment. It's going to be extremely effective."

Henry has always known how to act with circumspection. No good throwing a tantrum and saying—how dare you jettison Walpole, I insist that you reinstate Walpole. Henry has sensed an immovable force, where Delia Canning and her team are concerned. Make a fuss, and he could risk being dropped entirely. It is exasperating—and undignified—to be beholden in this way to these—well, apparatchiks, if one is honest—but there it is. Best to appear compliant, and then if—when—his performance is judged an unqualified success he will be in a position to exert pressure next time around.

"Somewhat perverse," he told Marion, over Corrie's Irish stew. "These people—a perverse choice, to my mind, but I dare say something can be made of it. You're not eating, my dear—not unwell, I hope?"

Marion was not unwell, but the Irish stew is a particular horror. However, Sunday lunch at Lansdale Gardens came as something of a respite, after a trying week. The Poles were undermanned, one of them nursing an injury, a large bill had come in (second demand), and there had been this dismaying business of George Harrington's secretary.

Marion had phoned, yet again, in pursuit of Harrington himself. She had dialed the direct number, but the call had been answered by an unfamiliar voice.

"Mr. Harrington's secretary is not available."

"Oh. When will she be back?"

A fractional pause. "I'm afraid I can't tell you."

Marion had persisted. Tomorrow? Next week? Is she ill? "I'm afraid I have no information."

Four days later there was still no information. Irritation turned to unease. What is this? What is going on? Harrington's last tranche of cash was now all spent; Marion had paid the Poles for the last three weeks, settled such bills as she absolutely must, and was now piling up her overdraft. The bank was reminding her of this. With relish, she felt.

Why had she never got hold of Harrington's mobile number? Oh, but she had tried to, she now remembered. At that lunch. She had said, at one point—"Wouldn't it be sensible if I could reach you directly if I need to?" and he had said that he was so often on the move, in some other time zone as like as not, better to get on to Judy, she's always available, she can always get a message through.

Huh. So where is she? Where is he? What do I do?

"Do?" said Jeremy. "She'll turn up, won't she? On holiday, I expect. Overdraft? Darling, you're talking to the world expert on overdrafts. I've had more overdrafts than you've had hot dinners. Treat it with disdain. An overdraft is just an attempt to hobble a really enterprising, creative person. Listen, sweetie, I am quite desperately in need of a break. I'm quite desperately in need of *you*. There's a clearance sale at this mansion in Shropshire next Saturday. Let's have a weekend in the country. Come on—you deserve it."

Marion had always been careful. She had balanced the books, had seen to it that money out was matched by money in. And now suddenly her formerly stable small overdraft had hurtled upward—£28,647 and counting. A consignment of expensive hand-made tiles had just been delivered to the flat—another bill; the Poles must be paid at the end of the week.

"I'm sorry, I have no information regarding Mr. Harrington's secretary."

"Forget about it," said Jeremy. "Put it out of your mind, darling. *Enjoy*—we're having a spree, a jaunt. And I'm *not* driving too fast— this is how I drive, that idiot was *crawling*, I had to overtake. Apparently this Shropshire place belonged to some sort of eccentric collector—bags of interesting stuff, there should be. The grapevine says art deco a specialty—great! I can unload all the art deco I can lay my hands on. Let's find something for you, too—a pretty piece for the showroom. Oh, cheer up, darling—of *course* you're in the mood for acquisition. One's always in the mood for acquisition. Did I tell you I've sold that carved overmantel? Couple doing up a pad in Bishop's Avenue—thrilled with it. Three grand—actually, I'd have settled for two and a half. So that's helped with the cash-flow, for the moment. See? Something always turns up, when you think the going's a bit rough. And I've got rid of the Irishman and taken on a boy as work experience—son of someone I know—so I needn't pay him at all, as work experience, it's a snip. How long will he last? Well, until he susses out that he's not experiencing much, I suppose, and then I can always find another. I should have thought of this before—the Irishman was money down the drain. Listen—I've booked us into this heavenly sounding pub—gastro, of course, and all beams and inglenooks and log fires. On me—my treat, thanks to the overmantel. So we'll have a lovely bibulous evening, after I've spent the rest of the overmantel on lots of gorgeous art deco—and then a happy night, won't we, sweetie?"

"Oh, wow!" said Jeremy. "Look at that stained glass! I've got to have that. And those chairs. And I'm sorely tempted by the lamps. Yes, I *know* I'm reclamation, not an antique dealer, but one's entitled to move upmarket from time to time. Customers get excited, too, when they spot something like that in my place—they think they've made a find, and end up paying more than they would in Kensington Church Street. Let's hope there's not too much by way of competition—I've seen one or two of the brotherhood prowling around, giving me shirty looks. God, why can't I live like this guy did—own a place like this, oodles of money, just spend it on good stuff, and sit around enjoying it. It's so bloody unfair, isn't it? Instead of which, one works one's butt off getting and spending—ooh, that's Wordsworth, isn't it? I'd forgotten I knew it. That's what comes of a posh education—little snippets of culture surface from time to time. Gosh—*look* at that gorgeous little table—now *you* should try to get that, it's just your style. There! I'm putting a big tick against it—I shall *make* you bid. I *am* enjoying this—it's just what I needed, after that beastly business with Stella, her storming past me, refusing to speak. Do you think I should have another go? I just feel that if I could only have five minutes with her, talk reasonably, get my point of view across. Oh, *sorry*, darling—I meant to put Stella on a back burner this weekend, and I have, thanks to you. You haven't got an overdraft, and I haven't got a divorce-crazy wife—there! We're going to sit in the front row when the auction gets going, and sweep the board. Should I go for that heavenly screen? Well, all right, only if it goes for a knock-down price, which it won't with the brotherhood here. But I'll have those William Morris curtains—they won't be interested in them. And the cushions—people are after fabrics these days, I'm finding. We'd better take a look at the carpets. This *is* fun. Why don't I always have you with me on days like this?"

Because, thought Marion, I am your mistress and a part-time one at that, and you are obsessed with preventing your wife from divorcing you. Which makes our connection wobbly, to say the least. And I have got more to think of than screens and pretty tables, right now. I am in debt to the bank, and am myself owed money by a man I am apparently unable to get hold of, and I don't know what to do about the Poles—do I keep them and go on paying them myself, not knowing if I will get reimbursed, or do I lay them off and risk losing them? Harrington may suddenly surface, all will be well, and I shall need to get the project moving and will have no Poles. What do I do?

"What one will have to do," Henry told Rose, "is go along with what they are proposing, and lend it one's own style—give it some authority. To that end I shall read up on topics with which I am a touch unfamiliar. They wish to home in on the low life of the period—very well, I must do so myself, eh?" A chuckle.

Have fun, thinks Rose, who is pondering Tube connections from home to Richmond, and when she should leave in order to be there by eleven.

Anton is doing the crossword. He sits on the Tube, with furrowed brow, anxious to have one clue at least completed before he meets her. It is the quick crossword, the easy one—surely he will manage something.

"I am no good," said Anton. "I have not done any. I try all the way, and not one." He showed Rose the pristine page, smiling.

Both were smiling, hugely. They had smiled their way along the platform, spotting each other from afar.

"We'll do it together, later. Actually, probably not—it's too nice a day for crosswords. Aren't we lucky!"

It is, it is. A blue and green spring day, sun with his hat on, birds jubilant, trees in lavish leaf. Rose was carrying a basket, in which was the picnic. A modest picnic, but choice: smoked salmon sandwiches, quail eggs, lettuce, grapes.

Anton had brought a bottle of wine. He took off his rucksack to show her. "It is from my country. One of the boys go home last week, and he bring it back for me. I hope you will like."

They made their way to Richmond Park. He told her that his mother had received the coat and scarf and was delighted.

"I tell her you help me and she say I must thank you. She say it is the best coat she have, ever."

"My pleasure," said Rose. "A lifetime's shopping experience came in useful, for once."

Anton was surveying the park. "I think here there is no shopping. Not even Starbucks."

"That's why we've got the picnic. But we have to earn it first. A mile, at least."

They walked, briskly. Anton was interested in the deer. "The book say this was always a place for deer—deer for the king to hunt, in old times. Look, over there, that one, that man one . . ."

"Stag."

"Stag. He has . . . eight wife. And he have to keep them all for himself, I know. They are like that at home. Fight other stags to keep for himself."

"What a life," said Rose. "Nothing but eating and fighting, and all to make sure your genes get carried on." She caught his perplexity.

"Genes . . . oh, help . . . the things we've all got that make us what we are, absolutely different from anyone else, and that we pass on to our children."

"Yes, yes. Like I have dark hair from my mother, and I need glasses for read, and I have tall from my father, and good with numbers, like him. And you? You have from your mother brown eyes, I have seen—what more?"

"Hay fever," said Rose. "It's starting up now. Any minute I'll be sneezing. You know—in spring, from the grass, the pollen."

"So for that you not say thank you to her. And from your father?"

She thought. "I don't know, really. He was clever—very clever. So's my mother, but he was clever differently—very applied, and bursting with energy."

"So you have clever, and I think . . ."

"No," said Rose. "I'm not like them, that way. I'm . . . practical. I can get things done, but I don't have their sort of mind."

"I think you do, like your mother. Same way of talk, sometimes. Same way of see, perhaps."

"Nonsense, I'm not a bit like her."

He was laughing. "I knew you say that. Nobody think they are like their parents. Everyone think we are quite different."

She smiled, shook her head. "I dare say you're right. And all this started with the stag."

"And he think nothing at all. Not—I must make child—just, I must have many wife and fight other stag."

Rose sneezed. "There—I told you. This place is steaming with pollen."

"You want to go somewhere else?"

"Certainly not." She fished in her pocket. "I've got this stuff—that'll help. We should go that way, I think—up the hill."

He told her that when he was a boy he had been taken to hunt deer, once, by an uncle. "We shoot. That is how I know what they do—he tell me. We shoot one and his wife cook and we eat, and I did not like."

"The meat? You didn't like the meat?"

"No, I did not like the killing. I liked to see the deer, not to kill it. But I could not say that, because that would be—not like a man. So I must enjoy. After that I never do it again—shoot."

"I've never killed anything," said Rose thoughtfully. "Oh yes—mice. In traps. And I didn't like that at all."

"If we do not like to kill," said Anton, "in other times—old times—we would be no good. We would not eat."

"Quite. Made helpless by Tesco and Sainsbury, that's us. I don't even know how to clean a chicken—you know, take out its insides."

"Fish, I can do. I have go fishing too with my uncle. That I did not mind. And . . . clean, after. Cut open—take out."

"I've never done *that*. Gone fishing. I must have the wrong kind of uncle."

"And I did not mind that we kill the fish. Not like shooting the deer. Why is that?"

"One doesn't *relate* to fish, exactly. Whereas deer are—cute, pretty."

"So in other time I would have to eat only fish," said Anton.

"And I would starve." Rose laughed. "And be overrun by mice. Actually, it wouldn't be like that at all. We would both have had uncles—or parents—who would have taught us to be appropriately bloodthirsty. We'd have killed without a thought."

"I think I prefer now. With Tesco."

"Lunch, in fact, is Waitrose. Talking of which—do you think it's time to look for somewhere nice to have it?"

They chose a place with an agreeable view, and settled down on the grass. Rose unpacked her basket. "There—smoked salmon. I hope you like it."

"And very small eggs. I have not seen those before."

"Quail eggs. Considered a delicacy."

Anton opened his wine, and filled paper cups. He sighed—a rich, luxuriant sigh. "This is—how can I say?—today is—I think I am in heaven." He turned to look at her, raised his cup of wine. "Thank you, for make heaven." He looked away, quickly, waved a hand at the park—the trees, the grass, the deer. "Now, when I am at the building site I think of this."

Presently, they walked again. Faster this time, intent upon covering ground, talking occasionally, then falling into an uninhibited silence. Rose thought, when you are able to be with a person and there is no need to talk, something has happened. She felt exhilarated—by the exercise, the intensity of the spring world around them, by his company. When they paused for a rest, sitting for a while on a bench under a huge oak, she told him about holidays in her childhood.

"Mum and Dad liked to walk. We did some of Hadrian's Wall once, that's up in the north, country that's very—wild and open. The opposite of this, really." After a moment, she added, "You'd like it. I wish . . ." Her voice trailed away. She rummaged for a tissue, felt him looking at her, blew her nose, looked back, and saw that he knew what she wished.

There was a silence. He said, "Perhaps one day I go there. When I am an accountant. With some money, and a car." He smiled.

"Mum says your reading gets better and better."

"Yes, I think so. A little longer, and I start to look for a job."

"Good. Great. Actually, I can't quite imagine you in an office. You don't seem an office kind of person. But not the building site, either—definitely not that."

He laughed. "Oh, I am an office person. But only because I have to be. Because that is what I can do, always—good at that, so that is how I can earn money."

"Well, I'm one too, of course, in a very small way. Any accountancy is done by me, and I'm *not* good at it. Luckily, it's just sorting his bills and writing out checks for him to sign."

"How is your office? What is it like?"

"Why?"

"Then I can think of you there."

"Oh . . . It's a small room looking out over the garden. Desk, and filing cabinet, and a brown armchair I don't much use. And a print of eighteenth-century London over the fireplace."

"What do you see from the window?"

"Grass that needs cutting—that reminds me, I must ring the contractors. A couple of trees at the end—there's sometimes a squirrel that jumps from one to the other. And pigeons, always."

"Now I see it," he said gravely. "Good."

They sat in silence. She got up. "Let's walk."

The day had tipped from morning into afternoon and now, as they walked, it became late afternoon, the sunlight softer, the shadows longer. They were heading toward the road that would take them back to the station.

"We go, I think," said Anton. "We go, I am afraid." He bent to pick something up. "How do you call this?"

"An acorn. You know—from oak trees. Left over from last autumn."

"Acorn. There—another word."

"Not a very useful one."

"You never know when you may need." He held the acorn in his hand, closed his fist over it, put it carefully in the pocket of his leather jacket. He looked at her, smiling. Did not look away. Nor did she. For seconds. Too long. Not long enough.

A little breeze had got up. Rose put an arm into her jacket, began to shrug it on. He reached behind her to help, then his hand lay on her shoulder. For a moment, for an everlasting moment, so that she would feel it still on the way home in the Tube, sitting there distracted. This can't be, mustn't be. This must not happen. But it has.

CHAPTER TWELVE

Henry was beginning to flag. He hadn't realized that filming was such a laborious process. He hadn't realized that it involved so much standing around doing nothing. He hadn't reckoned with endless discussion between the director, Paula (the tall, fair woman who had come to Lansdale Gardens), the cameraman, the sound man, the boy Mark, a further acolyte whose role was not entirely apparent. He hadn't understood that they would spend the day roaming London in pursuit of suitable locations at which to film a snatch of Henry talking about the seamier side of eighteenth-century London life with, if possible, an emotive accessory to hand.

One of these, a *Big Issue* seller, was being difficult. He was prepared to act as a backdrop, but only at a price. The price had just gone up; he had whipped out a mobile phone, presumably in order to contact a colleague about the going rate, and was now holding out for thirty.

"Thirty *pounds*?" said Henry, incredulous. "Just to stand behind me when I talk?"

So it seemed.

In Henry's view this particular *Big Issue* seller was more of a Dickensian than a Hogarthian figure. The Artful Dodger incarnate. He said so, but nobody took any notice. Eventually, a deal was struck.

Henry was placed at the right angle to the *Big Issue* seller and filming, at last, took place.

Once again, he fluffed. There were never more than a few sentences of the script to be delivered at any one spot, but somehow he could never get them into his head. He had not written them in the first place. That is to say, Mark had written them, they had been sent to Henry ahead of the day as a courtesy; Henry had made a few adjustments and amendments, most of which had been ignored.

"OK," said Paula patiently. "Let's go again."

They did. And again. The *Big Issue* seller was doubled up.

They moved on. Paula had been keen to find some prostitutes. But where? "It's a bore. Since they cleaned up the King's Cross area you don't know where to find them. At least I don't. Oh well, we'll have to do without. But I want some really rough types—though not necessarily today. Knife crime, if possible."

Mark suggested the emergency entrance at one of the main hospitals, on a Saturday night.

"Now *that's* an idea. But would we be allowed to film?"

"I can always get on to their PR people and try."

Henry listened aghast to this exchange. They were now outside a branch of the Royal Bank of Scotland, where a young man sitting cross-legged with a dewy-eyed dog across his lap had attracted the crew's attention. "Nice," said Paula. "Go and talk to him, Mark."

Mark came back, shaking his head. "It's forty, or he says he'll have to be moving on. I'll need to get some more cash." He disappeared into the bank.

Henry sat down on the bench at a nearby bus stop. His knee hurt. His feet hurt. He had a headache. He wished he had not after all decided to leave Rose behind; she would have been moral support. He could have complained to her. The cameraman was saying that street people just weren't as thick on the ground these days, were they? A problem when you're looking for background color for a project like this. The sound man went to get coffees from the Starbucks across the road. Henry clutched a horrible plastic cup and eyed the wretched script once more—set out in large font and triple spacing in deference to his eyesight. He thought of those young chaps whistling up hillsides while holding forth about the Middle Ages, and wished them luck; he knew now why he had settled for a life of desk-bound scholarship.

Filming took place alongside the young man and the dog, after cash had changed hands. Henry gazed anxiously at the camera, willing the right words to flow.

"Youth was short, in eighteenth-century London. Brief, and . . . and precarious. The fortunate few found an apprenticeship. The rest . . . um . . . the rest . . . oh dear."

"Cut," said Paula.

He tried again. ". . . The rest fought for survival, the flotsam and jetsam of the city, many forced into crime and prostitution."

The dog had risen from the young man's blanket and now started to bark. The young man yanked at its lead: "Just fucking shut up, you."

"I think we'll move on," said Paula. "I'm not sure I care for this location, anyway."

By late morning they were outside a shopping mall. Mark had found street musicians here on a reconnaissance trip, and it was thought they could be an interesting accompaniment. However, they were not to be seen today.

"Sorry," said Mark. "I should have booked them."

But Paula's attention was focused on a group of youths milling around outside a DVD outlet: "Now *those* would be good."

The youths were all hooded, shouting, and barging into unwary passersby. "Hmmn," said the cameraman. "Might not be entirely cooperative."

"Henry could engage with them," said Paula. "We could have him go up, say something. If it got out of hand—well, pull out."

Mark was murmuring that he wondered about health and safety. At that moment the youths noticed the camera and began to advance, yelling obscenities.

"Maybe not," said Paula. "OK—we'll break for lunch."

A pub was found. Henry did not care for pubs. He never went into pubs. He had expected something rather better: Rules or Wiltons. But at this stage any respite was welcome. The place was fairly crowded and the group split up; Henry found himself alone with Mark, who was being gratifyingly attentive. He had brought Henry a glass of red wine and the menu: "I'm afraid it's not exactly haute cuisine, but some of it sounds possible."

Henry was gracious. "The plaice and chips, I think. They surely can't go too far wrong with that."

Over food and drink Henry expanded. He was in reminiscence mood and found Mark a most appreciative audience: "That's so fascinating, that you knew Harold Wilson so well . . . Isaiah Berlin! Goodness!"

"Dear boy, one has made it one's business to know people. I used to lunch with Macmillan from time to time. Let me tell you about that . . ."

Mark was not a boy but rising thirty. He did not so much listen now as assess. The Henry who is talking—unstoppably—is quite another Henry from he who has just hesitated, fluffed, dried: "You have to understand that Bowra had his limitations. A conversationalist—yes, indeed—an entertainer, even, if one wants to be slightly snide, and don't get me wrong, one relished his company, but where his scholarship is concerned there are those who are disparaging, dismissive even. Now you may have heard that . . ."

Mark had not, and had no need to. What he now understood was that when it came to discussion—and denigration—of personalities Henry was an ace performer. Rubbish with a script, but can he talk! Let him loose on his own ground and you'd be away.

He said, "Did you ever come across A.J.P. Taylor?"

Of course Henry had known Taylor. And Trevor Roper. Historians a specialty. "Now, Geoffrey Elton . . ."

Mark sat back, complacent. He could see that this program would probably be dumped, and anyway he had his own agenda. He was finding Delia Canning tiresome to work for, he had a line to a producer at an independent company, and he had an idea to pitch. He smiled encouragingly at Henry.

Those designer tiles. The customized lighting system, also newly delivered and unreturnable—another hefty bill. A further week of the Poles. Marion watched her overdraft spiral out of control.

"Mr. Harrington's secretary no longer works here." The voice is entirely neutral. Or so it would seem.

Marion said, "It is essential that I reach Mr. Harrington. Can you tell me where he is?"

The voice cannot. "I'm afraid I have no information as to Mr. Harrington's whereabouts at the present time."

Marion said, "I don't believe this."

There is a fractional pause, a distant exhalation, possibly a sigh, as though the voice may have gone through this before.

"I'm afraid I can't help you."

Indeed, who is to help her? Not the bank, which squats there smugly piling up the figures. Not the nice Poles, who do not know what looms, and work away, smiling a welcome each time she arrives at the flat, which blooms with Farrow & Ball and the choicest of fittings. The Poles ply Marion with coffee or tea, whistling as they work. The one with the sprained ankle is hale once more, and assiduous: "Power shower good. See!"

Nothing like this has ever happened. Clients have behaved as clients should. They have paid up, they have paid on time, their checks have not bounced. Marion realized that she has had ludicrous faith; she has believed that you can trust people—most people—the people with whom you have dealings; she lacks the essential skepticism that drives business. She remembered an accountant who once said laconically: "I always assume the other guy is bent until he proves otherwise."

Who is Harrington? What is Harrington? Above all, where is Harrington?

"Scarpered, I should think," says Jeremy. "Made off with the takings. Which bank did you say he was with? Ah, them. Still trading, I think, but you'd better watch the press. Don't *worry*, darling. It'll get sorted somehow. Now, I know you're not supposed to be my agony aunt, but I've had this idea. It's Stella's birthday on Saturday, and I'm wondering if . . ."

Anton texts Rose: Is not heaven now like Sunday but I can think of it. I have bought very small eggs—quail, yes?—to remember. Today I read front page of *The Guardian*—except hard words. I must buy dictionary. Which is best?

Charlotte was reading *What Maisie Knew*. It was perhaps an indication of progress that she was able to venture into deeper waters. No more magazines, no more rereading of P. G. Wodehouse. She had to ask Rose to fetch the book from her own house. Rose said: "Some people would be needing their spare glasses, or that blue cardigan. You need a book. Of course."

"A deficiency?" said Charlotte meekly.

"Not at all. The need defines you, that's all."

Defined by a need for Henry James. Oh dear. Actually, it was not so much Henry James that she had wanted as a novel that would feed thoughts about the versatility of fiction, prompted by that conversation with Anton about the need for story. Story, yes, indeed, but the fascination of story is what it can do. Henry James can tell it through the eyes of a child, and make you, the reader, observe the adult chicanery and betrayals of which the child is unaware. Charlotte needed to remind herself of the sleight of hand whereby this is done. She sat in Rose's garden, reading. A blackbird sang, piercingly; bees rummaged in the flowers; her hip was not hurting, or only a bit. Tra-la.

Rose texts Anton: Cook quail eggs three minutes only—in boiling water. Eat in private—don't waste on the boys. Hard to say which dictionary. You need to see some. Perhaps more shopping?

The flowers caught Stella off guard, wrong-footed. There was this delivery man at the door, with a huge bouquet, and of course she took it. Brought it in, wondering vaguely—who? Fought off the cellophane and the raffia bow—lovely huge bunch of peonies and lilies, her favorites—found the envelope and the card.

"Happy birthday, darling. Thinking so much of you. Hope you are doing something nice. Wish I was doing it with you. Please—have dinner with me next week? All my love, Jeremy."

She wasn't doing anything nice. It was Saturday, so she wasn't going to the surgery. Presently she would fetch the girls from their music lessons. Make lunch. Ferry the girls to and from homes of friends. Make dinner.

She arranged the flowers, placed the vase on the kitchen table. They lit up the room—extravagant, voluptuous, eloquent. She put Jeremy's card in the waste bin. Five minutes later she took it out. Read it again. Put it on the dresser.

Marion had put the phone down on Jeremy. At least, she had put it on the table and could hear him bleating on from there.

I do not give a hang whether or not you send Stella flowers for her birthday. I am not interested in your negotiations with your wife. Truth to tell, I'm not sure how interested I am in you. It may soon be time for us to talk about this.

Marion was interested in George Harrington. Or rather, the black hole into which George Harrington had disappeared. She was compelled to take a bleak interest in her bank statement, in those bills, in the problem of the Poles.

"Are you out of your mind?" says Gill, hectoring Stella from forty miles away. "Have *dinner* with him?" Her voice is quite hoarse with indignation.

Stella holds the phone away from her ear. "Well, I just thought . . . Maybe just to hear what he's got to say . . ."

"*Flowers!* I think I should come over, Stella. I can tell you're in a bad state."

"No, no," says Stella. Somehow, she feels she'd be better without Gill just now. Actually, she doesn't feel in a particularly bad state.

"Anyway," says Gill. "You can't. See him. Not while the divorce negotiations are under way."

"*Can't?*"

"Definitely. Just ask Paul Newsome."

Paul Newsome makes a kind of hissing noise—a breath drawn in through the teeth. It is the sound a builder makes, inspecting dry rot, or a mechanic, staring at the innards of an ailing car.

"Inadvisable."

"Oh," says Stella. "Oh, I see." Then, nervously, "Why?"

Paul Newsome sighs. ". . . compromise our position at this delicate stage . . . expose yourself to disagreeable confrontation . . . insidious demands . . . special pleading . . . pressure."

"Yes," says Stella. "Yes, I see. Well, I suppose . . ."

She puts the phone down. The peonies and the lilies bloom away, on the kitchen table; the room is rich with scent.

Charlotte found herself much appreciative of *What Maisie Knew*. Even the most convoluted of Henry James's sentences are easily accessible. I must be getting better, she thinks. Mind and body both.

She surfaces from Maisie's story to consider her own—wayward, fortuitous, with none of the careful grooming of fiction. She thinks briefly of her mugger, now vanished into his or her own impulsive narrative; serial assaults upon elderly women, or merely the occasional raid when needs must? One will never know, which is probably for the best. She remembers hearing of some scheme whereby offenders and victims were brought together, presumably in order to induce guilt and regret in the offender, achieve forgiveness, or—worse—that questionable condition known as "closure." She has not the slightest desire to meet her mugger.

Rose comes into the room, staring at her mobile.

"I am actually enjoying Henry James," says Charlotte.

"What?"

"Henry James. Enjoying."

"Oh," says Rose, who has not heard.

I would very much like dictionary shopping, says Anton's text. When you are able to. Quail eggs were very good. I think I am the only worker on the site who eat quail eggs for lunch.

Stella dithers. She is in a state of acute dither—no, terminal dither. She reads Jeremy's card again, puts it into the waste bin, retrieves it, returns it to the dresser. She reads it once more, is going to tear it up this time, put a stop to this silliness; she reads again, twitches her head from side to side, does not tear it up.

She sniffs the lilies half a dozen times a day. The peonies have great blowsy silken centers; they are luxuriant, complacent. Does that Marion woman get sent lilies and peonies on her birthday?

Marion bites the bullet. She must sack the Poles. The amiable, harmless Poles. Oh, they will find another job, but it is tough. They have given nothing but satisfaction.

She calls the nephew; she explains, grimly. "So if you could come round, this afternoon. I want to be able to tell them exactly what has happened, why I've got to do this. I'm so sorry about it."

When the nephew arrived, Marion took him to one side. She set out the situation, which he accepted at once, apparently without surprise.

"The guy's made off? Dodgy, I imagine. Hope he hasn't stung you for too much."

Marion was not going to elaborate on her affairs to a seventeen-year-old schoolboy. "So could you explain to them that I'm just not able to finish the job, to keep them on. It's absolutely no reflection on their work. I'll be happy to give any references they'd like."

The boy said thoughtfully, "Interesting, a City type like that going AWOL. I'd love to know what he's been up to." He addressed his uncles in Polish—crisp and succinct, no messing, this is how it is. There were mutterings of dismay and regret; the elder Pole laid his hand for a moment on Marion's arm, with a murmur of sympathy, shaking his head. She felt even worse.

"Don't worry," said the boy. "I can fix them up with something else soon enough. We've got a pretty good database now. Actually, I'm thinking of moving them into commercial contracts—long-term stuff." He spoke like some plantation overseer. "I take it you're giving them a reasonable pay-off?"

Marion nodded.

"Good. We can work out the details."

At last, all three left, the Poles slung about with their bags of tools, their work kit. There was much shaking of heads, voluble expressions of regret. Marion kept saying, "I'm so *sorry*." "No matter," said the Poles. "No matter." The boy advised Marion to get on to Interpol: "They may have something on your guy—very likely, if he's dodgy."

Alone in the flat, she looked around—at the meticulously selected shades of Farrow & Ball, the halogen lights, the power shower, the Miele kitchen appliances. What would become of it now? To whom, indeed, did it belong? Not to her, that was for sure. All she could do was lock it up and leave it. If a man owns a property worth a couple of million, does he not at some point lay claim to it?

Henry stared in disbelief at Delia Canning's letter. He put it aside, picked it up, read the letter again and it still said the same thing.

Rose came into the room. "That Mark is on the phone—the television person."

Henry scowled at her. "I do not wish to speak to him." He waved the letter. "I have just received this from Ms. Canning. Apparently the project has been canceled. Aborted. They have pulled the plug on it. My time has been wasted. I do not wish to speak to anyone from Ms. Canning's office."

Rose said, "Actually, he's not phoning from there. He says it's a personal matter. He seemed to . . . to think you might be a bit reluctant."

Mark had not thought—he knew. He knew all about the letter because he had read it in Delia's office, and had anyway been present when Delia viewed the results of that day's filming: "Say no more. We can't use him. It was worth a try—but no."

Delia might not be able to use Henry, but Mark reckoned that he could. Mark had his own fish to fry, in the form of a proposal to a rival concern for a film about the presiding figures of history: Macaulay, Carlyle, Trevelyan, Tawney, Namier et al. Working title—merrily— *The Dinosaurs*, though one would have to come up with something else if the project took off. Which was a bit of a long shot—this was an arcane subject for an increasingly philistine medium, but worth a stab. It would be amusing to work up, and the material could always come in handy for an article, or even, one day, a book. Mark saw this stint in the world of television as a flirtation. He had every intention of making his real career in academia, as soon as the opportunity arose to get going. No messing about with an assistant lectureship somewhere in the sticks; a proper job at a Russell group university, or nothing. It was a matter of biding his time, and keeping up his contacts with a few people who might help, in due course. A chair by the time he was forty, that was the idea. Vice-Chancellor somewhere, perhaps, eventually, if one could be bothered with the admin.

". . . *entirely* understand your feelings," he said to Henry. "Between you and me, Delia is known to be a bit . . . well, inconsistent. Judgment not always spot-on. But the thing is, this might all work out for the best. There's a scheme I'd rather like to run past you, an idea I've got in which . . . well, in which, to be frank, you might play a rather crucial role. I wonder if I could come and see you?"

Henry grunted. He was feeling bruised, humiliated. One should never have let oneself in for this sort of treatment at the hands of some jumped-up young woman. And now here was the boy, who appeared to have defected, and was saying pleasingly critical things about Canning. What was all this about?

"We'll have to see what my diary looks like," he said. "Have a word with my secretary—she takes care of that."

CHAPTER THIRTEEN

George Harrington made the six o'clock news—the tail end, admittedly, merely a coda, but there he was: ". . . investment banker George Harrington has been arrested in Bermuda, charged with insider trading."

Marion heard it in her kitchen, distractedly chopping an onion for soup, her mind not on soup at all but on the bills, the bank, the bills. She heard it, subliminally, and then registered properly, and the knife fell from her hand.

Oh.

Insider trading?

Which is . . . ? I know—to do with shares, buying and selling. You've bought or sold when you have some insider information, so you're cashing in, and that is illegal.

Arrested.

George Harrington is in prison, which means forget trying to find out where he is, in order to have a chat. You are not going to be having a chat, either now or in the foreseeable future. George Harrington has neatly removed himself, or been removed. At some point he will emerge, and there will be a court case, and either he'll go back to prison for rather longer, or he won't, but in any event I am not going to be able to seize his attention, so forget it. I shall have to discover how I go about trying to get what's due to me, which will mean endless letters, and probably a solicitor, and it will take forever. Which leaves me, right now, alarmingly overdrawn, and nothing coming in until some well-heeled and reliable client turns up.

How can a man *do* this to someone? To me. Easily, it seems—because George Harrington and his like do not operate as I do myself, and as do practically all those I have come across, in a nice do-unto-others-as-you-would-be-done-to-yourself way; his is a climate of *sauve qui peut*, and never mind anyone else. George Harrington will not be giving me a thought, if he ever did—except as someone who was useful.

Thank you, Uncle Henry, for George Harrington. That blessed lunch in Manchester, at which I should not have been.

Marion had not intended to tell Henry about Harrington. She was prompted to do so over Sunday lunch, a lunch that was the last thing she needed right now, but Henry had been insistent: "I need some company, my dear. And Corrie has promised oxtail stew."

The prompt was Henry's extended grievance, which lasted through the tomato soup (tinned) and well beyond the oxtail stew: ". . . dumped, frankly, and one is not accustomed to such treatment. I should never have got involved with those people—exposed myself to such behavior. And all because of that Manchester business." With uncharacteristic candor, Henry had been explaining why the humiliation of the occasion had made him feel that he needed to restore his reputation. "If that lecture had gone as it should have gone, it would never have occurred to me to make myself available for *television*."

He's complaining about Manchester, thought Marion. What about me? And so she had talked of Harrington, of the flat, of Harrington's defection. Henry was shocked and, to his credit, sympathetic. "Outrageous. A man without a moral compass. Some kind of banker, you say? One has never dealt with such people, except of course for necessary services. You must take legal steps."

"Yes," said Marion wearily.

"The present Lord Chief Justice was a student of mine, briefly. I could have a word."

Marion said she doubted that the problem was within the remit of the Lord Chief Justice. "I'll get it sorted, Uncle Henry. Eventually. Somehow."

"We are both the victims of circumstance," said Henry. "I have the greatest mistrust of circumstance, whether in private life or public affairs. History is bedeviled by circumstance. Ah—here's Corrie. Am I right in thinking it's the rice pudding, Corrie? Excellent! Progress is forever skewed by circumstance—the unforeseen event, an untimely death, the unpredicted circumstance, and the course of history would be one of seamless advance. Without the Manchester circumstance you and I would be carefree."

Insofar as I ever am, thought Marion crossly. Has Uncle Henry ever lived in the real world? "Just a tiny helping, thank you, Corrie. Delicious, but I've eaten so much already."

"However, as it turns out, circumstance may also have thrown up something useful. There's this boy, what's-his-name, Mark something—well, young man really, I suppose—worked for the Canning woman but seems to have left her, came here a couple of days ago, and I believe he may have made quite a promising suggestion."

Mark had arrived in midmorning and at once set about establishing himself with Rose: "I'd *love* a coffee, how sweet of you, but only if Lord Peters is having one. This is such a lovely room—so atmospheric—I adored it last time I was here. Books do furnish a room, don't they?"

No one had ever called Henry's study lovely before. Gratified, Henry gave Mark a tour: the inscribed copies, the Gillray print, the bust of Walpole. Rose withdrew to make coffee, having got the measure of Mark. On the make, she thought. Heaven knows what he's doing here, but no doubt we'll find out.

In fact Mark was not entirely sure himself what he was doing here. His initial enthusiasm for the founding fathers of history project had already withered somewhat after he had floated the idea with the producer in question and failed to arouse any sort of response. Mark was not a man to waste time on unprofitable ventures. He was already wondering if it was not the moment to chuck television and get back onto the academic ladder. He had thought of canceling his date with Henry, and then some instinct told him that it might be expedient to keep up the connection.

Once settled in Henry's study, with Henry in full spate about his newly discovered—or rather, rediscovered—contempt for the popular medium of television, Mark considered Lansdale Gardens and perceived that Henry was not short of a bob or two. This was of academic interest only; Mark was not concerned with money for the sake of money, merely as the necessary prop for what you wanted to do, and that, in essence, was to make a name for yourself, probably in the university world.

Mark had, of course, an eerie affinity with Henry himself, and would have been offended to be told that. Like Henry, he recognized determined application to an area of scholarship as the route to distinction: make yourself the ultimate authority on something or other and you were away. It didn't terribly matter what, but you needed to be sure there weren't too many people in there already. He was thinking of taking over the Scottish Enlightenment entirely—flood the market with articles, then a book (beef up his thesis, so not too much extra work), elbow out the competition by hinting that all were superannuated hacks. This would take time, during which he needed an academic post, or funding in some other form.

Henry was satisfied to learn that Mark too was disillusioned: "Quite right to get out of that world. Amusing for a bit of youthful experience, I dare say, but no place for a serious-minded man. Now when I was your age I had of course my first Fellowship . . ."

More along these lines. Mark realized that Henry had entirely forgotten that there was an ostensible reason for the visit, and was quite happy to treat it as a social occasion with no particular purpose, which was just as well. No need for explanations. Henry was talking now about My Memoirs.

"I shall of course concentrate on the memoirs now that I have disposed of Ms. Canning." Henry paused, and looked inquiringly at

Mark. "Did you say you had some project in mind—I'd rather forgotten, remind me . . ."

Oh dear. Mark regrouped, with smooth efficiency. "I'm fascinated, of course, with the prospect of the memoirs. I was wondering about doing a piece for one of the papers—a taster, as it were."

Henry, of course, thought this an excellent idea. He warmed to the theme. He got out the typescript of My Memoirs. He explained the extent and range of the archival resources on which they were based—the shelves of files and boxes stuffed with papers. He led Mark over to the file cupboard, to view. He pulled out a file, at random—letters and other documents spilled to the ground. Mark gathered them up.

Henry tutted and shook his head. "One can never *find* anything, that's the problem."

"Really?" said Mark. Thoughtful. Very thoughtful. No, I can see you wouldn't be able to. Interesting.

Over the next half an hour or so Mark assessed the potential. He displayed a constructive interest in Henry's papers: "Of course with proper cataloguing . . . if you had a comprehensive index, then retrieval of any specific item would be simple . . . an orderly system could help your own approach to the memoirs."

"Quite," said Henry helplessly. "Quite so."

"If I could assist in any way . . ." murmured Mark.

And thus was the arrangement born. Mark had done a quick investigation of the shelves and reckoned that he could get this stuff sorted within a few weeks, couple of months max, if he went hard at it. But he would not go hard at it. This would be an on-going process, a lengthy and time-consuming process which would fund Mark's own, concurrent work. He could fiddle about with Henry's papers, in a leisurely way, for part of his day, and get on with the Scottish Enlightenment during the rest.

He explained the complexity of the task to Henry: "A modern database requires meticulous presentation . . . fortunately I do have some experience . . . an archive of this importance can't be dealt with in a hurry."

Henry liked the idea of a database. He eyed the file cupboard, and saw it transformed into a streamlined twenty-first-century research facility. He saw My Memoirs float forth from it, to critical acclaim and resounding sales.

It took Mark a while to get across the idea that he would need to be paid for his services. He murmured something about funding, a term with which Henry was not familiar. When the penny dropped, Henry brushed the matter aside as a mere technicality: "But of course, dear boy, of course. Whatever suits you. Sort something out with Rose."

Mark saw at once that this would not be a good idea: ". . . far happier if you yourself could suggest an arrangement." A sum was arrived at that was rather more than Mark had had in mind.

"Excellent!" said Henry. "Now when can you start?"

"Archivist!" Rose slammed the lid on the saucepan. The cat bolted from the room in protest. Charlotte kept silent; wisest not to risk comment.

"And will I get hold of two dozen box files, and will I clear the lobby so he can use it as his work center, and is it all right if I call you Rose, Mrs. Donovan? Please yourself. It's Henry now, I note, no more Lord P. Got his feet properly under the table, he has."

"Young?" ventured Charlotte.

Rose sniffed. "Thirty acting twenty-four. Boyish charm." She wrenched open the oven, banged a dish of lasagne onto the hob. "*Gerry . . . supper . . .*"

The cat returned, sheltering behind Gerry. Rose piled lasagne onto plates. "He needs surface space, and I'm stupid enough to remember that trestle table in the loft, so it's 'Oh, Rose, you're brilliant, shall we go up and get it?' And 'The lobby's a bit *dark*, Rose, would there be a table-lamp I could have?' And he dumps his stuff in the cloakroom where I fall over it."

"Who?" said Gerry.

"His lordship has employed an archivist."

"Ah." Gerry went no further, scenting a problem.

"Database! Since when does he need a database? Perfectly happy rooting about in the file cupboard."

This is about territory, thought Charlotte. Her territory has been invaded. Is it Lansdale Gardens that is her territory, or his lordship in person?

"*My* files are in perfect order," said Rose. "If he lays a finger on those there'll be real trouble. The last ten years are immaculate."

"I wish I could say the same," said Charlotte, seeking to cause a diversion. "When I get home I plan a major search-and-destroy operation. Incidentally, to the garden gate and back without the crutches this morning!"

Rose glanced at her. "So?"

"Just . . . progress," said Charlotte humbly.

Rose attacked her lasagne, without further comment. After a minute, she said, "Dictionaries. Which do you reckon is the best?"

"Ah," said Charlotte happily. "Now Chambers has its fans, but I suppose in the last resort the Shorter Oxford . . ."

The bookshop has many dictionaries. A shelf of dictionaries. Rose and Anton cruise dictionaries, taking down now this, now that.

"Too heavy," says Rose. "You can't lug that around."

"Lug?" says Anton. "That I do not know. Carry, I think? Yes, I need a dictionary very much."

"Maybe this . . ." Rose is on the verge of selection. They consider the choice, heads together.

"I try a word," says Anton. "Say to me a word I do not know."

"Oh, goodness . . . Charismatic."

"How do you spell?" Anton turns the pages. "Yes. Here. 'Charisma . . . a special personal . . .'"—he struggles, valiantly, wrestles his way through—"'. . . quality or power that enables an individual to impress or influence many of his fellows.' Now I say to the site manager, 'It is a pity you are not more charismatic.'"

They are both laughing. A passing head turns; can dictionaries be so amusing?

And Rose knows that dictionaries will never be the same again. Dictionaries will be forever imbued, sanctified, significant, suggestive. They will not be just themselves, but this moment, these moments, being here, like this, in this place, her and him, in this now. She will always have this now, tethered to Collins and Chambers and the Shorter Oxford.

Charlotte was quarreling with Henry James. That is to say, she was finding James's sentence constructions a bit too much, on a warm afternoon in the garden. Get to the point, man—stop piling on another phrase, another qualification, another flourish. Yes, I know it is unique, admired, an intriguing labyrinthine process, but today I am not receptive.

She put down *What Maisie Knew*, and picked up the mug of tea that Gerry had kindly brought. He was in his shed, attending to that table. She could hear woodwork sounds, and his radio—there was cricket on somewhere.

And where had Rose gone, this Saturday afternoon, hurrying off with a preoccupied look, saying that she had some shopping to do?

Charlotte sighed, engulfed by a wave of discontent. When will *I* be off somewhere once more on a Saturday afternoon, or indeed any other afternoon? One was not exactly skipping hither and thither, pre-mugging, but well able to come and go, walk to the bus-stop without a second thought, make a trip to the garden center, or into town for a spree to the Royal Academy or Tate Britain. When will I cease to be tethered, hobbled, grounded?

Stop whingeing. The hip is improving, you know that. Crutch-free to the garden gate now—a stab at the corner shop tomorrow.

"Not Starbucks," says Anton. "We go somewhere else, yes? Perhaps this place—how do you say it?"

"Euphorium. Odd name for a café-cum-bakery. It means—oh, being in a heightened state, being very . . . uplifted, happy."

"Then I think this is very much the right place." He turns to her and smiles. That smile. He puts a hand under her arm to steady her up a rather steep step. They stand at the counter and contemplate apple tart, chocolate tart, strawberry and cream tart, chocolate éclair.

"Cappuccino, please," says Rose. "And . . . no, I mustn't, I'm getting fat enough as it is."

"You are not fat. And I shall have strawberry and cream tart."

"Oh, all right. They look irresistible."

Once served and seated, Anton reaches into his rucksack for the dictionary. "How do you spell this irri—irrisist . . . ?"

"*No*," says Rose. "If you're going to dive into the dictionary every time I open my mouth we shall never have a conversation again."

"All right." The dictionary is returned to the rucksack. "So I dive instead into strawberry and cream tart. That is good way to speak? Good colloquial? See, that is a word I know."

"It'll do."

"I learn from the boys. In the flat, in the evenings. They tell me what is colloquial speak. Street speak, they say. Most is bad words. But I say now, 'Cheers, mate' and 'see you later.'"

"A long way from *Where the Wild Things Are* and *Charlotte's Web*," says Rose.

"Children book, crossword, newspaper, advertisement . . . my nephew street speak . . . I learn from all sort."

"Across the board," advises Rose. "That's polite colloquial."

"Thank you. I should make list—two list, polite and not polite."

"I made lists of words when I was about fourteen. I remember doing it. New words. Grown-up words. Show-off words."

"What words?"

"I'm not telling you," says Rose. "Or that dictionary will come out again. I was trying to impress my parents. It wasn't easy, being the child of teachers."

"Your mother is so clever teacher. She teach without you know you have been . . . teached."

"Taught. Oh, *listen* to me . . . I'm doing it too."

He laughs. "But you must. I would do the same, if you try to speak my language."

She sighs. "Do you feel . . . do you sometimes feel that there is . . . that there's a sort of wall between us because we don't speak the same language, think in the same language?"

He looks at her. An intent, considering look. "No," he says. "There is no wall. Where is the wall?"

The garden shed had fallen silent. Presently, Gerry emerged, looking disconsolate.

"I've done something stupid. Mucked up a perfectly good piece of wood. Miscalculation."

"How annoying. Have another cup of tea, to steady the nerves— and I'd love one too."

He came back, with tea, and sat beside her. He picked up Henry James. "I've never read him, I'm afraid."

"An acquired taste," said Charlotte. "I go off him at times, and then find myself back on. This afternoon I'm off, for some reason. Interesting, the way a relationship with a book, a writer, can be a bit like real life relationships, with friends." She thought of Gerry's friends—the two or three that she had met. Alan, with whom Gerry occasionally played squash. Bill, to whom he gave a lift on choir nights. And there was an old college contemporary who visited once in a while.

"Friends . . ." He considered. "I find mine stay much the same."

"That's to your credit. My relationships have waxed and waned. I am guilty right now about an old friend I rather keep at arm's length."

"I don't have that many," said Gerry. "Rose . . . Rose is forever on the phone, or meeting up with someone."

"Women," she told him. "That's women. We're much more intimate. We tell each other things, confide, all that. We associate. Well, men associate, but not in the same way."

Gerry looked faintly perturbed, as though stepping onto dangerous ground. "You may be right."

"What do you talk about with . . . Alan, say, or Bill?"

"Oh, I don't know . . ." Contained panic now, definitely. "Current affairs, that sort of thing. Work, sometimes. The cricket, if there is any."

"Exactly. Focused. Practical. Men are more serious than women. Women's talk is more haphazard. And confidential."

"Some men," said Gerry, rallying. "Some women."

"Oh, of course. A wild generalization. A travesty. But there's still a point."

"Haphazard . . ."

"Talk for the sake of talk. Unconsidered."

"Plenty of men I know . . ."

Charlotte laughed. "I think I'm winding you up, Gerry. At least I've taken your mind off the carpentry. And all prompted by Henry James."

He picked the book up again. "Who is Maisie?"

"A child. And what she knew—or didn't know—is a teaser. I've never quite been able to work it out. I suppose that's one reason it's a book you go back to."

He gave her a sideways look. "So maybe you should try out that old friend of yours again, too?"

"Touché," said Charlotte. "Well done. Would it be binge-drinking to have yet more tea, do you think?"

He held out his hand for her mug. "Feel free. And we can go on with this haphazard talk." Another sideways glance, with the hint of a grin.

Rose and Anton are walking toward the Tube station. She slows up as they approach a green space with seats. "Shall we stop for a minute or two?"

"You are tired."

"No. Just . . . there's no great hurry."

They sit. "Tonight I dive into the dictionary," he says. "My nephew and the boys, they dive into beer and street speak. I learn important words."

"Will they laugh at you?"

"Of course. But it is nice laugh—I am the uncle, I do uncle thing, like read books and now buy dictionary. They are . . . they are . . ."

"Indulgent," says Rose. "And *no*. No dictionary."

"Later, then. Later I look for this word and I think of . . . now. I think of you."

"Yes," she says. "Yes, I'll be thinking too." She looks away.

He lays a hand on her knee. Withdraws it at once. They sit in silence for a moment. Moments.

"It is the end of the afternoon," he says. "I do not like now the end of the afternoon. It is a bad time."

"But we had a good time."

"We had a *very* good time."

"Some other afternoon," she says. "We could . . ."

"There can be other afternoon?"

"Yes," she says. "Yes."

And later, in the wasteland of a sleepless night, she thinks: Can there be another life? Could there? Don't think of it. Don't.

CHAPTER FOURTEEN

Jeremy made sure to be at the restaurant first. He wanted to be sitting there, watching the door, when Stella came in, so that he could get to his feet, and stand waiting for her, looking . . . well, looking thrilled and welcoming, and, one hoped, a welcome sight. He had chosen the venue with care—an Italian place where the background music was unobtrusive, and there were dimly lit secluded corners. A courtship restaurant. He had taken Marion there once, early on. No matter. She hadn't cared for it—something wrong with the decor.

He saw Stella arrive, hand her coat to the man, glance around. She was looking so pretty. Never seen that dress before—gorgeous color, suits her a treat.

She joined him: "Hello." No move to kiss him, so he made no injudicious lunge at her cheek, just smiled, pulled back her chair. "Stella . . . This is wonderful."

Discussion of the menu. "Fritto di mare? You used to love that. I thought a frascati to drink—or would you rather red." The wait till food came, with chat about the girls. Stella was stiff, cautious, holding back. He raised a smile with a family joke about Daisy and her passion for shopping.

Food. Frascati. And she was starting to thaw. He told her about some bizarre customers he'd had lately. The woman who collected vintage deck chairs actually raised a laugh. He told her about the sale at that Shropshire mansion, and the pile of William Morris curtains for which he'd entered into a bidding war with a hard-nosed woman dealer (one didn't mention that Marion had come along on that occasion, of course): "I was absolutely determined that crone wasn't going to get them—I knew her of old, she lurks like a spider in an awful dive in Hackney, and the stuff was super, much too good for her. You've always liked William Morris, haven't you, darling?"

She was responding. A definite thaw. She told one or two little anecdotes of her own. They were having a dialogue. No mention of the matter in question—the matter possibly in question, reconciliation. But no mention of divorce, either. They were a couple enjoying a meal together. Lovers, perhaps, to a casual observer. At one point he took her hand for a moment, and it was not removed. Not immediately.

At the end, bill paid, coats on, he said, "Can we do this again, darling?"

She looked away, fiddled with a button, hesitated. "So long as Gill doesn't know. And . . . and Mr. Newsome."

Jeremy was about to say, "It's none of their bloody business." Then he saw how this could be interesting. He nodded. "Of course. It's just between you and me."

And so it all began. A lunch. Surreptitious phone calls. Texts. Once, they walked to the river, hand in hand, and he kissed her on a seat on the Embankment. Still, nothing was said about the future. Fine, play it by ear. And in the meantime, there was something distinctly enjoyable about the present.

It wouldn't do for Marion to know about this. Jeremy had the feeling that Marion was getting more perfunctory about their relationship; he wouldn't put it past her to dump him. And he didn't want that; he needed her. Of course, she'd known all along that he was determined not to let Stella divorce him, and that was one thing, but for her to sense that he was having . . . well, a rather delicious sort of *affair* with Stella was another. She'd slam the door on him.

Clandestine meetings with your wife were titillating—no getting away from it. The whole situation made Jeremy feel boyish, rather naughty. And it had lent Stella a new charm. She was so attractive; he fancied her something rotten, and was dying to get into bed, but that meant taking her to the flat, which was a decidedly unromantic site. He'd have to think about this.

Marion had had to extend her overdraft. She had had to go cap in hand to the bank. The figures terrified her. Never before has she been in this situation, or anything like it. And all because of a wretched man she had fetched up lunching alongside on an occasion she should never have been at in any case.

She took legal advice. The advice was exactly as she had anticipated. She did indeed have a claim, a considerable claim, but one that it could take years to pursue. The legal adviser would make some checks on George Harrington—"We can keep a tab on him, at the very least"—but could only recommend patience. Resignation, more like, thought Marion.

In the meantime, money was going out—hemorrhaging out—but not coming in. The trophy wives were still not making over a sitting-room or a bedroom. Marion tried a mailshot to old clients, to remind them of her existence, with enticing suggestions about new fabrics she had sourced, new wallpapers.

She was tired, stressed. I need a break, she thought. A couple of days away, diversion, stop thinking about this all of the time. Where? Who with? Well, Jeremy, I suppose. He'd be pleased, anyway—it's not usually me who suggests an outing. She rang him.

"This weekend? Oh, darling, I can't. Would you believe it, I've got a consignment of stuff coming in from a sale in Cheshire—I must be here, sort it and so forth. *What* a bore."

Marion was surprised; she felt a bit let down. Not like him to pass up a jaunt. Oh, well.

I don't know what's going on, thought Stella. Why am I feeling like this? All sort of . . . stirred up. Excited. I must be mad. What am I *doing*?

"Actually," she said to Gill, "don't come over. I'll be away this weekend. That old school friend of mine has invited me—Mary. The girls? No, the girls aren't coming. They're going to friends—it's just a couple of nights."

"Your husband's continued intransigence . . ." wrote Paul Newsome.

Henry was finding that he rather enjoyed Mark's presence at Lansdale Gardens. The mornings were enlivened by Mark's occasional deferential inquiries, as he emerged from the lobby—now called his office—with a file in his hand. "I'm just wondering if it might be an idea to open a database listing your contacts chronologically—might make it easier when doing a search or a check."

Henry had run for cover at Mark's initial suggestion of an online system. "No, no, no, dear boy. I can't stand those screens. Paper. I've got to have paper in my hand."

Mark was all compliance. "Of course—I *quite* understand. We'll set up a nice traditional card index, cross-referenced to files. And may I just say how *rewarding* I'm finding this. But one does need to take it slowly and carefully—with an archive of this depth and variety one has to be so sure not to miss anything."

Henry purred. Rose, bringing letters to be signed, slammed them down on the desk.

Mark too was entirely satisfied with the arrangement. His Lansdale Gardens mornings were nicely funding afternoon work fine-turning his thesis for potential publication; a monograph, probably, with a couple of articles before long to arouse interest—get one's name established as the coming man, where the Scottish Enlightenment was concerned. The cataloguing of Henry's papers was a task that could be made as leisurely as one liked. The old boy was obviously only too pleased to have someone dancing attendance, all you had to do was butter him up fairly regularly, and learn to go selectively deaf when he got into reminiscence mode. Quite enough about Isaiah Berlin and Maurice Bowra, thank you very much. Though, that said, it was wise to lend half an ear—you never knew what might turn up. Mark was a born opportunist; his progress to date had been owed to a mixture of natural talent, application, and the recognition of any promising moment. His entrée into the world of television had come about because Delia Canning came to give a talk to a college society when he was finishing off his thesis, and he had made sure to go up afterward and tell her that he had been so fascinated by what she had to say, such an insightful account of documentary film-making. Etcetera. Hang around her long enough to be sure that he had left an impression.

And so it was, thank you, Delia, for Henry Peters. Delia was of no further interest, as far as Mark was concerned, but she had been nicely useful, as it turned out.

Mark was finding that Henry's papers were a midden of academic gossip and infighting, heavily mulched with similar material from the world of public affairs—the whole larded with serious scholarly stuff, notes and articles and notes for articles and booklists and catalogues. And the whole mass crawled with people—names, names, names: students and colleagues and friends and enemies and those in high office and those who had aspired to high office and all those with whom Henry had at one time or another exchanged compliments or insults or simply drunk a few bottles of claret. Hence Mark's thought about a database—get this bunch sorted once and for all, dead or alive.

He began to enter names as he came across them, as they lifted from the morass of files: the writer of a letter, the recipient of a letter, colleagues, students, persons discussed or praised or reviled. Early on, he came across the communication from the Labour elder statesman that has prompted Henry's blizzard of proposals to newspaper editors. Mark read this with slightly raised interest but perceived—unlike Henry—that this ancient political scandal had no staying power. He did not, of course, know of Henry's efforts, but was himself keeping a vague eye out for useful fodder. Somewhere in here there might be something of real potential, but this was not it.

"Paris!" Stella had said.

"Is it too much of a cliché, darling? I just thought—Paris in the spring with you, what a heavenly thought. So easy—Eurostar, you're there in a trice. So I've booked—took a gamble. Is it all right?"

One of those furtive phone calls, that had been—furtive on Stella's part, making sure the girls weren't around, feeling guiltily that Gill would somehow know about it, by some osmotic process, the airwaves leaking the conversation.

And now here they were, in this gorgeous little bistro on the Left Bank, not far from the hotel, where they had done no more than leave their bags, check out the room, and at the sight of the double bed Stella had felt herself blushing, for heaven's sake. As though this weekend were some adulterous assignation.

"Ah—canard à l'orange. One of your favorites, isn't it? Or do you fancy the fish?" Jeremy was solicitous, attentive. She was reminded of . . . oh, goodness, of right back when they first went out together, and she'd never met anyone like him before, funny and fond and different. Other men paled by comparison, as they did again now. Somewhere far away, Gill was scolding; Mr. Newsome admonished across his desk.

Jeremy was on a high. *Such* fun. A spring evening in Paris with a pretty woman, and the fact that she was his wife made it all the more intriguing. Of course, Paris is always magic. Does it have that effect on Parisians? Are they on cloud nine all the time? Probably not—the effect has been cleverly groomed for the tourist trade. That, and French women. The girl over there—wow! And her at the next table— fifty if she's a day, but look at her! And, actually, Stella's holding her own nicely—super, that black dress, shows off her figure. Forget French women—we do our own, thank you.

The dress had been a bit of an extravagance—Stella had found she hadn't a thing to wear, really not a thing, and Paris is rather special, after all. So there had been a hasty raid on that favorite boutique, and the dress *was* pricey but so exactly right. And here was Jeremy being so appreciative. And such good company—she hadn't laughed like this in ages. What a lovely evening. But what is going *on*? What are we *doing*?

She said it. Over coffee, in a sudden moment of disbelief, of panic.

"What we're doing, darling," said Jeremy, "is just having a lovely time. And in a minute we're going back to the hotel to have even more of a lovely time, aren't we? But first we'll walk along the Seine for a few minutes—let's spin it out. And what shall we do tomorrow? Versailles? The Pompidou? I've always loved the Cluny Museum."

He wasn't entirely clear himself what they were doing. Reconciliation? Romance? Whatever, it's a whole lot of fun. Why spoil things with introspection?

Marion found that she was missing the Poles—their cheery camaraderie in the Hampstead flat. The flat itself had left a void in her life—no major work project, very little work at all, indeed. The media told her that she was a statistic, a victim of recession, alongside factory workers and civil servants and all those who could not get on the housing ladder or pay off their credit cards. In her mind's eye, recession and George Harrington were lined up side by side, grinning.

Not my fault, she told herself. I am still good at what I do. I am merely a statistic, and the fall-out from some piece of financial chicanery. She hoped that Harrington was in a peculiarly insalubrious lock-up; no more Brittany scallops, John Dory fillets, tian of smoked chicken.

But in the meantime the overdraft growled away, and cash did not flow. What to do? Realize assets? Diversify? Her only asset was the house—both home and business center. Diversification was a challenge. How? Into what could she diversify herself? She rang Jeremy, needing company, and suggested he come round that evening. She bought salmon, the first of the season's strawberries, an expensive cheese; sucks to the recession.

Jeremy was apparently in high spirits. He brought wine and a rather jarring exuberance: "Isn't life wonderful!"

Marion, who had not been feeling that it was, stared at him. "If you say so. Did you get your Cheshire sale stuff sorted?"

"Cheshire? Oh yes, yes. Shall I open this?" He waved the bottle.

Over the salmon, she said, "I'm thinking of diversifying. More by way of retail, while there are so few commissions coming in. None, to be precise. I'm wondering about sourcing abroad—trawling French *brocantes* and markets. Actually, it's something we could do together—there'd be material for you, too."

Jeremy frowned. "Well, it's a thought. Of course, the euro's quite strong at the moment. One would be paying more."

She had expected greater enthusiasm. "I've this idea of turning the showroom into much more of a retail outlet—specializing in French provincial."

He was doubtful. "You'd find it quite an undertaking, darling. And is there the space?"

"I might think of expanding. Take on a bigger outlet."

Jeremy pursed his lips. "Hmmn. Bigger overheads."

"This isn't like you," said Marion. "I've always seen you as a go-for-it man. Or do you reckon I'd be setting up in competition?" she added nastily.

He was affronted. "Hardly! Just, I wouldn't want you to come a cropper."

"I already have. I've got to think about some self-help. The bank . . ."

"Oh, never let a bank get you down. You can always string them along. Don't *worry*. You'll have some lovely big commission arrive any day now—just you see." He had had enough of this theme, that was clear—the exuberance took over once more. He began to talk about the Cluny Museum in Paris, for some reason, those amazing tapestries, how he'd had the idea that he ought to get hold of huge blown-up images of old tapestries and line the walls of the warehouse, create atmosphere, it would be fabulous . . .

Marion heard him in silence. She was beginning to regret the evening. One should have borne in mind that empathy was not Jeremy's strong point.

Mark's work on the files continued, in a leisurely way. Out of the midden there would lift a voice, every now and then. A clear voice from

1965, or 1979, or 1985—complaining or maligning or arguing. One particular voice caught his attention: "... shameless ... whole passages virtually replicated ... theft of intellectual property ... plagiarism, frankly." Plagiarism? Really? Mark read on, and then reread, with more than casual attention. The writer was a well-known historian, writing to Henry in the late 1970s. He was commenting upon the recently published work of a fellow historian, whose book, he alleged, bore an uncanny resemblance to an earlier publication of his own on the same subject. Both men were now dead, but their respective œuvres were still seen as standard sources. Mark considered, now distinctly interested.

More fun if they were still alive, of course. One could really stir things up. Even so, there was scope here for a titillating piece in one of the scholarly journals—cast doubt on a standard work, question an established reputation, get one's own name into the public eye, or, more important, into the eyes of academia. Henry would have to be compliant, of course.

Mark showed the letters to Henry, who was mildly surprised. "I'd entirely forgotten that fuss. Old George Bellamy going on about Carter, which of them owned nineteenth-century parliamentary reform studies. Not my field at all, of course, but one's opinion was rather sought after. Bellamy wanted me to get up a crusade for him against Carter."

"And did you?"

"Good heavens, no. Far too busy."

"And did he?"

"No, no. Hadn't the guts. Spineless fellow, Bellamy."

"*Was* it plagiarism, do you think?"

"Oh, possibly," said Henry cheerfully. "Plenty of it about. Why do you ask?"

Mark told him, up to a point. This idea for a rather fascinating article for one of the journals, using the letters to cast doubt upon the reliability of Carter's classic work on the Reform Acts. Generate a controversy.

Henry was intrigued. "Carter's reputation wouldn't survive. I never did care for the man, I have to say. I suppose one's name would have to come into it?"

Indeed. But this would be entirely advantageous. The archive would be mentioned—a trailer for My Memoir. Appetites would be whetted, potential publishers alerted.

"Marvelous idea, dear boy. How good you're being so careful about checking the materials, and found this."

Mark inclined his head in graceful acknowledgment. His plan, he explained, was to structure the article as a general discussion of plagiarism which would lead up to this challenging and relatively recent instance, inviting readers to reconsider the status of an established authority. The ensuing correspondence could run for months. Did Henry feel that he should go ahead?

"But of course—in the interests of scholarship." Henry beamed. "I think we need a glass of claret to celebrate this. Ask Rose to bring some through."

Paul Newsome was becoming—not exactly restless, that was not his style—but more pressing. "In the continuing absence of any cooperation on your husband's part, I am bound to consider the possible efficacy of a direct appeal to him from yourself. I am well aware that hitherto I have advised strongly against any contact, but given this position of stalemate, we may have to reconsider the options."

Stella read the letter with alarm. She was to tell Jeremy to find himself a lawyer, and get going on the divorce?

Paris had been amazing. So . . . well, romantic. Of course, Paris is romantic anyway, it apparently can't help being so, but she had a feeling that somehow right now even a weekend in Swindon with Jeremy would have been romantic. She wrote Paul Newsome a holding letter saying it was possible that her husband was out of the country on business, he sometimes had to make a trip abroad to inspect possible purchases. When next she spoke to Jeremy she told him what the solicitor had said, and they had a laugh.

Gill was another matter. She had noticed some euros on Stella's dresser.

"Where are these from? It's ages since you've been abroad."

Stella prevaricated. ". . . came across them somewhere. Thought I might as well get them changed." She felt herself blushing, and knew Gill had seen. Her face glowed. Gill stared at her.

"*Where* was it said you went that weekend—when you didn't want me to come over?"

"That old school friend of mine, you know . . ." No good, she is rumbled. The treacherous euros pulsate upon the dresser.

"Stella," said Gill. "You're not having an *affair* with someone, are you?"

No, no. Heavens, no. What an idea!

The blush deepened. Gill's stare was more intense.

"You do realize, don't you, that any misdemeanor of your own would *absolutely* compromise the chances of a satisfactory divorce— a divorce in which we get the best possible settlement for you and the girls?"

Stella protested. No misdemeanor. No way had she misdemeanored. No, no.

"So long as you're quite clear about the consequences." Gill was still suspicious, accusatory. Thus, in their childhood, had Stella been unable to lie herself out of some minor peccadillo. She would be watched, now. Gill would have her covered, she would have to account for every move.

She told Jeremy.

"God, that sister of yours! But what a hoot—she thinks you're having an affair! Well, you are, aren't you?"

Suppose I just *tell* her, Stella had been thinking. And Paul Newsome. But if I do, that means I don't want a divorce anymore. I'm taking Jeremy back.

Am I?

"*What* fun," said Jeremy. "Well, let her suspect away—it's no skin off our nose. Listen, darling, I've had an idea. Can you get up to town for a night this week? I thought we might do a show—I feel like a really cheesy musical. You could park the girls with friends, couldn't you?"

Goodness knows how long this can go on, he was thinking. Should we just have a good talk, she and I, and agree that I'm moving back home, all is forgiven? That's what I wanted, isn't it?

Isn't it?

CHAPTER FIFTEEN

"Anton has changed his day," says Charlotte. "He was coming tomorrow, but it seems he has an interview for a possible job. That's good, isn't it?"

"Mmn." Rose is apparently immersed in the shopping list that she is compiling.

"His reading really has come on in leaps and bounds. It's remarkable."

"Mmn."

"I would think he has a good chance of a proper job now."

"Mmn. I dare say." Rose frowns at the list, adds an item.

Charlotte is puzzled. A miasma of embarrassment hangs in the air. What is this? Is she tired of having him come here for the lessons?

"If we're in the way," says Charlotte, "I could always meet up with him somewhere. I can get to the library now, you know—we'd be fine there."

"Oh, for heaven's sake, Mum. And you shouldn't be doing the library on your own—it's too far. I've told you I'll come with you." She goes to the fridge. "Why are we always out of cheese?"

"I just heard your mobile ping," says Charlotte, trying to be helpful.

I think Victoria and Albert Museum would be good, says Anton's text. Irresistible. See, I know now this word. I dive every night in the dictionary. No, plunge. I plunge. So we plunge in Victoria and Albert Museum on Saturday.

Charlotte feels that a return to her own home is perhaps now a viable possibility. Before too long. It is no good pretending that she is self-sufficient once more—she cannot get in and out of a bath, stairs remain an undertaking, shopping and cooking would be a challenge. But she is inching toward that complacent state before her life collided so briefly with that of that vanished stranger, the person who decided that he (or she) could not go a moment longer without taking possession of Charlotte's bag.

That state now seems complacent because she had been living in her own home, she could do all that was still within her powers, crutches were things you occasionally saw others using, and felt vaguely sorry for them. It also seems both yesterday, and quite a while ago. One thing old age does is play tricks with time. Time is no longer reliable, moving along at its inexorable pace, but has become febrile, erratic. Mostly, it accelerates. Charlotte read a book recently called *Why Life Speeds Up as You Get Older*, by a psychologist, which attempted to explain the phenomenon—for phenomenon it is, apparently, universally reported. One persuasive explanation has to do with the changed nature of experience itself; when we are young, novelty abounds. We do, see, feel, taste, smell newly, day after day; this puts a brake on time. It hovers, while we savor each fresh moment. In old age, we've seen it all, to put it bluntly. Been there, done that. So time whisks by. Ah, that's why—those interminable days of childhood.

Whereas, now, Charlotte is stuck on this brisk conveyor belt that moves unstoppably ahead, and we know where it is going but no need to dwell on that. Suffice it that time is tediously predictable—except, of course, when it chooses not to be: in the wastes of a sleepless night, or on a day when pain has kicked in good and hard, and each hour is a test of endurance. And its performance means that she has been at Rose's house for no time at all, but time that has been punctuated by perversely dragging hours.

Today is one of those days, because pain is putting on a bravura act. Her back hurts, and her hip chimes in sympathy. Remember it is not always like this, she tells herself sternly. Tomorrow may be quite different. Tomorrow may be all song and dance, figuratively speaking. Think positive.

It is lunchtime. Rose will not be back till later because she is meeting up with her friend Sarah. Charlotte makes herself a salad, sits down to eat it and attempts some positive thinking. Thought drifts into recollection, as it so often does. But that can indeed be positive. By and large, good memory eclipses bad memory. Tom arrives; they are in the car, he is driving, he reaches over and lays a hand on her knee, which means: here we are, off somewhere, what fun, and by the way, I love you. Where were they going? This thought segues into another, in some mysterious process of free association; now she is pushing an infant Rose in her pram back from the library—her attention is distracted, and when she looks down into the pram she sees that Rose has got hold of the greengrocer's brown paper bag, there are squashed tomatoes all over Elizabeth Bowen and Iris Murdoch.

Why had these particular moments lodged? Well, lodge they have, and thanks be. Without them, one would be—untethered. What we add up to, in the end, is a handful of images, apparently unrelated and unselected. Chaos, you would think, except that it is the chaos that makes each of us a person. Identity, it is called in professional speak.

Savoring identity, Charlotte defies pain, which snarls on, but sulkily. She decides on a fruit yogurt, for afters.

"Do you remember being in love?" says Rose.

Sarah reflects. "Dimly. Temporary loss of sanity, as I recall. One is well out of it."

Rose nods.

"Why? Oh, I know. You're going to write a chick lit novel."

"If only," says Rose. "No, just thinking . . . of things I had forgotten about."

"How many times, for you?"

Rose considers. "Two and a half. You?"

"I hope Gerry wasn't the half. Let me see . . . Three and two-thirds, probably. The two-thirds was the PE teacher at school, and I had glandular fever at the time, which may account for it."

"My half was my best friend's boyfriend at college. I succeeded in smothering the passion, for the sake of my relationship with her."

"What else have we forgotten about?" says Sarah thoughtfully. "Childbirth? Yes. Definitely. No idea what that felt like."

"*Being* a child?"

"Oh, that, absolutely. Aliens—children. We can't ever have been *them.* Goodness—most of life goes down some plughole."

"Just as well," says Rose briskly. "Overload—if you had to carry it all around."

"Instead of which—a few bits and pieces. How did all this arise? Oh—love. *That.*"

"That," says Rose. "Idle thoughts. Whose turn is it to pay for the coffee?"

"I think I have not this job," said Anton. "It is with a small firm and they have other people they see. But the interview go quite well, I am not ashamed."

Charlotte beamed. "Good. Excellent. You'd hardly expect to strike lucky first time. Put it down to experience. So what have you been reading?"

Anton pulled a face. "Not interesting reading. I am reading tax regulations. I must know more about UK tax if I am to be a good accountant. So it is goodbye to stories, for now."

They had moved from children's fiction to short stories. "The trouble with the novel," Charlotte had told him, "is that it goes on and on.

Your reading improves by the day, but you still have to work hard at it. You aren't ready yet for on and on. *War and Peace* all in good time, but not yet. You need—actually we all need—to achieve a conclusion, an ending." She had provided an anthology, with suggestions.

"But first I have finish a story, before I start the tax," Anton went on. "*The Demon Lover*. There is an ending, but you are not quite sure what happen."

"Quite," said Charlotte. "A ghost story, of a kind. Clever, isn't it? And ambiguity can be effective, for an ending."

"I am sorry? Ambi . . . ambiguity?"

"Where there can be more than one interpretation—understanding of what is meant."

"Ah. Of course." Anton considered. "And that is how it is in how we live—there are always more than one way to look at what happen."

"Exactly. And you don't come across endings, as such. There's a fearful term that's in fashion at the moment—closure. People apparently believe it is desirable, and attainable."

He smiled. "I think I would like closure with the building site."

"Ah. That's different. You want to move on—and away. And you will. But you won't get rid of the building site—it will remain part of your experience, always."

"That is fine," said Anton. "If I not have to lift and dig anymore, and get dirty, and if I have closure with the site manager."

"You will. You're practically there. And with that in mind, I thought that today we'd tackle something even more exacting than tax regulations. The Conservative Party Manifesto, which I happened to notice in the recycling box. If you are going to spend much longer in this country you need to know something of the language of politics."

"The trouble with the V and A," said Rose, "is that one never knows where to begin. There's so *much*."

They stood in the entrance hall, their bags checked, their voluntary contributions contributed.

"Together we can do anything," said Anton.

She stared at him. "What?"

"I'm sorry. It is in my head. What I read with your mother. Political speak. In those rooms are Japanese and Chinese—perhaps we start there? Yes, this is ambitious. Yes, it is optimistic."

Rose laughed. "I hope I'm not going to spend *all* afternoon with David Cameron. My mum has the oddest ideas."

"No, it is good. I learn a new way of talking. But I think politicians talk the same everywhere. They make promise."

The museum teemed with visitors. "Actually," said Rose, "we need to get up into one of the quieter areas—maybe leave Japanese, for the moment. Textiles? That's costumes, and stuff like that."

Anton looked dubious.

"Ceramics? Pots and china."

"That I would like. I have a friend at home who makes pots."

The ceramics galleries did indeed turn out to be less frequented. Rose and Anton wandered alone past case after case, in which were gathered the crockery and the ornaments from everywhere, and every age, the plates, bowls, jars, tureens, vases, figures. The eye was caught by color, by shape, by glaze, by all this variety and ingenuity. They stopped, time and again, to admire, to comment, and came to rest at last in a far room which offered a comfortable seat from which you could contemplate more homely and local material—seventeenth-century English. Light flooded down from a domed skylight above; it was very quiet, there was no one else around.

"This is a good place," said Anton. "It is just for us." In front of them was a case in which were ranged, it seemed, whole dinner services—plate upon flowered plate, someone's once familiar domestic furnishings. "People have use these, do you think?" he went on. "Or they just have for to look at?"

"Some extremely careful washing-up must have gone on," said Rose.

"They are beautiful. All the flowers, and the painted people. That bird. My friend make only brown pots. Nice. Nice shape, but only brown."

"The seventeenth century did brown too," said Rose. "Look—over there."

"I feel as though there are many people in here," said Anton. "All the people who make these things, and use them. Very quiet people, like ghost."

"And just the things left. Much tougher than we are. Even china. Odd to think that my Habitat mugs will outlast me—not that they'll end up in a museum."

"The mugs with blue and gray pattern? I drink tea in one yesterday, with your mother."

Rose nodded. After a moment she said, not looking at him, "In fact, I didn't say to my mother that we were going to meet up here today."

"I think I know that, so I did not say." Then, quietly, with reluctance, it seemed: "She would not—understand?"

A silence. Rose said, at last, "No. It's that she *would* understand." And then they looked at one another.

Rose said, "Maybe we should move on. Enough ceramics."

"You do not want to talk . . . about this?"

She shook her head.

"No." He took a sharp breath; he laid a finger for a moment on her wrist. "No. It is perhaps better not to talk. Only—I want to tell you that when I am with you I begin to feel that I can perhaps live in this country, make a new life here. So I thank you for that. I thank you for . . ."—he smiled—"You are kind to a foreigner, and I thank you."

"*Don't,*" said Rose. "You know it's not like that."

A silence. "No, I think it is not. But I must tell myself that."

Footsteps. They were no longer alone. Two women were inspecting salt-glazed dishes. Rose got up: "Let's go—we've hardly seen anything yet."

In Jewelry, they considered art nouveau brooches. Rose thought: It is out now—not spoken, but out—and so nothing can be the same. She wanted to take his arm, to behave like other couples, and that was out of the question, quite out of the question. How can you feel happy, but also entirely sad? she wondered. Well evidently you can.

In Glass, they studied an engraved Venetian goblet, and Anton thought fleetingly of his wife, who had been irrelevant for a long while now. She hung there for a moment, a reminder of lost emotion. I had forgotten how to feel, he thought. Until now. I had forgotten what it was like to feel. And now I am feeling what I must not feel.

Later, they sat in the courtyard, with coffee and a snack. It was sunny, warm; Victorian brick glowed all around, children paddled and shouted in the great central pool, people sprawled on the grass. Voices rang out.

Anton said, "So many people. So many language. So far, I hear French, German, Japanese, Italian."

"And Scandinavian of some kind, just behind us. The museum is polyglot. There's a good word for you—speaking lots of languages. I'd forgotten I knew it."

"So I say to the site manager that his building site is polyglot. I think he will tell me to—get stuffed. And that I learn from my nephew. It is rude, I think?"

"Fairly rude," said Rose. "It depends who says it to whom. Between friends it would be acceptable, just about, if joking."

"The site manager is not my friend, and he does not do joking. So it would be rude. But there is so much rude on the site nobody would notice."

"If I may say so, I think you've become slightly obsessed with this site manager—with how much you don't like him."

"That is because he is somebody who have come into my life by accident—he should not be there."

"You could say that of me, too," said Rose, staring out across the courtyard, at the arched windows, the twisted columns, the Grecian frieze figures.

"He is a bad accident. You are . . . you are the good thing that has happen." He smiled.

That smile. She had to look away again. "All meetings are accidents really, I suppose. They might never have happened." Marriages, she thought.

"Oh yes, unless you believe in . . . how do you say? . . . what is going to happen anyway, it is going to come, it have to come."

"Fate. Destiny."

"Is that how you say it? And no—I think I do not believe in that."

"I suppose it would be worse if one did. No escape. As it is, you can always hope for a bit of luck."

"And I have luck. Today. That I am with you at this nice museum, and I think that there is much we have not yet look at." He pushed his chair back. "So perhaps we see some more? And I will forget the site manager and perhaps next week I will have luck with the job interview. There is another—I told you, I think."

She got up. "Yes. You did."

They moved away. Into Islamic, into Chinese. With all that was now understood, but unspoken.

Rose stares at her mother, not seeing her. Rose is elsewhere, floating free.

"Lucy rang," says Charlotte. "She wants you to ring back."

"Lucy?"

"*Lucy.*"

Rose stares on. A second. Two seconds. Then she crashes back into her own kitchen, her life. "Oh," she says. "Did she?" She gulps down her breakfast tea, gets up. "Thanks. I'll ring her."

The house closes in on her. The family. All of it.

"And another thing . . ." says Charlotte. But Rose has left the room. Two minutes later she returns—coat on, bag in hand.

"Another thing . . . I'm so sorry, but I've broken a mug. One of the Habitat blue and gray ones."

Rose laughs.

"Well, I'm relieved it's funny. I was afraid you treasured them."

"Not particularly. I had no desire to bequeath them to Lucy." Another laugh. "I must dash, Mum. I'm late, and Henry's always sitting there waiting. So much fuss about My Memoirs—huh! That Mark has been a pain. See you later."

Charlotte bins the broken mug. Why the laugh? She's odd these days—some Rose I don't know has surfaced. But who knows their own child? You know bits—certain predictable reactions, a handful of familiar qualities. The rest is impenetrable. And quite right too. You give birth to them. You do not design them.

Is she worried about something? Probably—most of us worry much of the time. The human condition. Lucy? James? Some problem there? No, she'd have said. A minor worry, let me hope. And now here am I worrying about her. Of course—human condition stuff again. On the Richter scale of worry, child-worry peaks at ten. Money noses in at five or six. Health zooms up and down, depending on severity of threat. The one or two of household inconvenience is mere indulgence. Give me a leaking pipe any day.

Old age worry is its own climate, she reflects. Up against the wire, as you are, the proverbial bus is less of a concern: it is heading for you anyway. The assault upon health is inevitable, rather than an unanticipated outrage. You remain solipsistic—we are all of us that—but the focus of worry is further from the self. You worry about loved ones—that tiresome term, as bad as closure—you worry about the state of the nation, about sixteen-year-olds sticking knives into one another, about twenty-year-olds who can't find a job, you worry about the absence of sparrows and the paucity of butterflies, about destruction of habitats, you worry about the decline of the language, about the books that are no longer read, about the people who don't read.

All of which is entirely unproductive—self-indulgent, maybe. Leave the knives to the police, the habitats to the environmentalists. If people don't read, that's their choice; a lifelong book habit may itself be some sort of affliction.

Charlotte clears away the breakfast things, feeds the cat. Gerry has gone to work, Rose is on her way to his lordship. The morning lies ahead, yawning. What to do? Pain is muffled today, thanks be. A trip to the library, despite Rose's strictures?

Anton plays poker with his nephew and the boys; he loses, disastrously, and forfeits a six pack of beer. The boys remonstrate, telling him it was his own fault, he wasn't concentrating, he played a crap hand, and Anton concurs, laughing. His back and his legs ache, as always after work, and it doesn't matter.

Don't think of her, he tells himself. But that is no good—of course he thinks of her. Of what was said, of what was not said. This won't do, he tells himself, you know it won't do. And of course he knows, and that makes no difference.

It is like feeling well again after a long illness, he thinks. But much more than that. Coming alive again. I had forgotten . . . not just what it was like to feel, but that feeling existed at all. It is like coming out into the sunlight.

He sends the nephew for some more beer, proposes another game, and plays with steely attention. This time he trounces them. There is much hilarity. What's got into the uncle? they say. First he's in a trance, then he's like a man possessed. He's got something on his mind, they say. Come on, Uncle, give—what's going on? Have you won the lottery? Are you planning to liquidate the site manager?

Rose types up the morning's dollop of My Memoirs. Or rather, she types, pauses, stares out of the window. Don't think of him. Yes, think of him—because I must, have to, can't help it.

And it is not, in any case, thought. He hangs there in her head—his face, his voice, the way he looks at a seventeenth-century plate, that finger on her wrist. He fills her mind; he takes up all her time.

No. Stop it. Grow up, Rose. This isn't happening, can't happen.

Can't it? It happens to others. Another life. A different life. Him.

She types: ". . . my intermittent association with Harold Macmillan prompts me to . . ."

Anton turns to her; he smiles. Again, and again. He says, "You do not want to talk . . . about this?"

The door opens. Here is Mark. "Oh, Rose—I mustn't butt in, but you're taking a break anyway, I see. Where do we keep spare wallet files?"

Rose tells him that as it happens there are no spare wallet files right now. She suggests Ryman's.

CHAPTER SIXTEEN

At Lansdale Gardens, database creation was now on hold while Mark worked on the plagiarism article: "I feel that this is rather a priority, as a teaser for the memoirs—we want to start whipping up interest."

Henry concurred entirely, and was himself setting to work with renewed enthusiasm. However, there was a certain disagreement about the eventual placing of the article. Henry did not seem to understand that this challenge to the reputation of a dead scholar was unlikely to grab the attention of the broadsheet editors.

"But why not? I thought that was the idea?"

Actually, the idea all along has been to generate a nice little dust-up in a heavyweight journal which would have Mark's name conspicuously attached, thus raising his profile and, with luck, lodging the name with a few of those influential in the academic world. No need for Henry to realize that.

"Popular exposure . . . ?" wondered Mark, frowning. "Isn't that a bit—well, tawdry? I do feel it's more appropriate to make a splash in one of the scholarly outlets. And we need them on board for the memoirs, in due course, don't we?"

"I take it one's name will be—prominent?"

"But of course. That's the point."

Henry beamed satisfaction. What luck that young Mark had come into his life. Though Henry couldn't now quite remember how or why he had. Oh yes, something to do with all that television nonsense. A good thing that never went any further; one had been on quite the wrong track there. No—the memoirs, that was the thing. "Off you go, dear boy. Get going on this valuable work."

Henry reached for his pen and a clean sheet of paper. Trevor-Roper today; some reflections on the man and his work. What a mercy the fellow's dead—no holds barred.

Mark, in contrast, was not inclined to write a word until he had some indication of interest. You don't waste effort. Accordingly he set about drafting an enticing proposal, and wrote a few letters, which he planned to follow up with a phone call or two. Mark knew himself to be good on the phone, and with any luck he'd be able to maneuver an invitation to drop by the editor's office. Only after that would he get going on the piece. Meanwhile, what was in theory Henry's time would be devoted to Mark's work on his thesis. The old boy was never going to know what exactly Mark was tapping away at on the laptop, in the Lansdale Gardens lobby.

Marion was sitting at a pavement table outside a coffee shop near to Hatton Garden. On her lap was her bag, not trusted to the table or the chair alongside her. Inside the bag was a small jewelry box, and, within the box, the most valuable items of the jewelry left to her by her mother: a pearl necklace, a diamond ring, diamond earclips, a diamond and sapphire brooch.

When do I wear them? Practically never.

Will I miss them? Not really.

So do I mind? Well, yes. They were hers.

She had already cruised past the Hatton Garden jewelry outlets, without going into any of them. The process repelled her: producing the box, laying out the contents for the inspection of some hard-eyed guy on the other side of a counter. The proceeds of the sale would barely make a dent in her overdraft, but she would feel that she had done something. A panic step, not rational—she knew that.

She sat there, putting off the moment. And was overcome suddenly with a sense of desolation. Here I am, she thought, getting middle-aged, beset by financial worries, my personal life centered around an entirely unsatisfactory lover. And I am about to sell my mother's jewelry. She was on the edge of tears. She fished for a tissue, dabbed at her eyes.

"Marion!"

She looked up.

"Marion! *What* a lovely surprise!"

"Laura!"

"Oh—*how* good to see you. What *luck*. I've got a solicitor appointment but I'm early. *Don't* tell me you're about to rush."

"No, no—I'm in no hurry at all."

Laura Davidson and Marion had been at art college together—best friends, indeed. They had always kept up, but Laura had been living in America for the past ten years, married to an American artist, and they had rather lost touch. Laura was a craftswoman—enamel work her specialty, though she also did glass engraving and some jewelry making. She was tall, blond, merry, and occasionally raucous—somewhat Marion's opposite. They had always felt that they complemented each other nicely.

Laura sat down, ordered a flat white, at once filled the pavement with talk, swept aside any inclination to despair. "So how *are* you? How's interior design? And listen, let's get it over with—I'm divorced. So snap! And it's not that *bad*, I'm finding. I'm sniffing the air—and, boy! is it good to be back this side of the pond!"

She was living in a leafy cathedral city, it emerged. "And I just love it. I've got a ducky little terrace house, and I've leased a big warehouse just near that's going to make a fantastic studio when I've got it properly set up. I've got all these plans . . ."

The leafy cathedral city seemed a touch unlikely, for Laura. Why there? Marion inquired.

Because Laura's brother was there, it seemed. A schoolmaster. "His wife died last year, poor darling. And his kids are gone and he's lonely and anyway we've always got on." Laura laughed. "We can prop each other up in our old age. But what about *you*?"

Marion began to talk, slowly and with restraint. And then the restraint deserted her, and it all came out. Everything. George Harrington. The overdraft. Recession. Even Jeremy.

And her mother's jewelry.

Marion opened her bag. Opened the box, shielding it from observers.

Laura looked. Closed the box. "Put it away," she said. "Marion, you are not doing this. You absolutely are not selling your mother's jewelry."

Marion sighed. "But . . ."

"There's some other way. There's got to be some other way. Listen, this needs thought. Come and stay the weekend. Just drop everything and come Friday to Monday and we'll think together. I'm not much good at money but I'm brilliant at ideas." More laughter. "Some of them fall to pieces but others take off. I had a whole craft commune that got going in Vermont. Anyway . . . come. You will, won't you?"

Marion found that she would.

Jeremy was put out. "You're away this weekend? What a bore, I need company. I need *you*. I'd thought we could do a film. Can't you cancel? No. Oh, well. Look—I'll call next week."

Marion sounded a little distant, he thought. Must see her—don't want her going cold on me.

Stella, on the other hand, was nicely warm. The thought of Stella perked him up again. They were talking regularly; there was a scheme afloat for a jaunt to the Cotswolds.

"Here we are," said Laura. "My bijou home. Your weekend task will be to advise me on what to do with the floors. And the downstairs loo. But this afternoon we'll do a walking tour of the city. And Nigel is coming to supper."

Marion found herself relaxing, in Laura's breezy company. The overdraft receded, and the empty order book. The leafy cathedral city appealed to her: quiet streets, that green central precinct. Laura's little house in a peaceful cul-de-sac of pastel-colored stucco houses—sugar pink, almond green.

And the warehouse that would be a studio. Laura strode around, waving her arms: "Enameling at that end, the kiln in the corner. My jewelry bench along here. Glass work on another bench under the window. Masses of shelves. And there's room to spare. I might look for someone to come in with me. I've heard of a girl who weaves—needs somewhere for one of those whopping great looms."

Back at the house, Laura made supper. "No, you can't help—the kitchen isn't big enough. Just sit. Talk." She clattered about, asking questions. "Were you making lots of money? I mean, before this recession business. Enough? Well, that's all any of us need. Do you enjoy it? Is London life fabulous? And, Marion, one thing—I may be out of order here but it seems to me you need to ditch this Jeremy. He's obviously more pain than pleasure."

"I believe you're right," said Marion.

She sat there, attending to Laura's discourse. And not attending.

Do I enjoy it?

Is London life fabulous?

She said, "My London house is worth quite a bit over a million pounds."

Laura dropped a saucepan lid. "Wow! This one was about two hundred thousand. Are you pulling rank?"

"I'm saying this because I've just realized I shouldn't be thinking of myself as in a financial hole. I'm *lucky*. I'm loaded. I just need to look at things differently."

"It's called lateral thinking," said Laura. The doorbell rang. "Here's Nigel. Let's laterally think together tomorrow."

Later, Marion lay awake in Laura's pint-sized spare room: it needs some clever lighting, and a blind not curtains, and I'd have different paintwork. Having redesigned the space around her, she returned to the financial hole, which conceivably was not.

Marion's London house—both home and business—had been bought with money left to her by her mother. It had seemed a lavish purchase, twelve years ago, but was now valued even more lavishly yet—a substantial mid-Victorian property in a well-regarded but not particularly grand part of London, but then every building in the city has now, it seems, a fairly startling price tag.

Marion did some sums, lying there in this peaceful little house, in which she had just passed such an agreeable evening.

The proceeds of my London house minus the George Harrington deficit, in other words the overdraft, would equal enough to buy a place like this—right here, maybe—leaving around three quarters of proceeds of London house as capital sum. Which could generate—well, not enough to live on in the manner to which I am accustomed but a sizable contribution.

And I would not have sold mother's jewelry.

But I would no longer have a business. I would not be Marion Clark Interior Design but Marion Clark with a small house, no longer in London, and with not enough to live on in comfort, and so in need of further occupation/employment/ whatever. But Marion Clark Interior Design was on the skids anyway, doing no more than landing me in further debt.

So?

Such a good evening. Laura can be so funny. And what a nice man, her brother.

Mark's initial approaches to the editors of a couple of journals struck silver, if not gold. His proposal has been carefully worded, promising a piece that would be a general discussion of academic plagiarism—the way in which various scholars had allegedly ripped off one another—but centering on this intriguing question of Carter versus Bellamy and the disputed ownership of nineteenth-century parliamentary reform studies. An arcane matter, to most people, but not to those concerned with historical scholarship.

Two editors e-mailed Mark to the effect that they could be interested to see the article in due course.

Not good enough. Mark was not inclined to settle for less than a firm commission. He picked up the phone.

His first target gave in after a few minutes of Mark's charmingly silken pitch: "Well, yes, OK—call by if you like . . . I can't make any promises."

No, thought Mark, but you will.

"I'm thinking of giving up my business," said Marion, over Corrie's bread and butter pudding. She was irritated that Mark was present at a Lansdale Gardens lunch. This was a new departure; she had anticipated a private chat with Uncle Henry about her possible plans, and now here was that Mark, evidently firmly ensconced. "Moving out of London," she went on. She spoke of the cathedral city. Henry remembered that he had known the Bishop at one point: "Or it may have been a previous man. Either way, I'm sure I can arrange an introduction—you'd want to get to know some of the cathedral people."

"It's not definite, by any means. Just—I've been beginning to feel a bit stale, there's not a lot of work around anyway, time maybe for a change of direction."

"So wise," said Mark. "The great thing is to be flexible, isn't it?"

Marion eyed him sourly. What do you know about it, at your age?

"Young Mark here tried out television," said Henry. "Jacked it in—quite right too. Busy on my archive now, of course." An avuncular—proprietorial—smile.

A graceful nod from Mark. "A big undertaking. One can't rush it, with such an archive. But so fascinating."

The file cupboard? thought Marion. Archive? Pushing it a bit, isn't that?

"Though right now," Henry continued, "Mark is engaged on a piece of work inspired by the archive that we feel will set the academic world by the ears." He expounded, at length. Marion stifled a yawn, battling the bread and butter pudding. She considered Mark: he's got his foot in the door all right. Uncle Henry must be paying him—he doesn't seem the type to be putting himself out for love. Well, if it makes Uncle Henry happy.

". . . so there it is," said Henry. "A nicely provocative idea, don't you think?"

Marion agreed. "Fascinating." She saw Mark watching her, with the hint of a smile. Rumbled, she thought—he knows perfectly well I wasn't taking in a word. A smooth operator.

She said, "You must be appreciating Corrie's cooking, Mark. Nicely unusual, for nowadays?"

"I think vintage might be the word," said Mark. No smile; perfect sobriety. All right—well returned, but don't think we're in collusion— I'm not entirely sure I like you.

Henry was puzzled. "Vintage? Yes, Corrie really knows how to cook. I'm delighted to be able to share her talents. I'm sure there'd be a spot more of the pudding. No takers? Well, there's some Stilton, I know. Neither of you? Then I shall be abstemious too."

Mark said, "I had a peep at your Web site, Mrs. Clark. Most impressive. Such lovely rooms. Quite unlike anything I've ever known myself." A little laugh.

She eyed him. Am I being sent up?

He added, hastily—catching her look, "I mean, I've never lived anywhere that had been much *thought* about."

Henry chuckled. "Marion would love to get her hands on this place, but I tell her I'm beyond good taste."

"Lansdale Gardens is sui generis," said Mark.

"Or vintage, perhaps?" Marion inquired.

Marion's Web site is alluring, but it competes with very many others. The world of interior design is crowded; cyberspace is alive with images of exquisite interiors, the stalls set out by her competitors. Everyone is scrabbling for the trophy wives, the rich Russians, the Arabs. Marion is small beer by comparison with some of the big firms with their teams of consultants—the big stuff goes to them, anyway.

She has always depended on the more modest client looking for a new kitchen, a make-over to the living-room. In good times, even these would happily commit to an impressive spend, quite enough to keep Marion going, but now in this age of austerity the coffers have apparently dried up. People are making do with what they already have.

And could it be that she was in any case less enthralled by the work than she used to be? A new commission perhaps a chore rather than a challenge? The hunt for the perfect fabric less invigorating? And a selection of tiles or light fittings or taps or basins or worktops or kitchen cabinets inducing a sigh rather than eager anticipation?

A career break? Step aside for a while; regroup; look at ways of doing it differently.

Talk some more to Laura. And no harm in asking her about the pretty little house near her that's advertised.

"You're thinking of leaving London?" said Jeremy. "Darling, you must be out of your mind. Nobody leaves London and lives to tell the tale. We all aspire to London. Give up the business? What can you be thinking of? You're so successful, you've got a track record, this recession nonsense will come to an end, it's just a tiresome glitch, nothing to get fussed about, one simply has to ride it out. Not as keen as you were? Darling, you'd go stir crazy without the business, you're just feeling a bit stale, we all do from time to time. If I wasn't so hectic at the moment I'd sweep you off for a week in—no, not Paris—New York or somewhere. But I'm up to my eyes. Anyway, let's have no more of this out of London talk . . . Marion? Marion—are you there?"

"I'm still here." Only just, thought Marion, checking her bank statement, her mind on that.

"So what about supper tonight, and I can talk you right out of it. How about I come round to yours at about seven?"

"I don't think so. Look, Jeremy, I'll have to go—there's a call waiting."

What's going on?

Jeremy was put out. Put down, indeed, he felt. Call her back later?

Maybe not—that was the cold shoulder, that was. Well, she'll come round, won't she? Just needs a bit of space. Leave it for a few days. Meanwhile . . . meanwhile there's Stella, bless her.

Stella was in difficulties with Paul Newsome. His letters were insistent: ". . . implement my proposal that you discuss matters with your husband . . . speed up progress on the divorce . . . our proceedings at an unacceptable standstill."

And there was Gill: "You're spending the night in town? Staying with who? No, I've never heard you mention her before. I think I should come over, Stella—I feel you're overwrought. All right, all right . . ."

Stella did not like lying. Dissimulation did not come naturally. And she was not good at it; she could hear the suspicion in Gill's voice. Gill knew something was up.

This can't go on, she thought. And in any case, what *was* going on? I have got together with Jeremy. I seem to have—well, I have let him come back. In which case, should he not move back home? Or would that spoil things? No more of these somehow illicit meetings.

"Well, what do you think, darling?" said Jeremy.

He had no idea what he thought himself. The great thing, of course, was not to be divorced. Not to find himself with half the house and half his pension and half the car and so forth. And there was no mention of divorce now, from Stella; indeed, here she was, it seemed, wondering if he should come home.

He stared at her, across the table in the little bistro that had become their place. She looked charming—a top with a plunging neckline in a dark green that suited her perfectly, dangly earrings. She always dressed up for their meetings. After dinner, they'd go back to his admittedly grotty flat and make love.

Wouldn't it make more sense to be going back to the Surrey farmhouse, and the girls, and the Bang & Olufsen TV and the Aga and the

Delft tiles and the Welsh dresser and the Staffordshire pieces and all the other enviable things he'd picked up here and there and couldn't bring himself to sell?

What about Marion? There was bound to be a condition, to his coming home, and the condition must surely be no more Marion.

But was there, in any case, going to be any more Marion?

"Come and have a look," said Laura. "I know you're still undecided and you haven't even begun to sell your own place, but what's the harm? And I've had this idea—oh, I do love brewing up an idea!—I'm thinking, you could start up an advisory service, smaller scale than you've been doing, no showroom, just advising and sourcing. Actually, there don't seem to be so many people here who're into design."

Marion knew this. She had already checked. The leafy cathedral city had a few established interior designers, but not so many that it would be pointless to compete. A newcomer can arouse interest. Working differently, she thought, I might work afresh.

"Or," Laura went on, "there's the office space beside the warehouse. Going spare. You could think of a small showroom area, in time. Right next door to me—we'd have our lunch breaks together. Fatal—we'd never get any work done!" A gale of laughter. "And I'm friendly now with some local craft people, we're planning an annual craft week, there might be an opening for you there."

Marion listened, looking out of the window. London dissolved, and became an unknowable elsewhere, in which she was leading a new, unguessable life. Free of debt, free of George Harrington, and may he rot, wherever he is and will be, though conceivably he had precipitated a choice that should have been made in any case. I was stuck, was I not, just trundling ahead?

She returned to Laura's inviting flow: ". . . So, come down at the weekend and have a look. Oh, Nigel sends his regards, says if he can be of any help . . ."

CHAPTER SEVENTEEN

Mark was complacent. "Three thousand words. The lead piece for that issue, it will be. I just need to go over some references, and then I can get started. He was fascinated to hear about the memoirs, of course."

Not quite true, that. The editor of the learned journal had rolled his eyes at the mention of Henry's name: "Good Lord, is he still around? I had imagined him dead and buried, along with his line of history." Mark had had to maneuver with subtlety, indicating amused agreement while not entirely disassociating himself from Henry, whose patronage could not be jettisoned, not yet anyway.

"I'm wondering if I shouldn't contribute some kind of commentary," said Henry. "Add weight, don't you think?"

Mark did not. No way. "I feel we should save you up for the memoirs. Raise anticipation—your name will be mentioned, of course. Very much so. We want to use this as a sort of trail."

Henry frowned, but did not press the point. "You may be right. So you'll be getting to work on it right away?"

"Exactly. There's a deadline—not too imminent, thanks be. One doesn't want to rush this—it's too important, as an offshoot to the archive, and the memoirs. Of course, it means work on the archive will have to wait, for a while." Mark pulled a face. "I feel a bit frustrated there. But first things first."

And in fact, I can knock this thing off in a trice, he was thinking. And then back to the Scottish Enlightenment while I'm apparently fine-tuning it. And some more pottering around with the archive in due course, when I'm ready.

"Quite," said Henry. "And in the meantime, work on the memoirs is going most satisfactorily." He beamed at Mark: such an asset he has turned out to be, this young man. One is working with renewed enthusiasm, having him around. "Oh—we have company this afternoon. My niece is coming to tea. Join us. Corrie has made a Victoria sponge, I believe."

He was right. "Well, actually, no thank you, Uncle Henry," said Marion. "I've not long had lunch." She observed Mark, tackling a lavish slice. Have fun.

"So I hope you'll come to see me there," she went on, addressing Henry. "Everything is rushing ahead, and I should be moving in a few weeks' time. I could show you the cathedral, and my friend Laura says The Swan does a good lunch."

Genial acceptance. "I shall look forward to that, my dear. I dare say young Mark would escort me."

"Of course." A winning smile from Mark. "I'd love that. I haven't been there for ages. Such a pretty cathedral precinct, I remember. Is your house near there, Mrs. Clark?"

The purpose of Marion's visit has been to explain her plans to Henry, toward whom she did feel some sense of responsibility, as his only relative.

"But I shan't be that far from London, and I dare say I'll be coming up quite often." And this Mark is apparently well installed, she thought, so it'll be up to him to cope if there's some crisis. She enthused about her new home. "Tiny, after what I've got, but I just love it. Such luck, getting a buyer at once, for the London house. And Laura has been such a help, down there, finding a builder for me. And her brother too—sorting out a problem with the council, he's been so kind."

"We shall take a day off to visit you," said Henry. "Mark is of course hard at work on a rather crucial article. I should explain . . ."

A smooth interruption from Mark. "Actually, I seem to remember that Mrs. Clark heard all about that when last she was here. But yes, that's well under way now." Another smile at Marion: see, I've saved you from a further five-minute discourse. "Are you sure you won't try the sponge? Just a sliver?" Why should I suffer alone?

"Well, perhaps," said Marion. "But really just a small piece." All right—point scored.

"And the memoirs progress," said Henry. "So all in all this is a hive of activity. Rose is kept busy, one way and another."

Marion held her cup out to Mark. "Thank you, I'd love some more tea. Oh, yes—Rose. I thought she sounded a bit distracted when I rang. How is her mother, by the way?"

"Her mother?" Henry looked perplexed. "Oh, the mother. Yes, there was some accident, wasn't there?"

Charlotte was not too bad, as it happened. She was crutch-free now, around the house, the stairs were less of a challenge, she had managed a bath without Rose to help her in and out.

"Home next week," she said. A statement, not a query. Try it anyway.

"Week after next, just possibly," said Rose. "We'll see."

We'll see. How often have I said that? thought Charlotte. Now it's I who am seven, or thereabouts.

It was breakfast time—Gerry already gone, Rose about to go—checking her mobile, reading a text.

"Well, let's aim at that, not see." Must make my stand, seven or seventy-seven. "Anton this afternoon—he's always a morale booster. Though frankly I don't think he really needs me anymore. He's afloat on his own. Will you be here? I know he likes to see you."

Rose put the mobile in her bag, stood up. "I'm not sure. I may go into town with Sarah after work. See you later, anyway." She went.

This untethered look she has acquired. Never entirely with you. What's up?

Charlotte cleared the table, moved about the kitchen, rejoiced in these new abilities: I can put things into the dishwasher, I can change the rubbish bin liner, I can clean the table and the worktop. I am a free woman, or nearly so.

But what's up? Anything, or nothing? Stop looking over her shoulder, Charlotte. Mind your own business.

I understand, says Anton's text. It is difficult now at your mother house. Better perhaps you are not there. And soon it is Saturday.

" 'It is a truth universally acknowledged, that a single man in . . . in possession of a fortune . . .' There! It is difficult—much work with the dictionary, and only three pages. But I start."

Charlotte laughed. "Well, I never meant you to take literally everything I said. Whenever did I mention this?"

"Oh—back a few weeks. But I take notes always—write down names. This is a famous book, I think?"

"Very. Tiresomely so. The one novel everyone has heard of—a sort of prototype for fiction. Don't struggle on unless you're enjoying it."

"It is a good change from tax regulations," said Anton. "And the newspapers. I read much in *The Guardian* now, every day."

Charlotte sighed, smiled. "We must face up to it. You don't need me anymore, do you?"

He spread his hands. "Always I need—I want to ask you, what does this mean? Why do they say that? But I think I must not take your time—there are others who need you more. For 'I go to the shop,' 'I sit on the chair.' Or 'The night Max wore his wolf suit . . .'"

"That was an unorthodox departure," said Charlotte. "An experiment for an unusual student. I'm not sure I'll dare use it again. But I suppose you're right. The Bangladeshi ladies could come."

"When will you go to your own home?"

"Don't ask. Yes, do ask. Rose and my hip permitting, in a couple of weeks or so, perhaps. There can be someone who will come in daily, apparently, and help me do what I can't, and shop and so forth."

"Rose," he said. Half to himself, as though he simply wanted to say the word. "Rose. I'm sure she will arrange things for you very well."

"She does, bless her. I am lucky."

"You are. You are lucky, that you have Rose."

"She's out—you won't see her today. She said she might be."

He nodded. Fell silent for a moment. Then spoke briskly. "So perhaps the Bangladeshi ladies will come now. Or the builder. I remember the builder who cannot read. And the lady who does not really care if she read or not." He laughed. "And I thank you. I thank you with all my heart. Because of you I shall now I hope get a good job— a job I can like. Because of you I shall say goodbye to the building site, and the site manager."

"And because you've been so determined. That, most of all."

"And the stories," he said. "Because I must know what will happen."

"Indeed. Powerful things, stories. And now you're going to get on with your own story. Next chapter—accountancy job, flat of your own and no more slumming it with the boys. And I'm very glad that our stories happened to coincide like this—to bring us together. Even if we spin apart now." Spoken with warmth. I suppose I won't see him again, she was thinking. Pity. Then— "But keep in touch—let us know how things go."

He sat looking at her, as though he had to consider this. He half shook his head. "Yes. Perhaps. Yes. I . . . I have to think . . ." For a moment it seemed that he might be about to come out with something, then he shook his head again. Stopped speaking.

Charlotte was concerned. What have I done? Overstepped the mark in some way? Embarrassed him? She got up. "We need a cup of tea— come and give me a hand."

In the kitchen, she talked of what he might read now. "I've got my doubts about *Pride and Prejudice*. Why don't you try an Ian

McEwan—you said you've read him in translation. Or John Updike—
some transatlantic fresh air. Right—can you get a couple of mugs
from the dresser."

"These blue and gray?"

"Fine. Though I broke one of those the other day. Rose took it on
the chin—just laughed."

"She laughed?" He stood looking at the mug in his hand. "Then I
must be careful."

Back in the sitting-room, Charlotte talked book titles. Anton made
a list. Then, eventually, he got up, shouldered his rucksack. "So—I
go." He looked round the room. "I say goodbye, and thank you. Thank
you and thank you."

"I know Rose will be sorry to have missed you—she may not have
realized this would be the last time. I hadn't myself, really."

At the front door, further farewells. He was awkward now, diffident, his usual easy manner in abeyance. Always hard, saying goodbye, she thought, watching him go down the garden path, out of the
gate.

"Goodbye?" said Jeremy, incredulous. "Don't be silly, darling. You're
moving an hour or two from London, you're not going to Mongolia.
You'll be up and down all the time. It needn't make any difference
to us."

He knew himself to be flailing around. Here they were in her
house—removers' boxes all around, a most unMarion-like state of
turmoil—and she was talking like this. Breakup stuff. Move on stuff.
Feel we both realize . . . stuff.

No, no. This wouldn't do. Apart from anything else, it did the
morale no good at all. One was not about to be . . . dumped.

"I *need* you," he said. Which immediately sounded pathetic. He
saw it in her eyes, tried to retract. "We have such *fun* together."

Actually, not really—not of late.

"What on earth will you do there?" he said. "I'm not going to let
you just go off and fester. Look, I want to help you with the move, and

get you settled in, and then we can see how we feel about things."
That's the way—involve oneself, refuse to be sidelined.

Marion sighed. "Well, no, Jeremy. Thank you, but I've got some
friends there who are helping out."

"I can't believe this," he said. "After everything . . ." He sounded
petulant now, and saw her look change from one of tactful regret to
one of irritation. After just about landing me with a divorce, he wanted
to say. With that blasted text message.

A shrug from Marion. Well, not quite a shrug—a sort of shrug
expression. After what? she was perhaps thinking.

In fact, divorce seems to be off the menu now, though she needn't
know that. Stella . . . He found himself thinking fondly of Stella.

"You should sort things out with your wife," said Marion briskly.
"I rather feel you're on the way to that as it is. I think that's what you
need, not me."

He stared at her, churning. Don't you tell me what I need, he wanted
to say. And leave Stella out of this. It was you who got her into it.

Dignified withdrawal, it would have to be. "Well, darling, if this is
what you want. What you think you want."

Later, alone, he rallied. Injury and indignation were laid aside.
Stella, he thought. Looking gorgeous, the other night, and what a
good time we had. Maybe . . . maybe go home this weekend, if she's
comfortable with that, and I rather think she will be.

There—Jeremy dealt with. Now—the china. Can't let the removal
men loose on mother's Spode.

Superficially in control, Marion was in fact in some emotional disar-
ray. She had found the scene with Jeremy more upsetting than anticipated, had had difficulty keeping resolute, knowing Jeremy's capacity to
undermine resolve. We did have fun, at points; he's a charmer, but—oh,
feckless, I suppose. I should never have . . . but you do, you do. Anyway,
there, it's done, he'll soon be over it, despite the fuss. And the wife will
take him back. It was never my fault, he knew what he was doing.

She sat amid the boxes. What has happened? My life is in upheaval, and all because of a man I met at a lunch, and something called the financial downturn, and running across Laura in Hatton Garden.

Goodbye to this house. Goodbye to Marion Clark Interiors. Goodbye to lunches at Lansdale Gardens, though as Uncle Henry rightly says I shall be coming to London from time to time, and I'm not going to desert the old boy. Not that he hasn't plenty of support: Corrie and Rose and now this Mark in attendance.

Am I making a ghastly mistake? Am I going to regret this? But you have to be flexible, swerve off course if it looks right—I've not done it enough, I've just plowed ahead. And anyway I was swerved. Things happened.

Charlotte continued to think of Anton after he had left. She saw his life in contrast to her own. A man driven by circumstance. Well, I have had some circumstance too—very much so, just recently—but I have not had to shift country, shift culture, find a new life. Good luck to him—he deserves it.

The front door banged. Rose. Dumping groceries on the kitchen table, a brief greeting—preoccupied, it would seem.

Charlotte said, "Anton has been and gone. This was his last time. Sorry to have missed you, I'm sure. He . . ." Oh, but he didn't. Leave any sort of goodbye message. Forgot, I imagine. He did seem—stressed.

"You're through with him. Right. I've got some salmon for supper—Gerry's favorite."

"One wonders how things will go for him. Anton, I mean."

"Mmn." Rose stared into the fridge. "Ah, there is a lemon—I'd forgotten to get one."

"One would like to have known how his story continues."

Fridge slammed shut. "Tartar sauce, I thought. And there's still some of that cucumber pickle."

"Wouldn't you?"

Rose standing there, a lemon in one hand. Thinking, it would seem, about what is to be had for supper.

"Oh . . . I dare say. You and stories, Mum—an obsession."

Story? You live twenty years in a London suburb. Husband, children, house, cat—go to the supermarket. Then—something happens. A person happens, that's all. Him.

You do not mess up everything that has been important to you for most of your life because you are in love with an Eastern European immigrant you have known for ten weeks. You do not do that to Gerry. To Lucy and James.

Do you?

In his head, language flows, lithe and lissom, eloquent, all that he would say, all that he would like to tell her of what he has been feeling, what he has been thinking. Not the broken and faulty language that he has to speak here, but the real language that he does speak, his own.

He remembers the last time with her, a moment then, when he had shaken his head in frustration, and she had looked at him anxiously: "Is something wrong?"

"There is everything wrong."

Everything.

Stella tells the girls that dad will be home this weekend. The girls receive this news without undue shock, dismay or rejoicing. Since they are aged thirteen and fifteen their concerns are entirely local and immediate, and while they have appeared to register Jeremy's absence from time to time they have not much applied themselves to asking where he is, or why. They are focused upon the intricacies of their relationships with their friends, on the state of their hair, on the next visit to Primark. Jeremy is of interest to them, but is not a central concern. They do not know, and never will, that he was near to becoming a divorced father. OK—so dad will be home this weekend.

Stella cooks. She cooks up a storm. She makes Jeremy's favorites: the Moroccan lamb tagine, roast fennel, the pears baked in Marsala with raisins and pinenuts. It is harvest home, or the return of the warrior, or something along those lines, except that Stella is also somewhat apprehensive. Is this the right thing to be doing? Should she be allowing him back? She was going to *divorce* him, after all, and now suddenly she isn't.

She is scared witless at the thought of what Paul Newsome is going to say.

There has already been Gill. Gill exploded. "He's *what*? He's coming *home*? Are you out of your mind, Stella?"

Stella said that she was not out of her mind, not at all. She had been thinking things over (sort of true), she and Jeremy had had some serious talks (not true), and she felt that badly as he had behaved this would never happen again (possibly true).

Henry was much pleased with the progress of the memoirs. He was writing daily, page after page to be handed to Rose the next morning. He was recollecting not exactly in tranquility but with a complacent fervor. So agreeable to settle some old scores, put the knife in here and there, hand out the occasional bouquet. Of course, one had to be careful, double check on who was dead and who was not—there are such things as the libel laws, and you never know who might be lurking yet in some nursing home, prepared to leap out of the woodwork. By and large, though, his cast was safely laid to rest, and he could indulge in uninhibited remembrance.

Henry was well aware of unreliable testimony; he was after all a historian and not a bad one, even if his approach was now quite out of fashion. He knew quite well that his views were idiosyncratic and partial. Fine. The point was to get them on record, given that one was in a position to do so—happily—and those under discussion were not. So one owed it to posterity to set down one's version of Harold Wilson,

Harold Macmillan, Maurice Bowra, Isaiah Berlin and the rest of them. Henry saw himself as a twenty-first century John Aubrey—less fey, more considered. This work would perfectly conclude and embellish his list of publications: revelatory, provocative, entertaining.

"There you go, Rose—today's offering. Some rather incisive observations on Hugh Gaitskell—you'll be intrigued. Now, where is young Mark this morning? Rose?"

Rose had apparently never set eyes on Henry before, gazing vacantly at him. She surfaced, swept up the typescript. "I've no idea. Oh, here he is."

The front door opened, and closed. Mark had his own key now. He put his head around the door. "Good morning, good morning. Great! Another installment of the memoir, I see. Fascinating."

"Indeed," said Henry. "Gaitskell. Overrated, I always feel. A rather ordinary fellow, in fact. Rose may be surprised."

Mark smiled at Rose. "How incredibly lucky you are—getting a preview like this."

Rose did not respond. She left the room, with Hugh Gaitskell's reputation and the day's consignment of letters.

Mark was only mildly interested in the memoirs, from which he would probably need to distance himself, if and when they ever achieved publication. It would not do to be seen as a disciple of a super-annuated historian whose approach was now entirely discredited. But that was not a problem, at the moment. Right now he needed Henry, both for funding purposes, and in the service of the plagiarism piece, which would give his—Mark's—name needed exposure, and an entrée into useful academic circles. With any luck it would drum up contro-versy, and he could be right in there, making further elegant points. In fact, the article was finished—a final polish, and he could get it off to the editor of the learned journal, when expedient. A week, it had taken.

"And your own effort—how is that going?" Henry inquired benignly.

Mark frowned. "Quite tricky, getting the emphasis right. The his-torical use and misuse of plagiarism, the background to the Bellamy/

Carter dispute. I'd love you to look it over when I've got it into some kind of shape."

"Of course, of course." Henry beamed, and Mark headed for his desk in the lobby, and a productive morning on his interpretation of the Scottish Enlightenment, which would propel him toward professorial status. Mark's career would depend upon that shaky quagmire, the past. He also knew only too well that most testimony is unreliable. Again, fine. That's what history is for—a morass of contentious stories that may or may not have a measure of veracity but are there to serve as fodder for the keen forensic analyst of another age. Glittering careers have been thus fueled, and Mark had every intention that his should be one. After the Scottish lot, a hop across the Channel, maybe, for a go at the rich pickings of the French Revolution. By which time one would hope to be nicely installed at Warwick or York, or a stint maybe with an Oxbridge fellowship.

He settled at his computer, began to look over yesterday's entry, and was conscious of a presence. Rose—apparently searching for something in that bookcase by the door. Lansdale Gardens was full of errant bookcases, stashed away in odd corners. Crammed with unsorted books. Ah—now, there's a thought: get going on Henry's library, when one has done with the archive. Another few months' funding, that would be.

"Can I help, Rose?"

"Not unless you happen to know where Debrett's Peerage for 1975 is. He wants to look something up. Immediately."

"Let's have a look. I don't think I've seen it." Mark joined her in front of the bookcase. "A bit disheveled, I'm afraid—his library."

"Disheveled?" Rose appeared to be considering the word. "Well, it's not here, is it?" A little less offhand—less hostile, perhaps—than usual. I'll get round her yet, Mark thought.

He said, "You're so marvelous with him, Rose. Not the easiest of employers."

She looked at him. Quite a sharp look—I've gone too far, he thought. But no—a half smile, a shrug. She went.

———

"It's a lovely day."

"Of course it is a lovely day." He took her arm for a moment, steered her down a rough bit of the path—Hampstead Heath laid out around them, rich with high summer, with growth, with birds, with life. London a blue and distant complexity away beyond. "And we are being very English, that we talk about the weather?"

"I'm sorry," said Rose. "It's what you do when you're wondering what else to say." When there is everything to say.

He smiled. Understanding, she saw—understanding entirely. "So what is to be sorry? And it is a lovely day because it is Saturday. I have known all the week that Saturday would be good. On Wednesday there was rain, and with rain the site is mud, mud, mud. And I say to the site manager—on Saturday, sun. He is not interested."

"Well, I suppose he must spend Saturday somewhere."

"No. I think he exist only in the week. It is not possible have wife and family and other life. At the weekend—pff! he disappear. But soon, perhaps, I say goodbye to him."

"Another interview?"

"Next week. The last one—no. They give the job to someone else, but they are nice, they say I did well and they tell me another firm who will see me. So . . . I hope."

"So do I. Oh, I do hope . . . If we go that way," she said, "there's a good place to sit. I remember from when I used to bring Lucy and James here. Yes, up here. They used to climb on a dead tree."

A bench. They sat. "That very tree," she said. "The one lying on its side. Great for children to scramble about. Amazing—all those years ago, and it's still here."

"I think a dead tree does not go away. Unless someone take it to burn it."

"This is an environmentally correct tree, I imagine. A place for insects and birds. And children—as an afterthought."

"This is the best . . . park . . . I see yet." He gestured: the sweep of the Heath, the gray–blue city laid out on the skyline. "You take me always to a good place. And London have so many."

"Spoiled for choice." She saw the shadows of her children, young again, playing on that tree. And now to be here with him. You cross your own path.

"And you choose well." A smile. "So I have in my head . . ."—counting on his fingers—". . . Victoria and Albert Museum, Richmond Park, the park where . . . in the middle . . . with the dogs and so many people running?"

"Hyde Park."

"Yes. So all those I have, to remember. And the dogs—spaniel, I think? And . . . terrier and German Shepherd dog. And those deer and the quail eggs and in the museum a plate with birds on it. I see that still."

"And here," said Rose. "Here, you've got—we've got—green parakeets. Look—over in that tree. Little green birds."

"I think that is not a British bird?"

"No. Apparently they've escaped and bred and now there are populations of them."

"Ah. They are immigrants. But asylum seekers, or economic migrants, like me?"

She laughed. "Hard to say."

"So I have the parakeets now, to remember." He was silent for a moment. Then—"But, most of all, there is—you."

Quite silent now, both of them. She turned to look at him. "Anton . . ."

He put his arms round her. His hand was in the small of her back: gentle, firm, strange. Oh. And then he was kissing her, his tongue in her mouth: alien, warm, arousing. Oh.

Later, he said, "I am sorry. For so long I have wanted to do that." Moments later; a whole world later—a passage of time after which nothing would be the same.

She shook her head. Wanted to say—me too. Could not, must not. She reached out and took his hand.

He got up. "We should walk some more, Rose. Perhaps we will find more not British birds. The big ones that eat dead animals?"

"Vultures. I don't think so. Not even on Hampstead Heath."

They were walking now, and they held hands. Like other couples. Like that boy and girl ahead, like those two over there, not young, married probably but holding hands still. Everything was different, in a few seconds, with what had been spoken, what had been done.

Anton said, "Before I came to this country, I was in a very bad time. I think you know. My wife—who go. No job. And I thought—I can do nothing, or I can do something. So I do something—I decide to come here. Choosing—choice. We talk about that once, with your mother—remember?"

"Yes. I remember."

"I know now that I choose right. It is not easy here, for me. But it is better all the time. I begin to—to live again. It is like learning to read English—learning to live again."

"I'm glad," she said. "I'm so glad." Her hand in his, all between them different now. Easier—and harder. So much harder.

"Your mother teach—taught—me to read. You have . . . you have shown me I can live. I can want the next day to come, and the next. I can . . . hope"—silent for a moment, his hand tightening on hers—". . . and that is much, very much. But I know also that with you—that you and me—that there is not the next day, and the next, more Saturdays, more going to good places."

She said, "Anton . . . don't."

"But that is true, I must say it."

They stopped. Off the path now, away from others, alone under a tree, a great spreading impervious tree, that neither knew nor cared.

He took her face in his hands; he kissed her on the lips.

"You are married."

"Yes."

"So this is not good."

"No."

They gazed at one another. Rose saw an unimaginable other life, which could not be. Anton saw a woman with whom he could have been happy.

He said, "There are words that say the same in all languages. Three words."

"Yes," she said. "I know." *Don't say them. Don't. I couldn't bear it—to have that in my head forever.*

"I must not say, but I am thinking, Rose."

So am I.

She said it. "So am I."

He shut his eyes for a moment. A little shake of the head. His hands closed on her upper arms, holding her like that. "So . . . we think. And we know. And that must be all."

Beyond them, around them, the Heath went about its business: a dog barked, children called out, somewhere in the distance grass was being cut. Theirs was a moment suspended in time—private, isolated. After a while, he took her arm and they walked away from the tree, back down the path, back among couples, groups, a jogger, a child with a kite, back with the world. They talked, and did not talk. He told her more of the firm with whom he had an interview. She told him Lucy would soon be home from college. They talked of anything that did not matter, and walked on, and on, as the summer afternoon faded around them, dipping toward evening, the shadows became long, and time carried them with it, back into their own lives, away and apart.

CHAPTER EIGHTEEN

S o that was the story. These have been the stories: of Charlotte, of Rose and Gerry, of Anton, of Jeremy and Stella, of Marion, of Henry, Mark, of all of them. The stories so capriciously triggered because something happened to Charlotte in the street one day. But of course this is not the end of the story, the stories. An ending is an artificial device; we like endings, they are satisfying, convenient, and a point has been made. But time does not end, and stories march in step with time. Equally, chaos theory does not assume an ending; the ripple effect goes on, and on. These stories do not end, but they spin away from one another, each on its own course.

Charlotte is home. Grateful to Rose and Gerry; deeply grateful to be once more her own woman. She is mobile, if precarious, and there is Elena from the Czech Republic who comes in daily to minister, to shop, to do household chores.

Home, alone, she picks up the threads. Pain is contained, corralled, though breaking out from time to time. Friends and neighbors visit, she is not really alone, the world is all around, she lives in an insistent present. But her thoughts are often of the past. That evanescent, pervasive, slippery internal landscape known to no one else, that vast accretion of data on which you depend—without it you would not be yourself. Impossible to share, and no one else could view it anyway. The past is our ultimate privacy; we pile it up, year by year, decade by decade, it stows itself away, with its perverse random recall system. We remember in shreds, the tattered faulty contents of the mind. Life has added up to this: seventy-seven moth-eaten years.

Jennifer next door has brought her baby around to be shown off to Charlotte—sitting up now, the baby, cooing, smiling. The baby has no past, she lives from emotion to emotion, a sliding present—now I'm happy, now I'm not, now I'm hungry, now I'll sleep. But she is learning: hot, cold, sweet, sour, nice, nasty. Her hands learn; her eyes learn; her brain learns. This is called experience, and there is a whole mountain of it to climb, she is on the foothills, striving away; presently she will indeed start to acquire a past, a fledgling past, something that teases in her head. She will have, in time, a yesterday—eventually, last month, last year.

The baby bashes together two plastic bricks. Her mother talks to Charlotte.

"So how *are* you? If there's anything you need do please let us know."

"I'm fine," says Charlotte. "And thanks, I will."

She asks to hold the baby, and enjoys the feel of her solid little body, new-minted, ready to grow and to go. She thinks of her own, which is time visible. She is walking proof that time is real, time exists, she is a demonstration of the power of time.

And this is a story that will indeed end. But not for a while, she thinks, not for a while.

Marion Clark's marriage to Nigel Davidson was an appropriately discreet affair, given the circumstances—he not that long a widower, neither of them spring chickens—but was managed with a certain panache by Laura. The warehouse was decked out for the reception, the Italian restaurant round the corner took on the catering, and did a grand job.

For Marion, it was a quietly blissful day. She had never imagined that she would marry again; this had stolen up on her, ambushed her, and she was entirely happy. The little house would now be sold, as she and Nigel would look for something larger.

She had sent Jeremy an e-mail, explaining what had happened, but received no reply. And truth to tell she did not much think of Jeremy; he seemed now an interlude, an aberration even. And, surprisingly perhaps, she thought even less of George Harrington, who could be said to be a factor in her present joy.

And as for Harrington himself, somewhere in a prison cell, he sits amid a welter of papers, immersed in the preparation of the arguments that will convince a court of his innocence. Or will not, as the case may be.

It would be absurd to say that Jeremy and Stella lived happily ever after. They settled back into their marriage and did their best with it. Stella tried hard not to go off the rails quite so often, and managed with just the occasional wobbly. Jeremy put Marion out of his mind (not difficult, after that e-mail—*married?* Well, sod off then, darling) and determined on fidelity and making lots of money. None of this quite came off; in due course there would be a girl he ran across at an auction, and a rather delightful customer, and one or two other distractions, while the business took a nasty lurch when the bank began to talk really tough, requiring Jeremy's utmost skill and ingenuity to get them off the hook. Money was lost rather than made, but there you go, and anyway he was wondering about a move to the Cotswolds—reclamation alongside a guy who he'd met who ran a garden center and bistro, nice little enclave they could be.

Paul Newsome's bill was impressive.

Mark's article caused a considerable stir, in the backwater of historical scholarship. The Bellamy/Carter controversy simmered on for months, with Mark giving a judicious poke every now and then to ensure that his name remained prominent—making a new point, flourishing some further evidence. In the meantime, he got on with his own work, while slowly—very slowly—assembling Henry's archive: "One cannot rush things, with material of this importance." And then there could be the library . . . were further funding required.

In the event, Mark landed a job rather sooner than he had anticipated. A lectureship at Bristol, which would not suit for long but could be used as a stepping stone. And so it would go. He never did become a vice-chancellor—the admin would drive one mad—but a few well received publications and some assiduously cultivated contacts propelled him into a distinguished professorial chair at an early age. He always remembered Henry with affection.

Henry devoted himself to My Memoirs for some years to come. The pages piled up, duly printed out by Rose, who, as time went on, perceived more and more repetitions, confusions, digressions. "I can't see anyone publishing this," she told Charlotte. "I mean, I'm no expert, but even I can see it just doesn't cut the mustard. He's going to be devastated, poor old boy, when people start saying, no thanks. What do I do?" "Just keep him at it," Charlotte advised. And so Rose commenced a strategy of procrastination by stealth, a marriage of encouragement and cautious obstruction, whereby enthusiasm was followed by proposals for a bit more here, a bit more there. Henry took to reading aloud to her his daily offering, and Rose would comment accordingly. This worked very well: "I agree," said Henry. "One mustn't rush this. Possibly a seminal work, though I say so myself." The long shadow of Mark was helpful here, reinforcing self-belief. And so Henry wrote, and wrote, and time went by, until at last he wrote rather less, and took to reading and rereading in a desultory way, and eventually ceased to do even that, and Rose saw that the danger had passed.

Long before that—soon after Charlotte returned home—in Rose and Gerry's garden the cat died. Gerry found her under the hedge. She had been missing overnight, and he had been concerned—off her food for a while now, something not right. He went into the house for something to wrap the little body before digging a hole, found Rose sitting in the kitchen, doing nothing, with that abstracted look, and told her what had happened. She stared at him, and then, to his astonishment, burst into tears.

Rose sat at the kitchen table, weeping. She wept and wept, and Gerry put his arm round her: "I didn't realize you were so fond of her, Rose." Rose seemed to shake her head, reached blindly in her bag for a tissue, and went on crying. Gerry sat beside her. Presently she reached out and laid her hand on his knee, and they sat there for a long time, in silence, with Gerry both moved and perplexed, until at last Rose was apparently all cried out, and he suggested a cup of tea.

At Barnsbury Accountants his line manager is well pleased with the new appointment. Couple of months now, and he's doing fine. Amazing, some of these Eastern Europeans, how they apply themselves, adapt. The occasional difficulty with the language, but nothing to get too bothered about, and when it comes to the nuts and bolts of the job, no problem. Nice guy, too.

The boys hold a farewell party for the uncle, who is moving into his flat. Quite a binge—delivery of pizzas, plenty of booze. Several of the boys get nicely wasted, including Anton's nephew. Anton is more abstemious—genial enough, but perhaps a bit preoccupied. The boys tease him: "The uncle is thinking in numbers already. He's in his classy office now. He wants to talk to a computer, not to us. Come on, Uncle, we've got some vodka, specially for you."

Anton's flat is above a newsagent that is run by an Asian couple with whom he is on excellent terms. The wife brings up a savory offering in a plastic container from time to time, all smiles. Her husband is British born, son of Ugandan Asians thrown out by Amin, immigrants twice over, but he is a Londoner to the core. The wife is from Bradford, she explains, so she has had to adapt to down here. Anton can understand all this; identify, up to a point.

The flat is something of a haven. There is traffic noise, and the decor leaves much to be desired, but perhaps he will do something about that, in time. He can cook for himself, he has the choice of what to watch on television (and he begins to follow, to become addicted to a sitcom, to be absorbed in a documentary). He has arranged his possessions—the table for the computer, the shelf for his books. The dictionary stands apart, sacrosanct. He reads now, in the evenings, grateful for the solitude and the quiet. Eat, watch television, read— reaching frequently for the dictionary. He is occupied, but every now and then something shunts these occupations aside, something more insistent; he sits staring at nothing, he is somewhere else, another place, another time.

He has bought some new clothes. A couple of suits for the office. Good shirts. A sweater. Respectable shoes—throw away those that did duty on the building site.

But he still wears, mostly, the black leather jacket. In the pocket, there is an acorn. His fingers reach for it daily. It will be there for a long time to come.

And what of the mugger? The catalyst, he or she who set everything off, who sent them all on their way.

The delinquent—fourteen years old, male, as it happens, despite equal opportunities—was himself set upon almost immediately by a hostile gang and relieved of the £67.27, which were distributed among the gang membership and disposed of within the hour. The delinquent was much annoyed at his loss, but recovered within a day or two; so it goes. Beyond him, unknown and of no interest, he had left Char- lotte on her crutches, the embattled Daltons, Henry in his humilia- tion, Marion, Rose, Anton . . . Demonstrating that no man is an island, even a fourteen-year-old with behavioral problems.

AVAILABLE FROM PENGUIN

Family Album

All Alison ever wanted—to the point of obsession—was to create a blissful home for her six children. But when they return home as adults, family mysteries quickly unravel and long-suppressed secrets are forced into the open.

ISBN 978-0-14-311787-2

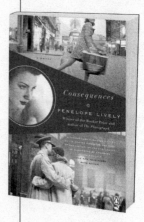

Consequences

In this powerful story of growth, death, and renewal, Penelope Lively chronicles the lives and loves of three women in one family's history and offers a profound reaffirmation of the force of connection between generations.

ISBN 978-0-14-311343-0

PENGUIN
BOOKS

AVAILABLE FROM PENGUIN

Making It Up

Making It Up is Penelope Lively's answer to the oft-asked question, "How much of what you write comes from your own life?" By exploring the stories that could have been hers, Lively fashions a sublime dance between reality and imagination.

ISBN 978-0-14-303784-2

The Photograph

The Photograph opens with a snapshot: Kath, before her death, at an unknown gathering, holding hands with a man who is not her husband. The photograph is in an envelope marked DON'T OPEN—DESTROY. But Kath's husband does not heed the warning, embarking on a journey of discovery that reveals a tight web of secrets.

ISBN 978-0-14-200442-5

PENGUIN
BOOKS